In a Suspect Universe

Albert Wendland

D G STAR BOOKS

Published by Dog Star Books
Bowie, MD

First Edition

Cover Image: Bradley Sharp
Book Design: Jennifer Barnes

Printed in the United States of America

ISBN: 978-1-947879-05-8

Library of Congress Control Number: 2018942307

www.DogStarBooks.org

Contents

Part I: Homeworld

Part II: Alchera

Part III: Elsewhere

Acknowledgements

I want to thank the following people who have all helped in their special way to bring this story into existence: Paul Goat Allen, Michael Arnzen, Michelle Babich, Timons Esaias, J. L. Gribble, Heidi Ruby Miller, James Morrow, Stacey Rubin, Bethany Vargo, a helpful guide at Mystic Seaport, several members of the Gallagher family, and all the wonderful faculty and students in the Writing Popular Fiction Program at Seton Hill University, whose community and shared talent are a continuing inspiration. Plus a special thanks to Jennifer Barnes and John Edward Lawson, the fine people ("writer's angels") at Dog Star Books, and to Bradley Sharp, visionary. Finally, and always, a deep love and appreciation for Carol, without whose generosity, support, and understanding these imaginary realms would never come about. I get to dream because of her.

At the end of *The Man Who Loved Alien Landscapes*, Mykol Ranglen was asked by Pia Folinari if he'd ever tell the "big story" she suspected he kept hidden in his past. He never said he would.

But this is that story.

It's annoying, alarming,
Sad, and perverse,
To learn one lives
In a suspect universe.

—from *Temporary Planets for Transitory Days,*
by Mykol Ranglen

Part I: Homeworld

Chapter 1: Storm Track

He fell from the sky in a burst of light. But he was no falling angel or god.

He was a man.

He crashed onto the hood of Riley's jeep, his face pressed against her windshield and his stark blue eyes staring into hers.

Riley hit the brakes. The vehicle plowed across the sand and the man tumbled away from view.

Shock kept her still. She had just missed death. Half a second more and he would have fallen through the jeep's open frame and thrust her head against the steering wheel, probably breaking her neck.

She leapt from her seat into the Great South Desert's first big storm of the season. Wind raked the sky with grit. The smell of glass and crushed stone struck her nostrils as dust blew against her.

The man lay on his side, sand pooling on his jacket and slacks. Blood stained his left shoulder. He stared at her as if recognizing her.

Then he flinched in pain and his head turned away. She reached under his arms and tried to lift him, yelling, "Get up! There's a storm coming!"

He winced, held his shoulder. But he stood unsteadily and followed her. He needed her support but he was able to stumble his way to her vehicle.

She pushed him into the passenger seat where he fell onto the cushions. She lifted his legs with his worn boots and set them inside. Luckily the door had been removed, leaving room for her to maneuver. She tied the safety harness around him. He gave her an enigmatic look of sorrow, longing, and resignation.

"Don't try to talk," she said, but the wind screamed over her words. She knew what was coming. She hurried to the driver's side, leapt behind the wheel and gunned the engine. The intake filters were supposedly good enough for this drastic weather. A Desert Ranging Vehicle was a capable tool for exploration and back-country travel, but she often abused it.

The man looked indifferent to the turmoil, caught in his own private grief.

She bullied the vehicle across the dunes while the sand rose in tornado-like columns. The towers strutted across the desert—vicious, destructive. When the pillars enveloped her, she had no visibility and she couldn't rely on the vessel's tracking device.

As the tornados retreated, she glanced behind and saw a great darkening pall, like a line of hills made from eddies and swirls—the stronger second wave of the storm. The outlying finger-like tornadoes preceded a shroud that people on Homeworld called the "devil's hand." The twisters plowed ahead like a rake while the bigger destruction bulldozed behind. She had to reach her shelter before the hand's "palm" covered her jeep—slapped down and squashed her like a lid.

She drove the vehicle as fast as she could. Her shelter sat at the top of a gully that sloped up to a rocky plateau. She charged for the chasm while frightened she might hit the walls, crippling her vehicle and burying it in the sand.

Her passenger glanced behind into darkness, finally showing awareness and unease.

She entered the canyon. The wind lessened. Her path sloped upward and she believed now she was in the home-stretch.

A great blackness swept over them.

She trampled the accelerator. The vehicle didn't move faster, just kicked up sand. She yelled in frustration, "Come on! Get me there!"

The darkness moved on. Maybe it was just an outlier of the main gale, a tornado blowing horizontally and not the "devil's palm" itself. They still had a chance! And the vehicle moved faster now with greater traction on the gravel pavement and rock of the gully.

After a burst of speed she saw her trailer and storage tents, almost hidden behind curtains of dust.

She quickly pulled into the fabric shelter where she kept her vehicle and other tools—she was concerned he would see them, would guess what she was doing. She jumped out to close the flaps but grit-filled air rammed against her, eye-searing, brutal, not the fine dust of a normal storm. It thundered over her and knocked her down.

The man pulled her upright, supporting her with his one good arm.

They looked at each other as the world's sands tore around them.

They tried to close the openings to the hut, but this was impossible. She shouted, "Forget that! Come in here!" And she led him through a cloth-covered framework that flapped madly, barely secured.

They reached the trailer. She opened the door and sand blew inside.

They shut the barrier behind them while the storm screeched, like metallic whips striking the walls. She knew the stabilizers might not hold. The whole trailer could tilt over and become buried.

They locked windows and doors. Wind crept in through unknown leaks and dust scurried across the floor.

The pall of sand at the storm's center now poured thickly over them, punctuated by bursts of lightning that stabbed from the darkness and flashed in the windows. Riley once had seen such a storm from high in an aircar. It resembled a huge dark-brown spider, striding on cords of lightning legs behind a sheaf of tentacle-like tornados. It terrified and thrilled her.

She and the unknown man stood together, facing outward, staring at the walls, caught in the center of an invisible battle. The besieged trailer rocked on its supports. The lightning pierced and thunder crashed.

They moved closer to each other.

Then, abruptly, the lightning stopped, the sand-pall thinned.

A soft light entered the windows.

After a long time holding her breath, Riley said, "Okay. That should be the worst of it."

The man collapsed onto the single couch. He looked broken, defeated, his face caked with so much dust he resembled the victim of a bomb explosion. His lips were cracked, his blond-brown hair filled with sand. He touched his shoulder and flinched. She again noticed how bloody it was.

"How bad is that?" she said.

"Not serious."

"Let me check."

"Really, don't worry."

But she could see a hole in the arm of the jacket—a bullet wound? She said nothing, but she got her medical kit and took out tweezers, gloves, sterile wipes, alcohol.

He opened his jacket, his shirt, and undershirt. He was dressed for a colder climate than the desert. The top of his arm was covered in blood. "The bullet hit you?"

He nodded.

She wiped the area and found a perforation wound, a shallow through-and-through with the exit larger than the entrance, superficial. It would ache a lot but no bones or arteries were hit. She applied pressure until any more bleeding stopped. "I'll clean and dress it."

He didn't argue. He looked embarrassed. A stoic calm settled over him even though he was in obvious pain.

She cleared the area of any dirt or threads from the shredded clothing, applied clamps that would close the gaps and then wrapped the arm in gauze. She cleaned the bruises on his face, neck, and hands too, which might have come from a fall or a fight. (She had seen the results of fights before.)

He didn't speak and his hands trembled. She assumed he was in shock—but shock from what?

"I have painkillers."

He shook his head, but then, after a moment, "Please."

She brought them and he thanked her.

The wind marauded around the trailer, scraped sandpaper nails against the metal. But the grit lessened, and the silence between them grew noticeable.

He spoke first. "How long have you been here?"

"You mean in this trailer?"

"At this spot on the plateau. We're at the top of the ravine, correct?"

"You know this place?"

"I came here once. When did you come?"

She hesitated. If he had been here before her then he might know what she had found. "Six months ago."

He looked disappointed. He murmured, "Six months." Then, "This trailer, it's been here that long?"

"Yes. Why?"

"No reason."

"Look, I have a *claim* to this place. I own habitation and exploration rights. There were no other takers."

"It's yours. I don't want it."

"But how did you—"

"I'm telling you I won't bother you. Just let me rest here a bit. I'm tired...and I hurt."

This last she felt was added to generate sympathy. "But then what? You can't just walk out of here. There's no place where you can go."

He closed his eyes, appeared to fall into temporary sleep.

She leaned closer.

His head jerked sideways and his eyes sprang open. He *had* been asleep. He was that tired. His ice-blue pools stared at her. And he said, "I'm not interested in your Airafane stonework."

This shocked her. He knew exactly what she had found.

"I saw the ruins when I was here the last time, which should prove I'm not

13

interested in them. I made no claim. Coming here now was just an accident."

She didn't believe him. "How did you get here? And why the hell did you fall out of the sky?"

"My aircar lost power and dropped into the storm. I had no control, so I jumped out. I was low enough."

She said nothing about the burst of light, that she heard no aircar or saw no wreck.

"Look," he added, "I promise not to tell anyone about your find. I know that's what you're worried about. Just let me rest here and I'll leave in a few days. I have a cache of supplies on the other side of the massif. I left them there long ago, with a locked DRV. If you take me to it I can drive off on my own. You won't see me again and no one will know you're here."

She leaned back and shouted at him, "*I'm not after Clips!*"

He remained calm, seemed unsurprised by the outburst. "Neither am I. So please . . . trust me."

She still didn't believe him. Everyone wanted Clips, the hidden Airafane trinkets from the past filled with their secret alien technologies, which led to incredible wealth for their finders.

But discovering one would make her too accessible, too public, too known. She did not want that.

"I assure you," he added, "just give me a few days to get back in shape, and then I'll leave."

His focus did seem far away. He was emotionally as well as physically hurt, preoccupied with something she believed had nothing to do with her.

But he also had a gunshot wound.

Still, she surprised herself. "All right. You can do that."

He looked surprised too. "So, you trust me?"

"No. But for now I won't ask questions. *Only* for now."

"Okay, that's fine." He reclined on the couch, closed his eyes, and immediately fell asleep.

After waiting a bit, she gave out a long and shaky breath.

The wind stirred outside, strained the cords and metal struts. Tendrils of dust slid around the room.

The man groaned a little, rolled over, settled more comfortably into his sleep.

A notebook fell from his jacket pocket.

The pocket had a flap but it became loosened when he pushed his coat aside for her to bandage the wound.

She stared at the book.

Then, after a minute or two, to make sure he breathed deeply, she lifted it away from him.

It was nothing special. A worn and well-used pocket notebook with black leather cover, the insides made of real paper and not hiding a disguised touch-screen or cellpad.

She opened it to a random page and read several hand-written lines, of a poem apparently.

I am destruction,
I am the storm,
I bring revelation
Of what lies hid.
Your world's unlikely,
Your time is false,
My new perspective
Comes dark from within.
You're alone and frightened,
Tormented, un-free.
Your life and your planet
Are suspect, my friend.
To this chaos, this blight,
You have no key.

The words touched her where she didn't want to be reached, where she kept her uncertainties and fears locked. He couldn't have known her when he wrote them, but they seemed to speak directly to *her*.

She turned more pages, stopped, read.

He slides his finger
Down her face
In a raw sensual
Arc of longing.
He touches her lips,
Lightly, lightly.
His fingers tremble.
His hands thus

Destroy all art,
Replace design
With pure sensation,
To love her in a language
That came before words.

The lines didn't use the personal "I" but she was sure he lived this experience, that he hid behind a vague third-person point-of-view to protect himself.

She knew that pose well.

Rage grew in her. She lived alone, and yet this man fell from the sky and almost landed in her lap. He spoke in riddles, wrote of terrors, and described a woman he obviously loved.

She read from one more page:

And now, after long years,
As I hear bat squeals
Above the roofs outside,
I realize—I know—
The secret of identity
That to our window
Night brings...
Our longing is blind,
But our longing has wings.

God*damn* it, she knew this too well. The secret of one's identity indeed.

She closed the book and slipped it quickly back into his pocket. His words had become too personal—too dangerous. She wanted none of this.

But a strange fascination welled up inside her.

She felt the planet turn, history crash, alien races war in the night, and her private sanctuary crumble around her.

For she knew now—she *knew!*—

Everything would change.

Chapter 2: The Amateur Airafanologist

Ancient galactic civilizations made Riley into what she was.

She called herself an Airafanologist. But she exaggerated.

The Airafane was the alien race that once inhabited this part of the galaxy, and Airafanology the study of their relics. It was no formal science since it had too little to work with. It was more an obsession with a dramatic tragedy from the galaxy's past. Amateurs rather than professionals indulged in it. They liked the romance of ancient archaeology, old secrets, terrors, triumphs—and buried treasure!

The Airafane met extinction in a series of wars with another vanished race called the Moyocks. When the Airafane realized they would not survive, they miniaturized blueprints of their technological discoveries in "Clips" (Carrier-Locked Integrated Programs), small units of concentrated information bound in crystals and reinforced by stasis fields. These then were buried in the subduction zones of scattered planets whose geologies ran on plate tectonics.

The Airafane did this so the blueprints would be hidden for millions of years, before returning to the surface through the convection currents in the mantles of the planets. They then could be found by later civilizations and used to recreate the technology. Earth had discovered FTL travel, antigravity, and the means to build a huge space habitat—eventually called Annulus—through such finds.

The discoveries changed human history. Many people argued they "saved" humanity because the Clips came—late-21st century—when Earth had nearly destroyed itself with unchecked population, dwindling resources, and environmental collapse. The Clips opened the universe to quick and cheap emigration, so people left Earth in waves.

At that point, the story of the Airafane became the story of Riley Campanara. As a child, she was abandoned.

Her parents were not cruel, but they followed a chance to search for Clips when they came to Homeworld. They believed it was wrong to take a child with them so they made arrangements for Riley to be cared for. They then left the planet and never returned. Human progress, once so proudly, or fatally, self-directed, was replaced by this new scurry to find Clips in order to advance the human race—or, more crudely, to make a lot of money. It became an obsession, which few people bothered to understand.

The children, like Riley, suffered most.

Maybe it was the fault of the horrible living conditions on Earth, or the new rampant freedom in space travel, but breaking all personal connections with the past was not so anti-social anymore—troubling many humanitarians. People even speculated that an evolutionary gene might have mutated (ideas fostered by paranoia about alien—or Clip—"intervention"). Ethnic and racial ties, traditions, families, even children, were left behind, as if some strange turning point in human development had been reached and uncritically accepted, making the phrase "post-human" more literal than it ever had been.

In the midst of so much social change, Riley needed a foundation, something she could depend on once she left the government home where she'd been placed. She became interested in studying the Airafane—maybe because her solitude was the result of that race's ancient decisions. She heard of the sites on different planets where ruins had been found, and she became enthralled.

Then, by accident (when crossing the Great South Desert alone, in a rootless gypsy wandering that was also a trait of post-Clip culture), she discovered a new Airafane site. Since these structures never showed up on satellite or aerial scans, it was possible to keep its location secret and study it alone.

This faux-scientific pursuit brought focus to her life, at least temporarily. If hard pressed she'd admit it was more an "escape" than a "finding." But she didn't care. She knew that when distance was no longer a barrier and the universe lay open to inexpensive forays, then anyone could indulge—in exploration, personal fixation, or offbeat pseudo-intellectual studies.

And this interest gave her one more attraction.

Since most site-oriented Airafanologists labored independently in remote places, Riley knew she'd be working alone.

Exactly what she wanted.

She was still resentful over her parents abandoning her, and when a recent lover also ran away to search for Clips, she lost desire to maintain connections. She didn't regret the latest departure—the relationship had been dull—but it added to a persistent self-impression of being a "discard," which both humiliated *and* inspired her. Instead of letting the label defeat her, she accepted its solitude and wore it with pride. Now a staunch loner, she lived in the desert and plunged into study of her private ruins, all on her own.

She found it ironic that, while the extinct Airafane led to her victimization, they also provided her with a purpose for her life.

Until now.

As she watched the man sleeping before her, in her recently rented field-study trailer, she felt threatened in more ways than one.

Was he running away or searching for something? Did his words make sense? Was he discarded too, like herself? He fell from the sky as if thrown away. She laughed at this but she was serious, for she didn't want to impose her own history onto him— or his onto her.

She let him sleep.

Setting up a cot for him would make the trailer too crowded and she didn't want to come across as overly inviting, so she let him stay on the couch.

She swept the sand and opened the door to the wreckage of her camp. The weather had calmed, the pink Homeworld sky now clear. The storms, often disasters at their peak, afterward became serene benedictions to a changed world, the dunes remade, the air mild.

She salvaged what she could of her fabric shelters. She had replacements since they weren't meant to outlast such weather. She righted all the blown-down equipment and moved back everything to its proper place.

Then she re-entered the trailer, to find the man trying to sit up.

He couldn't do this because two plastic braces, "zip-ties," thin but impossible to break, held his leg and his one good arm to the frame of the couch, which was made of metal and bolted to the floor.

"Sorry," she said. "Just taking precautions. I have a few questions for you."

His stunned face showed livid anger. "I thought we had a deal."

"We did, in order to get you to sleep. I added the ties while you were under."

He yanked feverishly at the restraints. "I would have co-operated with you. You didn't have to do this."

"I said I'm sorry. But we need to get a few things straight. I also have this." She pulled out a pistol, a small green semi-automatic with a black handle, from a holster on her back that had been covered by her jacket. She held it up for him to see, then put it back. "And, in case I do eventually free you—you'll need to convince me of a few things first—be sure you don't take it from me. It's programmed for the enzymes and DNA signature of my hand only. So, if you try to shoot it, you might blow your arm off."

His look was fierce. But he controlled his anger and settled into an awkward but defensive stance. "I guessed you had a weapon when you picked me up in the desert—I felt it behind you when you walked me to your jeep."

If true, his capacity for observation disturbed her, but she hid her reaction. "I always have it with me."

"Sentimental attachment?"

"It was a gift from my father."

"Your father gave you a gun?"

"He felt guilty when he left me. Never mind. You need to talk."

"I have little to say."

"Then start with your name."

"I would have given it to you. You didn't have to *shackle* me."

"Ha! 'Shackle.' I haven't heard that word in years. But...your name?"

He hesitated. "Mykol Ranglen."

"That's familiar."

"If you've studied the Airafane you've probably come across it. I've written articles."

Envy embarrassed her. He was an Airafane scholar as well as a poet. "That makes me more suspicious of your being here."

"I don't study the Airafane professionally. I've traveled a lot so I've seen more than one set of ruins. I write travelogue stuff."

"But there's something else about you. I can't remember..."

He looked uncomfortable, and from more than just the brace holding him. "I found the third Clip."

"What? You're kidding!" She didn't believe him, because only three Clips were known to exist—and here, in her presence, was the discoverer of one of them?

She remembered the name now. She once even saw a picture of him.

He added, "The Clip that's building Annulus."

"Yes. *Yes.* I remember now. They fought over it, didn't they?"

"Over who would be in control of building it and running it."

"And you felt no one should be in charge, right?"

"I objected. It didn't get me far."

"So...you're famous."

He said nothing but he looked offended.

"You of all people then should realize why I can't believe you're not after Clips."

"I didn't lie. I never want to find one again. And Clips aren't present in the ruins anyway, which I'm sure you know. They come up through seafloor spreading, far from the centers of continents like this."

"Yes, I know that, but all the idiot treasure-hunters don't. And the ruins are more accessible than the bottom of the ocean. So I need to be careful. That's why I carry the gun."

"Look, you'll either have to believe me or not. You can take your time and think about it, but this damned thing is hurting my arm—I'm wounded, remember?" He pulled on the brace. "And, by the way, what's *your* name?"

She made him wait a bit. "Riley Campanara."

"And you're here because…?"

"I'm the one asking the questions, remember?"

"Riley, we need to stop this. I *know* what you're doing here. You gave it away by being so close to the ruins, and for other reasons too."

She waited fearfully, making him argue his point.

"You're driving a Desert Range Vehicle," he said, "which is often used by archeologists. You're in a rented trailer that makes an ideal base camp. You have portable shelters for archaeological tools—shovels, strainers, a small assessing lab—which I saw when we came in during the storm. They look new but they're not top-of-the-line, and you're apparently staying here alone. So you're not professional—you'd have a team with you if you were. I grant you might not be looking for Clips—you say so, anyway, though no one would believe you, in the same way you didn't believe me. But you *are* trying to be an Airafanologist. Right?

Now she was annoyed. "You like to show off how perceptive you are."

"I'm a writer. It's my job."

"I told you I made a claim to this place. And *everyone* interested in the Airafane is an amateur. But I'm not lying to you—I'm no treasure-hunter."

"Neither am I!"

They glared at each other in personal stand-off.

"Riley, listen, the only way we'll get over this is if you trust me. I've already said I'm not here to bother you."

She didn't respond.

He made a fist in frustration. "Dammit, doesn't it bother you we're being so *predictable?* This is the way everyone comes together now—like soldiers ready to fight or run. You even brought artillery! Clips have made us so suspicious we're ready to kill each other…and we've just met."

She was shocked by his outburst, but she basically agreed. She remembered her parents and her ex-lover.

She then stated her *real* fear. "I think you're a government agent from either Homeworld or Earth."

He sighed, almost laughed. "That's absurd."

"They must review all property claims like mine in case something's found. The government wants Clips as much as treasure-hunters do. You could be an agent tracking down leads. Since surveillance drones don't work over the ruins, authorities would have to visit directly. You blundered in the storm and lost your aircar—or maybe that was even your *plan*."

"I'd be a very bad spy then. You forget that Homeworld took from me the authority to build Annulus, so I don't like its government. I almost started a public campaign against them but they quickly squashed it."

"An agent could call in troops to secure this site, take everything from me. I can't afford that."

"I agree—you'd have no protection if Clips were found here, if they even *thought* Clips could be found. But you won't get that suspicion from me. And thinking I'm from Earth is ridiculous."

"Their Federal Investigators go everywhere, making sure no world in the Confederation becomes too powerful." The lover who left her had been an Investigator and he liked to brag, so she knew this was true. "A newly found Clip would do just that."

"I don't like the Federals either."

"But you can see why I'm concerned."

"And you're right to stay that way—but not because of *me*." He tried to move to a more comfortable position but he was stopped by the restraints. "Will you please cut these off? I can't even sit up."

She considered.

"Have I tried to hurt you?" he said.

"You're not able to."

"You probably saved my life in the storm. I owe you."

She still considered. Then, after a sizable delay, she stepped toward the couch.

Before she reached it, the braces fell off and he sat up abruptly.

She jumped out of his reach, whipped out her pistol and pointed it at him.

He opened his right hand. A round plate sat in his palm. She recognized it as a laser device commonly used as a cutting tool, portable heater, light source, and weapon. He had severed the bracelets as she moved toward him. He now aimed the lethal instrument at her.

She could sense the red indicator beam on her face.

Neither of them moved.

"So, here we are," he said, "untrustworthy as hell. The typical post-Clip couple."

She didn't laugh.

"When you walked toward me I could have grabbed your arm after freeing myself, burned your eyes and taken anything I wanted. But—know!—I didn't do that."

Between her shallow breaths, she said, "That you *could* have done it is why I had to bind you."

"Let's not quibble. One of us will be hurt if we don't stop this. I made no move against you when I could have broken free. I'm not a Homeworld or Federal agent. I don't want to make a claim on your site. And I'm not after Clips. Besides this disk, I have no firearms or surveillance devices. I carry a Swiss Army knife in my left pocket, which I'll gladly give to you if you want it. So I'm not a threat."

That's not what your notebook said!

But she asked one more question. "How did you get that bullet wound?"

"I won't talk about that. You have to take me on faith. It's from nothing illegal."

He said this with such a calm firmness that she believed she'd get no more from him. Not for now, at least.

"Can we respect each other?" he asked.

"I want to be left alone, free to do my work. Just your being here disturbs that. And I don't want your problems becoming mine."

"I'll be here just a few days," he repeated. "I feel sore and I want this wound to heal. But after that, I'll be gone."

"I'll still ask you questions."

"You can ask all you want but I choose how to answer them." He lowered his disk and placed it on the table before him. "You can keep that if you want."

She dropped the gun to her side but she didn't put it in her holster yet. "A few days only. Then I'll take you out of here."

"Fine. Thank you." And once again he collapsed onto the couch. Sweat beaded his face and his breath came short and tense. He must have been hurting more than he showed.

"I'm getting something to eat," she said. "I might even share it."

"I'd love that. And I'll reimburse you for everything when I get to my cache."

"We're not eating together."

"Are we that bad a pair?"

"You found a Clip. You made our lives into what they are."

"I never expected that to happen."

"Maybe you should have." She stepped into the kitchen area.

But there she stopped. An overwhelming impulse boiled in her. She marched back to him and declared, to his startled eyes, "Maybe you're not a government agent. Maybe you're not after Clips—but only because you already found one. And maybe aircars do crash in dust-storms. But I know you're hiding something. I know you didn't come here because of any silly accident. I saw your face when you arrived and it showed more pain than that from a minor bullet wound. You *know* something. You *fear* something. And—" *And you want someone so badly you thought that even I might be her.* But she didn't say that.

He was too stunned to respond.

"There, how's *that* for powers of observation?"

She left him before he could react.

And before she was tempted to reveal any more of what she had learned from his notebook.

She yelled to him but didn't look back, "If you feel well enough, I'll take you up to the stonework tomorrow. We can compare notes, maybe get some mutual insights." She did want to learn from his reactions—and thus maybe find out more about him.

I'm an archaeologist, after all, she said to herself, to bolster her confidence. *I know how to excavate a ruin.*

But a part of her thought she was being cruel.

Chapter 3: Ruins in a Landscape

She awoke in darkness and thought she'd get up before her visitor had a chance to awake. She felt it best to let him sleep and then they'd both leave for the stonework after sun-up.

But he already was gone.

She was furious—he had "snuck off" without her.

She threw on her jacket, checked her pistol and hurried into the gulley that led to the plateau.

Lights hung along the trail. She restrung them yesterday after most were downed by the storm. He must have found the switch that powered them. They were just lamps to mark the path and they ran mostly on solar power, but still—what arrogance!

She should have left the zip-ties on him.

In the pre-dawn darkness she approached the ruins. Though hidden in a side canyon they still could be seen because of larger lamps she had set up there. He had lit these also, though they were not strong enough for night work. They showed off the mystery of the place more than its details.

Ranglen stood before the tumbled walls like a new conqueror, his feet spread, his shoulders straight as if wanting to dominate—or become—the scene.

She strode up beside him. "You couldn't wait? You had to come alone?"

He looked too engrossed to hear her anger. "Did you discover anything different?"

"No. Did you expect me to?"

"The site's beautiful. I remember its colors in the early sunlight."

"I have rights of exploration for two years. *Sole* rights."

"You're lucky. Keep the place secret. Once the word's out…"

"I know, I know. Someone will bribe an official and buy up the claim."

"If the government gets it they'll thank you generously, but then take over and say it's for your safety. They'd be right."

She reluctantly agreed but didn't want to show it, annoyed at *his* smugness as much as the government's.

Though the morning wasn't going the way she planned, the ruins still belonged to her, so she knew she occupied the emotional high ground. His coming here without her was not a defeat but a victory. It showed that not even he could resist the enigma, the fascination, the secrets that lay before them.

Arranged in a complex pattern of rooms, hallways, pits, and standing rubble, the rock walls lay dark, spotted with the tiny pools of light that did little to unveil the mystery in the shadows. The structure had no roofs, little design, few artifacts, and she had spoken truth when she said she discovered nothing different from the other Airafane sites scattered across planets.

Indeed, the ruins were *always* the same.

Exactly!

This impossible fact baffled scientists. Not only the original structures were similar, but the same amount of weathering, the same tumbled openings, the same half-standing walls, the same cave-ins of fallen material—all the sites were also similar in their amount, degree, and placement of ruination.

No one knew how this could be.

The only difference between them was that each structure was composed of the planet's local stone. The design never varied but the building material did, and it always matched the surrounding strata. Here on Homeworld, the walls were made of the same banded sandstone as the plateau, with the colors just as strong—though they couldn't be seen in this darkness and would become apparent only at dawn.

The sameness indicated the ruins had been planned. They were not "ruins." They had to be something else—stage-sets, common artwork, special effects.

But what was their purpose?

And the rock of the walls was *not* the same age as the local rock around the structures. The Airafane stonework was always older (if it could be dated at all), as old as when the Clips were first placed into the subduction zones of the various planets—when most of the continents on Earth, for example, were in different locations, and when the landscape neighboring the structures didn't exist yet.

So, though the ruins were made of local rock, they apparently were made long *before* the local rock even came into being.

Which made no sense.

Riley, like all amateur Airafanologists, hoped to find an answer, some new discovery at her own private site. But of course she didn't succeed. No one did. All her surveys, cataloging, scaled plans, measurements, excavations, ditches, pits, soil samples, siftings of earth, classification of finds, cuts and fills, core samples, laser ranging, metal detection, thermography, magnetometry, electrical resistivity, stratigraphy—the work more descriptive than analytic—had shown nothing. Though anyone finding an explanation would become famous, humanity still waited for an answer. And apparently would keep right on waiting.

She asked, "Did you find anything when *you* were here?"

"No. Nothing."

But maybe he said this a bit too quickly, or maybe she was just looking for it. "You did search, though."

"Because of my own curiosity, not to challenge any theories."

"Then why were you here?"

"I like empty landscapes."

When she didn't respond, he added, "As apparently you do too."

She understood, but she wasn't ready to talk about that yet.

"Look," he said, "I'm sorry for coming here before you woke up. I couldn't sleep. I needed one of your pain pills but I didn't want to wake you."

"Don't do it again."

"I promise."

She felt she gained a slight advantage.

He nodded at the ruins resting in their ghost-light beneath the brightening sky. "Do I get the tour?"

"You've been here already."

"We'll compare notes, like you said."

"Is your arm okay?"

"It aches, but I'm game."

Resigned, she led him inward.

Though the walls looked "primitive," the stones were held together by precision cuts, not by mortar, so the rock had a high degree of shaping. The number of stones was always the same from planet to planet, as well as the sizes. The round pits that appeared in the floor also never varied. They inevitably were called "kivas," but they had no connection to terrestrial Native-American sites. Such imposition of pre-Columbian notions onto alien artifacts was a major problem in Airafane studies. Still, the structures "looked" ancient.

Riley and Ranglen walked by markings, carved petroglyphs or the streaks of pictograms (which, Riley knew, were made from local pigments that had the same dating contradictions as the rest of the rock). The faceless figures explained nothing. They came with varying numbers of limbs, in exterior coverings that could be flesh, hide, clothes, carapaces, shells, or spacesuits, and they were sometimes adorned with long strips of feathers, antennae, barbs, or knives. Other designs suggested "blueprints" with strangely Byzantine or Hindu patterns, at least according to some researchers. All these vague and random connections confounded attempts at identifying anything. Wall-openings contained cobble-like fused agglomerates that might be artifacts, melted sculpture, or just debris—all of them, of course, identical at every site, and in the same state of arranged decay.

"Such great technology comes in the Clips," Ranglen said, "where the Airafane even included instructions. But you find none of that here."

"Yet the same technology had to be responsible for planting all these 'ruins' in the first place. So what was the point?"

"Maybe the Airafane followed a big master plan they established in their past. Maybe all the sites were built at the same time and then flown to different planets and placed their simultaneously."

"But simultaneity doesn't work across light-year distances—Einstein's relativity. And if all the ruins seem the same, then why is the building material made to look contemporary?"

"Maybe the ruins are monuments, constructed heirlooms to their lost civilization, packaged museums brought 'on the road'—like traveling circuses, meant to entertain."

"And baffle, confuse, distress and torment anyone who finds them."

"Some people like galactic mysteries, the deeper the better."

Riley snorted. She thought of other questions asked over and over. How did these identical constructions survive millions of years of continental drift? They weren't all planted on stable cratons at the centers of tectonic plates, though they were situated away from the colliding edges (at least on the worlds today).

And how did the Airafane know of the environment so far in the future in order to make the stonework resemble local rock? Did the building material change over the centuries, "update" itself and reprogram its composition? Were the walls sensitive to the eras of the people who discovered them? Did the expectations of the visitors define how the rock should be composed, in some weird macrocosmic version of quantum probabilities? And if the stone changed for each world, then why were the shapes always consistent, the artifacts and markings identical?

The two humans moved on through silent perplexities.

Riley noticed, or maybe imagined, that Ranglen stayed longer in certain rooms rather than others, seemed to look extra closely in specific locations. Of course she assumed he knew more than what he admitted, so she threw out questions in hope he'd reveal things. "You've been to ruins on other planets, you say?"

"A few. They're usually found in places like this—isolated, rocky, so the outline blends into the background."

"There are a lot of spots like that on Homeworld. It's still quite a coincidence that we both found this place. You don't believe they could manipulate probabilities over light-years, do you?"

"The 'Schrodinger-Macro-Airafane effect'? No. That theory always seemed desperate to me. It's not so much science as pure subjectivity. That's the problem. Everything we learn is subjective. We make up stories and hope they fit."

She made a wry expression. "So that's your contribution to our 'comparing notes'?"

"We have nothing *but* notes. There are no experts."

"What about that emblem there?" She pointed to a petroglyph that was similar to a Kokopelli figure, the hunchbacked flute-player of the ancient terrestrial American southwest, but different enough to make the resemblance just coincidental.

"Ah yes, Kokopelli. It drives people crazy. The Airafane lived during the dinosaurs—not the Ancestral Pueblo peoples. Others see Tibetan connections, Celtic, Greek, Assyrian, Japanese, the folklore of Australian aborigines—'Dream Time' and 'Sky Heroes.' What's your favorite?"

"None in particular." Or none she'd admit to, for she did feel connections to plumed Aztec serpents, the Popol Vuh or Mayan chronicle, and the Peruvian Oculate Being (whose oversized eyes and smiling mouth, with snakes crawling over its face, she saw in some of the figures). Though she knew she never could be original with these notions, she cherished hope.

"Everyone has something to add," Ranglen said. "But it's all random. How can you connect to a hundred different histories on fifty different worlds—and before the histories even *existed*? There are too many dead ends and too much disappointment."

"Do you think they preserve something about the Airafane past?"

"They're not explanatory or inclusive enough. They're hardly museum material, and not good history texts or 'exhibits.' The information in the Clips is different—it's *meant* to be used. But the ruins provide nothing."

"I sometimes feel they're here just to annoy us."

"The Clips give us wonders and the ruins give us ignorance—is that what you mean? But it doesn't make sense. They're like products of two different cultures."

"Maybe their definition of 'godlike' is to be all-knowing *and* all-vague."

"That makes for a god with a cheap sense of humor."

"Aren't most gods like that, overly ironic?"

He waved his arm impatiently. "We sound as desperate as the theories do. The suicide rate for Airafanologists is supposed to be high."

29

"Speak for yourself."

"People get tired of endless speculation."

She felt he was just closing off discussion.

They maneuvered more rooms. The sky brightened through tints of green to its normal pink.

Once more she tried to draw him forth. "You seem less 'inspired' by all this than I am. I'd expect you to be more obsessed. You found a Clip."

"I told you I was disappointed in how it was used."

"Is that why you're on Homeworld instead of near Annulus, to get away from reminders of losing control?"

"That's part of it."

The man makes a world but then runs away from it. And comes here to ruin mine. "Why did you leave this place?"

He didn't answer.

Ah. Caught you.

They walked on and came to the dropped pit of a "kiva."

"And what are these supposed to be?" she asked. "Storage bins for machinery, grain? Torture chambers? Swimming pools? Why would the Airafane arrive here in spaceships and then build stone pits?"

"Good question."

"Maybe it's because you can't 'touch' the promise of a Clip. It's too abstract. But you can feel a stone wall, run your fingers over it and sense it. Is this their way of letting us know their 'presence'?"

"That's anthropomorphic reasoning."

"The ruins invite us to think that way."

"Which is also an assumption." He looked scornful. "Let's keep walking. I'm tired of this place already."

Riley once had a friend who bought a new aircar every two years even though he couldn't afford it—he did this solely to prove to himself that his poverty could not take away his *freedom* to buy a new car. And sometimes Riley thought she behaved in the same irrational way, proving that her aloneness and private indulgence could not stop her from *choosing* to be alone, private, and indulgent. Like everyone else in humanity's more-than-abundant society (because of Clips), she needed activity to make her life valid. But how long could amateur Airafanology satisfy her? Studying these ruins provided no "end," no obvious reward.

"The sunlight should be hitting the walls by now," she said. "Let's go outside. There's something else I want to show you."

30

They left the ruins, crossed gravel laid down by an ancient stream, then walked farther onto the plateau. The clouds that formed at night above the cooler peaks dissipated and the sun sat low in its rosy sky. The dust that saturated the upper atmosphere caused the sky-color, along with the vaguely pinkish light of the K5 star.

In the bowl of the depression lay the ruins, the walls like a makeshift labyrinth or discarded honeycomb, built from the same layered sandstone as the plateau with its strong colors. Carmine, pink, black-brown, yellow-orange, gold, ginger, cherry, maroon, in lavish and overly exotic bands. Homeworld was known for such parti-colored rocks, "land of the melted rainbow" indeed. And this soft period of post-dawn light (and, later, pre-sunset) added a gentle painted overcoat that soon would be lost in the hothouse of day.

So the ruins fit perfectly into their setting. All the pinnacles and walls around them, the whole plateau's rolling surface of wind-eroded sandstone and limestone was layered with the same heated shades, darkened in spots with the manganese and iron of desert varnish.

Ranglen said in admiration, "You know how to pick your locations, Riley."

"There's more. It's not Airafane. I'll show you what *first* brought me here."

She led him between formations in tiers of color, past vegetation that looked pale in comparison—blond grass, ochre shrubs, spindly mop-like olive trees. The sun splashed warmth on everything and awoke a smell of fried butter and dusty cloves. A higher massif of dark metamorphic rock rose up inland.

"Do you do much exploring here?"

"I did at first, but I stick to just the ruins now." She thought the question suspicious but she didn't know why.

She guided him through a hidden alcove to the edge of a cliff. From there the rocks tumbled down to the dunes below.

"I hope you appreciate this," she said. "I've showed it to no one." *I've had no chance to.*

The desert lay beneath them like an ocean, its vivid orange waves stained with shadows that followed the raised curves of dunes. In the distance, rock debris of islands rose up like reefs. A few isolated yardangs, wedges and fins of emergent rock, sat like hulls of overturned ships, wide freighters or knife-edged yachts. The erg lay wide, choppy, crested, under an incredibly open sky. The horizon, distinct, would soon be lost in the heat haze of day, when mirages would erupt in a ring of rippling deception, like melted mirrors floating on the land. Then the rock islands would move and dance.

"When you walk across the dunes," she said, "you kick up dust that rises into the sky. Pink plumes from an orange sea." She wanted to prove she was poetic too.

Ranglen looked moved. "Thank you for showing me this. I never reached this spot when I was here."

"It's too hidden, too out-of-the-way."

"I can understand you liking the view. But don't you get lonely here?"

"In the city I felt worse, pushed aside. Here I feel part of something bigger. You *listen* more. Your mind's 'on hold,' ready for some bigger revelation. It's a mood of suspense, but you don't feel endangered, as if you're poised on the edge of something. It keeps surprising you."

He smiled at her.

"I'm talking too much."

"You're lost in landscape. I know that well."

Like a good journalist doing an interview, she had shared something private in the hope of getting a similar revelation from him—he should feel "owing" to her after this gesture. She had brought him to this spot to show it off but also to coax from him more information.

But he countered with his own question first. "When I fell from my car, why didn't you leave me there in the storm? For all your distrust—which I understand— why not just abandon me?"

"I never even considered that. You were in need."

"Well, I thank you."

"Maybe we're not as post-human as what we claim."

"Let's hope so."

Then she took a dangerous chance. "So I look like her, eh?"

His gaze hardened. But when he finally spoke he sounded normal. "I thought for a moment you were someone else. Just for a moment. You two don't look much alike."

"Wishful thinking?"

"Maybe," he said

She pictured herself: stark features, straight nose, well-formed mouth (at least she had been told that), handsome but not pretty, with long black hair tied in a pony-tail while shorter coils of it fell across her forehead. Her slim body stayed in shape from her work. Though she had plenty of physical self-esteem, she didn't think she could be someone's poetic muse.

She again tried to pull him off guard. "You had a rough experience before coming here, didn't you?"

He looked down, away from the desert. "You could say that."

She jumped into the opening. "Did it involve Clips?"

He finally nodded.

"And it involved a woman."

He didn't acknowledge this but he didn't deny it.

"So, it was a romance."

"Actually," he said, "it was more a tragedy."

She knew she had gone too far. "I'm sorry."

"Can we go back now?"

"I'd like to stay just another minute."

"Then I'll ask you a question. Why did your father buy you a green gun?"

She smiled. "He just gave me the money for it. I picked it out myself."

"Why green?"

"Well...I guess it seemed less threatening."

He laughed, maybe charmed by the answer. "I bet you're good with it."

"Take that stone there and throw it in the air." She indicated a thumb-sized piece of sandstone.

He lifted it with his good arm and flung it high.

In one effortless motion she reached under her jacket and pulled out the gun, unclicked the safety and shot at the stone just as it reached the top of its arc.

The rock burst.

The noise shattered the desert air. Echoes crashed among the distant crags, seemed to run up and down the chasms.

"Not bad," he said.

"I have time to practice."

As the echoes died, an ambiguous quiet settled between them.

I am destruction, she remembered. *I am the storm, I bring revelation of what lies hid.*

"Be honest with me, Mykol. Are we in any danger from what you've 'discovered'? Is there something I should watch for? Something you're not telling me?"

After several moments, he said, "I'm not sure. If we are, it's a peculiar form of danger, and hard to define. But...I *am* sure your little green gun won't help you much."

She asked him to explain.

"Let's say you're shooting at more rocks that you throw in the air, and you're very pleased with yourself on how well you're doing. But then, as you walk home, you find a woman hiding behind a boulder, and you discover it's not you shooting down the rocks, but her—that she's been doing it all along, firing at the same time so you don't notice. It wasn't your accuracy at all, but hers. And suddenly you feel that all your skill has been taken away, rendered false, unreal."

She listened closely.

"And then you walk on and find that she *too* was deceived, that a third person was hitting the stones. And then you walk farther and find someone else shooting the rocks instead of *her*. And then you go farther yet and find someone else after that. On and on, until everyone's deceived, and you have no idea who's really hitting the rocks—or if it's even just accidental, that so many people are shooting at them that one of the bullets *has* to hit. Or maybe the stones are just exploding on their own, from some personal whim of suicidal rocks. So no one's certain about who's doing what or what's going on."

She didn't respond, but she was feeling disturbed.

"So if you find all that 'dangerous,' then…yes, maybe you and I *are* both in danger."

She stared into the desert, then finally said, "So, this story you've been through that you won't talk about, it's neither a romance nor a tragedy. It's a horror story."

"That depends on how you define 'horror.'"

"You're playing with me, Mykol."

He stood up then, as if eager to return to the trailer and not waiting for her to accompany him. "It's not me who's doing the playing, Riley. It's something much larger." He looked at her closely. "And *that's* the part that's scary."

He walked away then and left her alone.

She followed quickly. She didn't want him in her trailer without her supervision. Did she trust him more now?…or everything else less?

Chapter 4: The Notebook

An uneasy truce developed between them, workable if not free of tension. She wouldn't let him stay by himself in the trailer so he accompanied her as she worked in the ruins.

Her current excavation was a trench outside the eastern wall, where she rigorously recorded the three-dimensional position of everything she found. So far nothing was unusual, all finds similar to those on other planets. She thought at one point she discovered signs of ancient plant-life which might suggest conditions when the ruins were established, but deep searching in paleobotanical resources showed that the pollen could not be ancient. Still, she dug, surveyed, ran augers and corers inside the trench and under the walls.

Ranglen helped but little conversation passed between them. He wasn't good with a trowel or hoe (his wounded arm didn't help), and too often he seemed preoccupied. He'd ask if he could wander off into the highlands. He always gave a specific direction, though he usually stayed away longer than proposed, saying he walked farther than expected. She had running spy-cameras back at the trailer that were part of her security system. She reviewed their scans when she was alone but she never saw him back-tracking to the trailer while she was gone, so she had no reason to think he lied.

Her feelings toward him were still unclear. She resented his secrets, his repeated choice to keep to himself, his superior academic knowledge and personal learning (he obviously knew more about the Airafane than she did but he didn't divulge it), and even his alienated solitude, though she herself shared it and understood its attraction. Thinking of him perhaps made her reflect too much on herself, on her own neurotic attraction to the site, on her unsuccessful emotional past, and on her current paranoid fixation with the gun, which she always kept handy. She didn't think it scared him much anyway.

She felt he believed he had the upper hand—that he only *chose* to leave her in charge. This infuriated her.

He said nothing more about when he would leave. He took his walks as if only to restore his strength. When he arrived, he had been despondent, but he grew in fortitude while keeping to himself, though he never returned from his treks with any sense of excitement or discovery.

She felt he was coming to a decision.

She gave up trying to trick him into talking. She lived in a tension between wanting full disclosure or total restraint. She was frightened of what he knew while longing to hear of it. From the start, she refused to be dragged into his murky emotional depths, for he obviously carried baggage. She had past entanglements of her own so she knew it was best to avoid his. But now she was curious, and she longed for revelations.

This strain was not altogether unpleasant. She wasn't sure now she wanted him to leave.

Then something happened.

They worked together one morning, she losing interest in the trench and ready to dig a new pit inside. Ranglen suggested some possible spots, but then he said his muscles were cramping so he wanted to walk. He indicated an outcrop-peak as a destination, viewable from the ruins. At his leisurely pace he said he'd take several hours to get there and back.

Riley said she'd return early to the trailer and that, for once, he could walk there after his hike instead of to the ruins. She had nothing in the trailer that would interest him anyway and all her private possessions were locked in a safe, but this restriction was her one means of maintaining some control over him.

After grabbing water and a wide hat, he walked off. She watched him, and even followed him a bit, just to be sure he did what he claimed.

She stayed longer at the ruins than expected, not returning to the trailer till late afternoon, so she assumed he'd arrive before long.

She fixed a sandwich, but then she realized she left the backup for her cellpad at the ruins. She worked strictly on hard-drives and copied everything into a separate storage-bank, not trusting satellite networks with their possible data surveillance. Since she needed the back-up for compiling her nightly notes, she'd have to go back to the ruins to get it.

She shoved her sandwich into the refrigerator and impatiently hiked again to the stonework.

The sun touched the horizon. She wasn't concerned about Ranglen losing his way in the dark. On a clear night the three small moons provided enough light to follow a known path. And since the trail from the outcrop passed the ruins, she might even run into him.

She reached the stonework.

But there, in the small light of early evening, she noticed an odd glow from within.

The sky-color had darkened to carmine and the rocks were still tinted gold, but a slight illumination could be seen among the walls—vaguely bluish, not the ivory or white of her own lamps. And it seemed more a spread-out haze than a point source.

Suspicious now, she left the path and approached the walls from a different angle. The glow came from a room not near the trench where she and Ranglen recently worked.

She remembered that the places he had suggested for new digs were all at the opposite end of the site, distant from where this glow emerged.

Had he tried to lead her away from the spot?

With surging doubts, she kept a screen of rocks in front of her as she maneuvered closer, not wanting to be seen. She reached a spot where she was concealed and yet she could spy through a gap into the room with the glow.

What she saw astonished her.

Ranglen stood beside a wide column of blue light that rose from one of the "kiva" pits, its width defined by the circular ring of stones defining the depression. The soft glow faded at the column's top, and it was not bright enough to provide illumination. The color was unlikely and the definition of the column almost too precise, about three meters in height and two meters across. It was luminescent and slightly translucent, like a glowing fog that vanished gradually at its upper extent.

At first she wondered what kind of light source Ranglen had placed inside the kiva—a glowing ring exactly wide enough to fill it. But she couldn't understand what he was doing. And the light seemed to have an almost material density, like a cylindrical wall. She wondered why it rose as high as it did and yet did not fade until the top.

He stood beyond the glowing cylinder with his back to her. He glanced behind him, apparently to make sure no one entered the room, then he pulled a small flat object from the stone wall. It was so tiny she could barely see it. But the moment he did pull it out, the column of light vanished.

A pale lantern, belonging to Riley but that Ranglen apparently borrowed, illuminated the room, just enough so she could see him. He glanced into the kiva. Then he faced the wall again and reinserted what he held in his hand.

The cylinder of blue light re-appeared.

Riley knew then—the light had to come from the ruins themselves. And he controlled it with whatever he held.

He had discovered something!

I'm here for months and find nothing, but he arrives and just after a few days makes the discovery of the century.

And he didn't even *show* it to her!

For all her anger she couldn't help feeling excited. This was a monumental breakthrough. But she was too conflicted to know what to do—too enraged to run in with congratulations but too thrilled to turn away in anger.

And she realized, vaguely, something was wrong.

He had kept the discovery *too* much to himself. She believed, and still did, his claim that he wasn't interested in wealth and glory. His weary demeanor, his sorrow and disappointment, maybe even his bullet wound, all suggested he wasn't concerned— but were all these impressions then false, part of a cover to keep his greed hidden?

Yet he didn't look elated. He was too focused. For just making a landmark discovery he acted more like a mechanic checking specifications.

She watched him glance into the light-column, then back to where he had inserted the...*yes*, it must be a *Clip!* It was just the right size.

Since the Clips and the ruins were both Airafane, maybe the stone wall recognized the Clip, accepted it.

Ranglen pulled it out and the column disappeared again. Then he turned it over and reinserted it. The light returned.

But now when he pulled it out a second time, the glow remained—for about fifteen seconds before it faded away.

And *this* time, Ranglen smiled.

Her thoughts churned in a growing storm. He had his precious secret after all. No wonder he asked to stay at her site. He needed to check this, to get his private Clip working. And then he'd ask to be taxied away without saying *anything* to her—taking full credit for the discovery and leaving her out of it.

Goddamn him!

But she held herself back from running in and confronting him, which is what she wanted to do—but not yet, not now. She needed to know more. She wanted control. She'd play his game for just another day to see where it led.

He stepped around the column and looked briefly in her direction.

She kept still. She was sure he couldn't see her.

Then she realized—he didn't have his jacket.

They had left for the ruins later than usual and the day already had been warm. She couldn't remember him bringing it with him. Maybe he knew he'd go on his hike so he didn't take it. It must be back at the trailer.

With his notebook?

She backed slowly away from her hiding spot, making no noise.

The moment she couldn't be seen from the ruins, she raced down the path and back to her trailer.

He couldn't have been working at this "experiment" for long. He hadn't been separated from her except on his walks, and then she always had stayed in the ruins. She would have seen him. Did he discover this the first time he was here? But then where did he get the Clip? For all the years of people studying at the other ruins, no one had discovered any.

Now there were *four* Clips in existence.

And Ranglen had discovered two of them.

Impossible!

She reached the trailer. She looked behind her before she entered. He hadn't followed.

She ran inside and scanned the room. She didn't see the jacket at first, but then she found it under the couch where he slept. It was almost hidden, but she recalled now he kept it there, always beneath him.

She pulled it out, careful to notice how it had been placed so she could put it back in the same position. She opened the flap of the breast pocket and reached inside.

She felt the notebook.

She knew she was crossing a fatal line, from where she could not return. But at that point nothing could stop her.

She peered through the window, looked for any approaching shadow.

Nothing, no one.

She opened the book and read the first lines she saw.

Its eyes are blank, its henchmen are brutes.
It's more a monster than validating myth.
Its food is human life, that's all,
A singular appetite hardly profound.
And though some still hear from it
Insight and lore,

39

We know what it really says:
"More!"
"More!"

The lines disturbed her. What force or creature ate human life, so casually and without significance? If this thing existed, what could it be?

A single line at the top of the page said, "Cannibal at the North End of the World."

So it must be only a metaphor, and she didn't care about poetry. Where were his *secrets*, his plans, his schemes? She wanted the dirt.

She glanced outside again. Still no sign of him.

She read from another page:

He dreams of ghost worlds
In a haunted universe,
Seeks private wonders
And planetary romance,
Caves, maelstroms,
Oceans with lids.
And when he's too focused
On only himself,
He wants to dissolve
Into alien landscapes,
Worlds unbearably,
Unthinkably new.

Writing about himself, probably—confession, autobiography, but why so vague for a personal journal? And what the hell is an ocean with a lid?

She turned more pages.

It's annoying, alarming,
Sad, and perverse,
To learn one lives
In a suspect universe.

More symbols and abstractions. She risked everything and was finding nothing. It made her more angry.

Another glance up the trail. No one.
She read,

How can I paint her,
Conjure her from memory,
Produce my failed
If timid copy?
Outline her shoulders,
Her neck, her face,
Highlight the glints
In her sable hair,
Relate the sound
Of her voice, her passion,
Depict her bottomless
Storm-fed eyes?

I cannot paint her.
I can only love her.
That is my statement.

More about "the woman." She didn't need this.
But it was hard to stop reading. What would it be like to be loved like that?

I want my gift to her
To be her own true self.
I want my masterpiece
To be my love for her.
I want her to cherish
What she is in my eyes.

She would've read more but she had no time. She turned pages and kept finding only...
Disappointment overwhelmed her—
These were his secrets! His confessions and love were his only real interests. Not what he knew, but what he felt. He had no field notes, maps, blueprints, essays or summaries of his findings in the ruins. He had only poems!

She read with no hope.

What mad underside
Of this planet beckons?
Why were we lied to?
Why do we get
These late terrors,
A dying race's
Primeval screams?
Why did they trick us,
Hate us, condemn us?
Why did they toy
With our wishes and lives?
Why help us, to destroy us?
Why dangle new worlds
And then draw them away,
Hide inside equations,
Justify torture
Through cosmic "laws"?
What's behind what they've done?
What's behind what *I've* done?

Did he refer to the Airafane, the Moyocks, others? Who could be so devious or false? Who tortures? Who screams? What did it mean?

Vertigo swept over her. She leaned against a wall, tried to settle.

But she turned one more page.

Nothing. Blank.

She had read the last entry. The one before it she saw on the first night. And prior to those were lines about the woman.

No grand secrets, no revelations of schemes or plots.

She flipped other pages but didn't stop to read. She had seen enough. She closed the notebook and stuffed it into the pocket of his jacket, which she then placed under the couch. She had wanted to make the discovery of the century but now it scared her. She wanted science, measurable insights, hard data, not some cauldron of intense emotion.

She looked up the trail and saw no one.

She didn't care now. He could come any time he wanted.

She sank onto the couch—*his* couch. She wondered if the woman he wrote about ever saw the poems. Did she learn how he felt for her?

What a stupid thing to think about, while he's out there demolishing everything in my world!

A bobbing lantern moved down the trail. She grabbed a treatise on desert excavation, moved to a chair and pretended to read it.

Ranglen came in, said nothing to her.

She stayed quiet.

The silence continued for much too long. "Enjoy your walk?" she said.

"Took longer than expected."

"Gets dark here fast."

"Yes, I noticed."

They spoke like two people in a worn-out marriage, trying to avoid the big threatening hopeless argument that simmered like a dragon in the middle of the room.

"I stopped at the overlook," he said. "I thought you might be there."

"I was busy."

"You missed a great sunset."

She hated talking about such trivia but she wasn't ready to confront him yet. She was still too shaken.

And she wanted to see the ruins for herself, check out the pit-room—find the slot in the wall, maybe even get the light-column to activate.

Ranglen lay on his couch. He reached under it and pulled out his jacket, draped it over him like a blanket.

So he knew the jacket was there. Did he leave it intentionally? Was she *meant* to find it and read the notebook? Was it all a set-up?

"I'll be leaving soon," he said. "I think I've bothered you long enough. I'm able to use my arm now. The day after tomorrow, if that's okay. I want to take one more walk—I've enjoyed them. Then, can you drive me a few kilometers to the other side of the massif? If you pull up a map I can show you where my supplies are. It would take just a few hours, so the whole trip won't consume the day."

Who's predictable now? You get what you want and then you leave. "Sure. We'll start early." *But I'll have some questions for you before then—some* real *questions this time!*

"Good. I want you to know I'm grateful for all this."

"No need to thank me."

"I'm turning in now. That walk was tiring."

He didn't ask about her obvious reticence that thickened the air. He leaned back and closed his eyes.

Then, with an attempt to occupy herself and yet continue her festering mood, she reached behind her back and pulled the pistol from its holster. She held it before her and contemplated it. Only the frame and the slider were green but those parts comprised the bulk of the weapon. The barrel was matte black, as well as the grip panels, the magazine release, the take-down lever, the safety decocker, the slide release, the hammer, and the trigger. She disassembled the major parts, looked down the barrel, adjusted the rear sight, pulled out the magazine, worked the slide (she did this loudly), reinserted the magazine (more loudly), and aimed at the lantern he had carried. She wanted to get a laser sight someday and wished she had done so already. She aimed at other objects, not trying to muffle the noise she was making, then she put it away with a vigorous snap.

His eyes stayed closed during all of this, but she was certain he wasn't asleep.

She smirked at the scene in her mind: estranged couple stews in silence till one theatrically examines a pistol.

She walked to the refrigerator and took out her sandwich. She carried it to her separate room and closed the door behind her, silently locked it.

She ate two-and-a-half mouthfuls. Then she stayed awake for hours.

Chapter 5: One Desert Night

Ranglen went for his walk the next day, early enough that he needed his jacket. He left Riley in the trailer, free to examine the ruins on her own.

She rushed up to them immediately in case he planned to stop there first, but she didn't see him. She walked among the crumbled walls to make sure he wasn't hiding, then she entered the room where she watched him yesterday.

She found nothing. No slot in the wall, no mark in the stones, no trace of anything new in the kiva. Only solid rocks, same as before, ever and always.

Maybe she dreamt it. Maybe his poems were just metaphorical excess. And even if he led her into reading them, what would be the point? They contained only emotional confessions. Why share those?

She tried to work more on the new pit but she didn't care enough about it now. All she did here seemed pointless. She had assumed she'd eventually come to this state but she had delayed it for such a long time.

Till *he* came.

But maybe she only deceived herself. Maybe it was somehow not his fault.

She hated such thoughts.

Because of her stubbornness she worked hard that day. Ranglen never came, and she didn't care now if he returned to the trailer first. He'd leave tomorrow, and—she was certain—tell her nothing, no matter what she asked him.

She could feel herself becoming resigned. She hated that too.

When the sun went down she returned "home."

Ranglen wasn't there. A note said, "I walked down into the erg. Can you follow and meet me?"

Of course she'd go. Even if the offer was a trap she had too much curiosity. Her resentment was stronger than her caution.

The sun set, but she could see his footprints in the patches of sand. They led downslope toward the open dunes. At times she lost the prints on the gravel and chipped stones, part of the old streambed delta that led from the canyon into the erg. But eventually she found him, sitting on a blanket near the top of a rise overlooking the desert.

It was smart of him to bring the blanket. The ground got cold at night so an insulating shield helped. And the rock island was a good place from which to watch the dunes—for feeling a part of them, not like her lofty cliff on the plateau. Here you could be intimate with the landscape.

Of course he'd come here. He knows these feelings and he's trying to distract me.

She walked up the slope and sat beside him on the blanket.

He said, "I had forgotten what it's like to be down here after dark. It's a different world."

Riley understood. The sky, for over an hour before turning black, would hold a slight bluish-green tint, making the stars shine blue within it. This afterglow was caused by luminescent dust that slid from the tops of the dunes—like ghosts sliding into the air, veiling the ridges in thin greenish clouds.

He said, with a wonder that sounded genuine, "The planet's haunted."

She had come there ready to fight with him, but she could sense the vista calming her. She didn't resist. Though people annoyed her, the desert she could always forgive.

"We lay claim to this place," he said, "but we don't own it."

"I have rights to only digging and exploring. I don't lay *claim* to anything."

"I didn't mean you. I can see you don't want to exploit it or change it."

"I don't want to live here or make this place mine. I'm traveling through it, just like you, learning from it. I might be gone tomorrow. No one should be condemned for what I do here."

She wanted these statements to be declarations, but her anger now struck her as tiresome. Maybe she did brood too much, hate too much. And it *was* his discovery, even if the ruins "belonged" to her.

He said, "When I sit here, I feel there's something out there, something alive."

And this was a subject she could talk about. "You don't find much life during the day," she said, "but you see traces of it from the night before: tracks of mammals, lizards, birds. Especially around water pools after rain. Nothing's dead here, only hidden. There's a reptile with webbed feet and a wide tail that *swims* through the sand. And another creature with transparent eyelids so it can see in a dust-storm."

"Did you know your voice changes when you talk about the landscape? It gets solemn."

"I can't help it. The desert holds too many stories. Piles of rock that look like tombs— that maybe *are* tombs. Drawings and paintings that can't be explained. Intelligent life never existed on Homeworld, but the drawings don't look Airafane. Some finds are like arrowheads or old tools, as if the desert was inhabited once and then suddenly abandoned. I've seen places resembling empty camps, as if nomads move across the dunes but are never seen. And I sometimes hear noises at night—like people walking, animals being driven, drums beating. I thought I saw torches out in the distance once."

"That's typical for any alien world. Your mind imagines things, plays at impressions, and the planet gives back your own thoughts, tries to make them real."

"People talk about colony ships sent out after the first Clip was discovered, that they were abandoned once they arrived here and the settlers moved into the desert, before anyone noticed or kept track. They might still be there, hidden someplace."

"This is why you and I came here, Riley, for just these kinds of mysteries. We know the desert won't give us answers, but that doesn't stop us. We want the *search*, the focus it provides us."

His words crept over her.

"You want to be 'unimagined' by the landscape," he said. "Reformed, re-defined. If we feel that a Clip can reboot history, make civilization become something else, then why can't we do the same for ourselves and re-construct what we are?"

But her anger returned. "I'm glad someone else shares these interests, Mykol, that I'm not alone. But it's time to stop. You're just avoiding telling me what you've found."

His face didn't change.

"The light in the kiva, the blue column, the Clip I saw you put into the wall. I'm sure it *was* a Clip."

His body seemed locked in a hard stillness. But he did nod.

"You want your ride to your camp, don't you? And you still owe me—for saving your life. So, what's going on?"

"I don't need you to drive me to my cache. That's why I took walks. I scouted routes across the massif. I can make it on my own."

"I promised I'd take you and I will. But I deserve an explanation."

He stared into the darkening desert, at the stray waving banners of mists—the ghosts. "Nothing I say could ever be enough, and frankly the less that's said, the better."

"Better for me or better for you?"

"Riley, please. What I'm doing is against the law. I don't want you involved. And I can't have anyone tracking me through you. If I could erase all your memories of me, I would. It's best you forget everything about me. Nothing happened. We never met."

"I can't forget this."

"You have to! If they—Homeworld, Earth, the Confederation—find out you're connected to me they could arrest you to get more information. You never were meant to see that Clip—don't mention it to anyone! If they learn of it you'll have an army here. They'll lock you up and take whatever they want from you."

"I don't care about Clips, and that kind of treatment is almost expectable. It's part of the game we're all playing. So you're not scaring me. I'm past being concerned. I just want to know what the hell you've seen."

"You don't realize what you're asking. I can't explain it."

"Those are excuses."

He looked up to the sky and pointed. "See that constellation there, shaped like an eel or a snake? It's called 'Draco,' or 'the Dragon.' It's similar to the one seen from Earth. Do you know the root meaning of the word, 'dragon'?"

She shook her head.

"Chaos. Disorder. The primal flux that came before creation."

"So?"

"*That's* what I've seen."

She shook her head with more exasperation.

"All right," he finally said. "Listen to me then, but none of this will make sense. I've seen the impossible. I've seen things come to life that could never be alive, that defied all laws of physics. I've seen legends walk out of myths, become real and attack people and even kill them. I've encountered landscapes that were so much a part of me and so familiar that they made me think my mind had turned inside out, that I was falling into a labyrinth made from myself, from my worst fears, which I couldn't understand or ever escape. I've seen longed-for fantasies come alive, but I've also seen monsters—miracles and disasters, the wonderful and the terrifying. I've been thrilled by new possibilities and then horrified they might come true."

He stopped, but only to take a deep breath. "I've seen all this, or maybe I've dreamt it. The difference isn't significant anymore. And it's too disturbing. You lose control. You misplace everything you thought was certain. I didn't want any of this but now I can't get rid of it. I think of it constantly. It's why I can't sleep. When I first reached you I was hopeless. I had lost all desire to try anything. But I want to go back now and restart worlds. I can do this, Riley."

He looked directly at her. "Yet I did not want *you* to be a part of it. I can sacrifice myself, but I won't have you doing the same. I won't be responsible for one more person and I don't want to hurt you. So forget about me, like everyone else has. You never knew me. You don't know me now. I have nothing to give you, because I can only *take* from you and destroy what is taken. Leave me this one moment of freedom where I don't owe anyone anything. I've enjoyed being here. I thank you for this time. But you deserve to be free of it—free of me. You have more to live for. Savor it. Keep it."

She didn't know what to say. His feelings overwhelmed her—and she even believed them. But she could find no logic to them. She stared at his face, filled with his bleak but determined energy.

"I've lived too long with this," he added. "I'm caught between facts and elaborate illusions, images, metaphors. I can't make distinctions. There *are* no distinctions. No standards, no laws. You don't want me talking about any of this. It'll drive you mad. It came very close to doing that to me—or maybe it did. So enjoy what you have here. Take advantage of it. But then…leave! You don't want to be around if anything's discovered. Nothing can help you then."

"What about you?"

"It's the price I pay for the knowledge I've gained. Don't worry about me. I have my own tasks."

"But your coming here wasn't harmless, Mykol. All I was doing, my work, my life—it's destroyed now, all my interest in it. The ruins, archaeology, I don't care about them anymore. You already know more than anyone. You've made this great discovery—*whatever* it is. So what's the point in my going on?"

"I'm sorry, Riley. I didn't know you'd be here. I never meant to hurt you. But you still have your life. And you're *free*. If you forget all you've seen of me, you can get back what's been disturbed or lost."

"No. It's gone."

"You still have *this*." He waved his arm at the night-shrouded desert. "Your fascination with this world, how you just described it. Hold on to this place."

"I'd never 'hold' it."

"I'm not saying for you to own it. Just be a part of it."

"But—"

"Wait…" He stared more intently into the desert. "Is that…?"

She followed his gaze. A wide curtain of darkness moved into the sky, occluding the stars. At its lower edge, in a line that stretched across the horizon, a layer of sparks crawled like a snake, tinted violet.

"Dammit! That's a storm." Riley was furious at herself. In her rush to get here she hadn't brought her cellpad with its automatic warnings.

"But the sky's still clear. There's no thunder."

"The storms come from electrical imbalance in the sand, not the sky, and you'll hear the thunder soon enough. Come on! We have to get back to the trailer." She hurried toward the gulley that led uphill.

Ranglen followed. "Aren't the ruins just as close?"

"They're too open. The trailer's our only chance."

They ploughed through the dunes onto the hardpack. She glanced across the erg and saw that the horizon looked nearer. Spicules of sand reached upward like witch's fingers—the coming tornados. The speed at which a storm arose astounded her, as if it had will and personal malevolence.

They raced up the chasm, the uneven slope agonizing them. The sands lifted and swirled around them even though the storm was kilometers away. Flashes bloomed in the heights, glows reflected from the lightning. Thunder reverberated through the ravine.

She didn't look back. She knew what the storm would appear like now—a fat mollusk with a face of tentacles.

Dust and ozone filled their lungs. They coughed, staggered, kept running.

They reached the clearing near the camp where the level ground helped them move faster. Noise grew—a sustained roar from the grit-filled wind, scraping against stone walls and howling like a flood in the narrow canyon.

Through eddies and curtains she saw the camp. They rushed on, past the blowing flaps of tents and screens.

She reached the trailer, pulled open the door and jumped inside, holding it open for Ranglen behind her. She turned to close the door after he ran through—

He wasn't there.

He had been with her when she reached the tents but now he was gone.

The pile-driving sandstorm rushed into the opening, knocked her across the floor and blew everything loose.

By leaning all her weight against the door she managed to close it. Dust obscured the room as sand fell across the furniture. She fastened the latch, hoped it would hold, left it unlocked in case Ranglen returned.

The walls vibrated and the trailer rocked.

What happened to him? He couldn't survive out there. If he fell, he'd be buried. He—

The ruins! He must have gone there!

But that was madness.

Yet if he got there before the main blast hit and he reached the center of the labyrinth, then the many walls might protect him, at least a little. And if he managed to cover himself in one of the kivas…

When they first ran from the sand dune, he had grabbed the blanket and carried it with him.

But the walls had no roofs. The lightning would be vicious. He still could be dead.

The trailer shook. Sand rose and filled the air. She coughed harshly and her eyes burned. She found and donned a breathing mask.

She noticed a mask already missing.

Ranglen! Of course. He took one earlier, kept it on him and must have used it now, after he left her at the trailer.

Did he know the storm was coming? Had he raided her cellpad and heard a long-range warning she missed?

An oxygen tank and goggles also were missing. Did he hide these in the ruins during his "walks"? Did he prepare this grand escape?

Her anger raged.

Loud booms of wind swept by. The trailer lifted, hung, fell, stayed at an angle as if one of the supports had collapsed. Furniture slid toward the lowered corner.

More noise, parts of her camp slamming about, the metal struts beating the walls. She fell to the floor, tried to find shelter under a table. Minutes of terror clamored by.

Then a sudden relative quiet.

As the storm weakened, she grabbed goggles and staggered up the sloping floor to the entrance. A part of her knew that aligning the trailer again would be impossible.

She couldn't leave until it was safer. But the storm weakened fast enough that she could soon follow him.

She remembered he wore his jacket down on the erg, so his precious notebook was with him too.

The storm abated enough now. She believed so anyway. She didn't care. She opened the door—to a quick blast of grit that pushed her back. She had been too eager and she should have waited. She shoved the door closed.

Frantic, she waited. Was Ranglen alive? Buried, asphyxiated, blind, dead?

She couldn't stand the wait so she opened the door again. Much howling greeted her but she could bear it now.

With her own mask, goggles, and hand-light, but no oxygen tank, she raced out of her shelter and followed the buried path to the ruins.

Her equipment lay scattered about, the damage worse than expected. She should have secured things better—again! She was getting lax. It was Ranglen's fault! She had become too preoccupied with him.

The wind scurried and teased. Palls of dust blocked her view, complicated by darkness and the loss of her guiding lights, all blown away. But the further she walked, the calmer the air.

She felt the weight of her gun against her back. Her father's cheap conciliatory gift. The thought made her determination grow.

She came to the ruins. She moved to the spot where she spied on Ranglen the night before. She looked into the room.

He was there, fiddling with his damned Clip near the wall—though she couldn't see it for certain. Dust covered everything, and a lantern he must have hidden there wasn't much help. She saw the blanket under which he must have sheltered. She saw more than one. How much had he prepared? The room was a mess and his clothes filthy but he wasn't slowed by what he was doing.

He glanced up to see if she stood behind him or had entered the room.

But she hid herself well. She was sure he couldn't see her.

The column of blue light appeared.

He glanced at it, then turned to the wall and pulled out the Clip—the fourth Clip ever discovered. How many of them did he intend to find?

The light vanished.

He moved out of view but soon returned, with one of her own carrying packs that looked full. He must have stolen it from her trailer. He threw it into the kiva.

And suddenly she knew what was happening.

She pulled out her pistol.

Fear, sorrow, anger warred in her. He had lied to her again. She felt like she did back in the government home where she was "cared for"—where the older children beat her and her "friends" deserted her—she, the discard, the abandoned, the fool.

She could shoot at him now, like she had shot at her lover, even shot at her father as they both left her. She only meant to scare them. She didn't hurt them, but they'd remember her. Oh yes, they'd remember.

But, like Ranglen, she wanted her grand escape too.

She lowered the pistol, put it away.

Ranglen put the Clip back into the wall. The column of light reappeared. Then he pulled it out again but the light didn't leave. He looked apprehensive and yet determined. He too was not himself. He stepped into the kiva and its glowing pillar, stood in the center with his arms to his sides. He looked frightened. But he had made his decision.

Now she made hers.

She jumped into the room, leapt into the blue column and landed in the pit beside him. She stood there motionless, inches away from him. She even tried to smile at him.

His eyes went wide, his mouth gaped. He stared at her in absolute horror.

Immediately she regretted her decision.

The light brightened.

They disappeared.

Part II: Alchera

Chapter 6: The Asteroid

Five months earlier—

Mykol Ranglen embarked on a dangerous and highly illegal personal experiment. It happened because he was angry.

While traveling alone in his small spaceship he saw in the forward observation port the newly built habitat-in-space called Annulus, rising in a rainbow arc from the hazy debris swirling around a newborn star.

It was almost complete now, its gently sloping dish-rim over 300 kilometers wide and glowing in colorful concentric rings—reddish desert, yellow prairie, an inner rim of green forest and blue lakes. Built from an asteroid by the Airafane nanotechnology that originated with the third Clip, it would soon become an incredible living space for human colonists.

And the sight of it should have thrilled Ranglen, since he *discovered* the third Clip.

But instead he was annoyed.

When he gave the Clip to Confederation officials, he felt he'd have influence over what it might produce. And when he learned the result would be a habitat in space, he vowed to keep it free of exploitation, over-development, uncontrolled economic growth. He wanted it to be more a natural park, a common playground where an enormous rainbow, the opposite side of the arc, would always glow with serenity in the sky.

His gift to humanity. "Ranglen World!"

Finding the Clip had been grandeur enough, but he also wanted to be recognized as the creator and bestower of this grand wonder.

But he was locked away from important decisions. His discovery was bought from him—though "bribed" might be the better word. His notion of a pristine landscape beneath stellar vistas where you could marvel at alien engineering would never come true. His material wealth was made secure, but his emotional fantasy shriveled and died.

"So much for *that* dream!" he muttered.

And thus, alone in his spaceship as he stared at Annulus, and in a certain retaliation, he pulled out the one thing he secretly *did* keep from his find.

He didn't know then he was about to discover something so dangerous, he would keep it hidden from humanity for years.

Clips came in octahedral crystals of a strong substance that resembled fluorite. Once broken open and the Clip removed, the material weakened and the crystal panes sometimes could be peeled away.

When Ranglen still had the third Clip he sliced a shard from the crystal and kept it to himself. He did this out of spite. He wanted *something* he could actually keep from the find.

And now he held it up before him, stared at it and gloated. At least *this* was still his!

But then, in one of those fateful events that prowled like sharks throughout history, he looked *through* it at the star-field before him.

The image was murky, the optics poor. But as he pulled it away and looked through it again, he thought he saw something he could not see without it. A small gleam, like an indicator light, in the dust-and-rock debris of the new sun's accretion disk.

"What the hell—"

If you looked through the shard you saw a gleam. Take the shard away—and no gleam.

A location indicator?

Ranglen knew the Airafane did not believe in coincidence. They were telling him something. This had to be important.

A wild giddiness flooded his nerves.

No one else had discovered this. If so, the officials would give as much importance to the crystalline containers as they did to the Clip. They took the crystals, of course, but they demanded only the Clips.

He trembled. He gripped his chair and looked behind his back. He checked for nearby flying drones to make sure governments weren't swarming to capture him.

But beneath this sudden paranoid terror, a boyish satisfaction leapt up inside him.

"Maybe *now* I'll get my just due!"

He laughed...quietly.

He flew toward the spot where the light shone. He maneuvered from above the disk's plane and saw that it indicated an asteroid.

Most of the accretion disk was composed of only dust and pebbles, but a number of island-sized objects, and even a planetary core or two, moved through the gossamer strands.

When he analyzed the asteroid's parameters, he saw that the density was lower than expected for its rocky nickel-iron make-up. He concluded, "It must have caves."

He jumped from the sound of his own voice. He was that on-edge.

But the chunk of debris did not appear porous—not like, for example, Hyperion, the spongy moon of Saturn. It showed the same battered-potato look of most asteroids, hard with rock and cratered regolith.

He was baffled.

Then he found an entrance into the interior that seemed too convenient to be normal.

It was large enough for him to park his ship inside, almost a cave but more an overhang. And from the chamber's far end, he could see a tunnel leading into the rock wall, big enough for him to walk through in a spacesuit.

"This can't be for real."

Ranglen normally didn't talk to himself—another indication of how much he was agitated. He had a feeling he was facing *destiny*.

He didn't like it.

With powered lights and a 3-D map-maker running on his cellpad, he gingerly entered the mountain-sized orb.

More astonishment. The caves were artificial.

He proceeded on, if nearly horrified.

The chambers were lined with tall trapezoidal frames of a smooth plaster-like material that buttressed and shaped the tunnels. The floors were surfaced with the same substance that thus provided walking pathways—in some places he even found steps, spaced for creatures the same size as humans.

He had no explanation for these tunnels. He first even wondered if some odd outer-space structure had wandered close to the embryo star and become encrusted with the nebula's remains, the rock built up around the linear chambers. But all the passages were empty. No instrumentation could be found, no controls, no artifacts— no plan, no reason. Once mapped, the nest of tunnels formed no recognizable shape.

But Ranglen was certain they meant something.

He knew they'd be destroyed eventually, buried inside the accumulating worldlets that would gather and sort themselves into bigger planets. The caves would be crushed from the hot pressure and weight around them.

But if the shard indicated *this* asteroid, then the Airafane meant that something was here. Ranglen trusted them. All signs argued that the ancient race faced their destruction at the hands of the Moyocks soberly and thoughtfully, that they had no time or inclination to play. Somehow this discovery was part of their plan.

He drifted along, in free graceful long strides from the micro-gravity.

Then he saw something on the floor, a small angular object that at first he passed over.

He came to a stop, slowly returned.

It was an octahedron of yellowish-purple crystal, two-to-three centimeters wide. It could easily fit in the palm of his hand.

Any member of current human civilization would know what it was. The container for an Airafane Clip! The most prized—and sought after—object in the galaxy.

Mykol Ranglen had now found two of them. He could not be so impossibly lucky.

And he knew he wasn't. The gleam that had showed up in the shard had *led* him here, and thus to the Clip.

Blood rushed to his head. His vision blurred. His spacesuit warned him about the racing of his heart, which he could hear beating frantically.

Of all the Clips discovered, he had found the third and now a fourth. But—and far more important—he had uncovered a means for *finding* Clips.

He was sole owner of the most valuable secret in the human universe.

He decided first not to reveal the discovery.

It was too big. Maybe in time, but not until after more history passed, to make sure civilization could handle the changes the first three Clips had wrought. Maybe on his deathbed—and he meant this seriously. He pictured himself reaching up with a dying hand and croaking to a doctor, "Wait, before I go, I have a small gift for intelligent life-forms everywhere. Please use it well…and, please, don't destroy yourselves."

Even if he waited till then, he still wasn't sure he could bear the responsibility.

As for the Clip, he decided he might wait a while on that too. When he finally did hand it over, he'd insist on strict anonymity. People wouldn't be happy with any one person finding two Clips. They wouldn't believe such an event was accidental. And the various governments would trust him least.

So he chose to wait. He didn't need the money, and notoriety he desired even less.

Besides, he could investigate the Clip *on his own*, find out what it did *by himself.*

This idea attracted him. Each Clip contained a different technological breakthrough. What would this one provide?

But—and here's where his worrying, hesitation and doubt, already extreme, intensified more—all the other Clips had been buried in the mantles of developed planets, and thus hidden away for millions of years until they were exposed by volcanism or erosion. But *this* one lay in plain sight. True, it eventually would have been hidden inside an evolving world, but it could not return to the planet's surface through seafloor spreading the way other Clips did. It would be too deeply buried for that.

Why was this Clip different?

There were only three others for comparison, but still—this Clip had its own separate story. Was it misplaced? Dropped? Forgotten? Discarded?

Clips were far too important to be lost. And the Airafane showed no sign of neglect—quite the opposite. Their plans worked for millions of years.

"Then maybe it was *purposely* left here."

For an awful moment, he thought he might be sick in his spacesuit.

It made no sense. Inside this asteroid the Clip would be destroyed or hidden forever—even with its stasis field it would become inaccessible, locked inside the planetary core. If it were meant to be destroyed, throwing it into a sun would be easier and more final. Even if it survived and was spewed forth again by a solar convection cell or flare, no one would be close enough to the star to retrieve it.

But his finding it, given the Airafane's usually simple logic, suggested it was *meant* to be found, and easily.

He closed his padded hand into a fist, clutched the crystal. "Whatever you are, you're mine for now—nobody's else's!"

This made him feel satisfied, but only momentarily. The object's difference still troubled him deeply.

He returned to his ship. He cycled through the airlock and placed the octahedron on a table—the ship had its own gravity kept at Earth standard (gravity control was a result of the second Clip).

He removed his helmet. He slowly stepped out of his spacesuit, prolonging the time before making a decision. Finally, calmly, he sat and stared at the octahedron before him.

He studied it for a long time.

"Okay, Mykol," he finally said, his voice sounding to him like someone else's. "Just what the hell will you do with this thing?"

To understand the rest of this story, it's necessary to know a bit more about Ranglen.

He lived alone. He had no family, no ties to his past. He felt separate from most people, from civilization in general, from its goals that he saw as too determined by specialized interests, by a drive for power or narrow-minded greed. He believed in human institutions but felt they were flawed from the start. Media was too selective, science too reductive (especially the soft sciences—for him, any view of social reality had to be as complex as reality itself), and education too much a form of class stratification based on proprietary powers of analysis and eventually money.

Though he related to people well enough he didn't see himself as "fitting in." What he enjoyed most was traveling to distant planets and exploring them on his own, and then writing about them. He was more himself and most happy in an *alien* landscape, more "at home" when most away. This contradiction both pleased and disturbed him. He dreamed of having a partner/lover he could travel with, who wanted the same life-style he did, but he was never successful in finding one and now he didn't believe it possible—he realized he wanted only a copy of himself, which was hardly inclusive or generous.

He was still young but already jaded, too disappointed with his civilization while feeling at fault for not being suitable for it. He saw himself with irony but not enough self-liberating humor to free himself *from* himself. He looked outward more than inward, wanting to bury his personal doubts in vast sublime planetary vistas.

Still, he knew he'd eventually give the Clip to the "proper authorities" and let them take charge. Though he didn't always trust those authorities, he did believe in the Airafane at least, who he felt must have been very conscientious and logical, a true mix of Roman engineering and Greek philosophy. When pushed into a corner, he'd admit he believed in humanity too. "What else have we got?" he often said. So it seemed pointless to be too critical of it. The Clips so far had been grandly advantageous for progress and growth, and though some people saw megalomaniacal schemes behind them, Ranglen never went that far.

And, finally, he believed in self-sacrifice, in giving back, even for those like himself who were isolated and unattached. He simply felt that most people didn't have much chance to do anything that demanded such heroism. But if the situation arose, and if the participants had a little time at least to *think* about their choices, then good decisions would generally be made.

For all his gripes and desire to "get away," he believed in people.

So maybe it wasn't just personal satisfaction, selfishness, or his anger at being excluded from planning for Annulus, that made him do what he did. Since this Clip was different, maybe it was *best* that only one person examine it, just in case something truly was wrong with it.

But then, he remembered, once his finding and deception were known, he could be imprisoned and maybe even killed.

"But I discovered it," he said aloud. "It's *my* responsibility. I should be first to see if it's dangerous."

Or was this only a damn-you attitude too intoxicating to resist? Maybe he just wanted to touch the mysteries of the cosmos *himself,* with no intermediary or protecting guard.

All this debate and counter-reasoning was not unusual for him. As said, he didn't like simplifications. He could feel—all at once—self-justification, curiosity, vengeance, and the simple longing for adventure before the established experts, or bullies, moved in.

He knew he *would* turn it over.

In time.

He had to decide quickly, before the courage *to* decide failed him.

"Debate's forever! Action is now!"

He grabbed the crystal, twisted it in his hands but failed to open it. So he got a vise, a small wedge and a big hammer and broke it open. His methods were crude. But the object within was near indestructible even without its stasis field, which apparently already had ceased. Maybe it never had needed one in the first place.

The well-recognized, tiny, gray, rectangular wafer sat inside.

A Clip.

The fourth Clip.

He placed it gently in his left palm.

Clips needed an energy source to do their work. But since energy was equivalent to mass, placing the Clip against any material, if rich enough with heavy elements, would provide the necessary resource.

Ranglen didn't use anything in his ship. He could have left the Clip on his table and let the table itself be consumed. But he didn't know how much substance would be needed as the nanotechnology went to work, a technology used by the three other Clips. He couldn't have large parts of his spaceship suddenly transformed, though he was sure that features built into the Clips prevented such catastrophes.

Still, better to be safe.

He found a metal shipping carton with flat sides. Then he donned his spacesuit again—annoyed now that he took the time earlier to discard it—and carried the carton and the Clip through the airlock. He placed the box on a relatively flat part of the asteroid floor near the entrance to the cave, flush to the ground in case the Clip needed more material than the carton could provide. It then could probe down into the asteroid itself. The Clip might consume the whole moon, but that would take time and Ranglen would be able to leave in his spaceship before that happened.

The rectangular Clip, a centimeter wide, three centimeters long, and four millimeters thick (the size and shape of a small stick of chewing gum) he placed face-up on the carton. Clips were slightly different on either side and the face with the greater number of marks was traditionally called the "top."

Then he waited.

After a week, he noticed that the Clip had bonded to the carton, and the carton itself had bonded to the rock floor beneath it. He couldn't move either of them.

He became excited, almost frantic.

After another week, he saw a roughly rectangular mound growing beneath the Clip, swelling upward from the top of the surface of the carton. It was larger than the Clip itself, maybe as big as an eye-glass case.

More weeks passed. The shape became detailed with tiny perforations and unknown instruments.

During all this time, Ranglen felt intense expectation, frayed nerves, and tightly-wired terror. He regularly monitored his blood pressure, heart rate, body temperature, pulse oximetry, respiratory rate. He didn't bother with cholesterol or glucose levels though he thought he maybe should. He didn't want to examine himself too closely. He was afraid of what he'd discover—he often believed he was going out of his mind.

Scared of other people finding him, he wanted to take the Clip away in his spaceship, far outside the planetary disk—into the dark between the stars. But then he worried he'd be *too* alone with it. What if something happened? He assumed the area around the asteroid, though not so dense with accretion debris that it was overly dangerous, was still thick enough to make difficult any random surveillance by scanning probes, radar beams, infrared detectors in search of energy footprints. But he couldn't be sure.

He checked often for any other visitors. He set up alarms that would go off when anything larger than a matchbox approached (it could be a spy drone). But since so much clutter drifted out there, these alarms went off constantly—driving him crazy.

He often checked the Clip for changes since he couldn't concentrate on anything else. In all this free writing time he got little work done. Even routine maintenance on his ship became difficult. He was exhausted from lack of sleep and food. Then he'd suddenly indulge in binge eating followed by nausea, or falling asleep on chairs or floors and waking up in agonized back-breaking pain.

Endless speculation—and bad dreams—wore him out. What if this Clip was programmed to invade the sun and make it go supernova, to inform distant stars that a civilization was ready for invasion? (The sun was too small for that, but it didn't stop him from worrying.) What if the galaxy needed signal lights, and blowing up solar systems would provide that nicely? What if the Clip carried ancient viruses that were so malicious they'd contaminate a whole cluster of stars?

He regretted his choice to do this alone. No wonder there were laws against keeping a Clip.

Then, finally, something changed.

A flat glowing square of light hung vertically in the empty space above the Clip, like a projection image in two dimensions. On it appeared diagrams and figures. It had no substance—you could wave your hand through it—but the flat screen glowed as if tangible.

Ranglen was almost too agitated to look closely at it. He forced himself to.

It showed a series of lines, curves, circles. An overhead diagram of maybe a set of rooms.

He recognized it immediately. A plan for the Airafane stonework "ruins" scattered on different Earth-like planets. They were the same on each world, so instantly identifiable.

A tiny light blinked inside a circle in a particular room. And, near it, a small rectangular icon moved back and forth, in and out of a wall. Ranglen recognized the circle as a "kiva." He also knew the rectangular icon. It represented a Clip.

"Okay, well, that was easy." But he shivered as he said this.

The instructions were amazingly understandable. Take the Clip to one of the Airafane stoneworks, on any world since no special planet was indicated (which perhaps explained why the ruins were all similar). In the designated room, insert it or place it at the spot on the wall specified by the Clip icon.

And then what?

Would something appear inside the kiva? A star-destroying weapon? The secret of force-fields? A treatment for cancer? Immortality?

All this was suddenly too traumatic for Ranglen. After he was certain the screen wouldn't change, he re-entered his spaceship, removed the smelly EVA suit and his grungy unwashed clothes, and lay on his bed to relax. He immediately fell asleep and didn't wake for twelve hours.

Then he showered, made himself an enormous meal, and managed to eat every bit of it.

Restored now, he returned to the Clip.

The image had changed.

The screen was now globular, larger, and it showed a three-dimensional star-map. Ranglen brought up similar charts on his cellpad and identified the stars. They all lay within the nearby stellar neighborhood in a globe 120 light-years across. Some of them had small glowing spots beside them that blinked.

Again, he was impressed with how clear the Airafane explanations could be. They used only visual symbols but the programs "taught" as much as they displayed.

The ease of getting the Clips to work was another reason why laws required they be given to officials.

Some of these stars Ranglen knew had worlds with Airafane ruins. So the image presumably was a map of all their nearby locations, several of which were still undiscovered. By opening the Clip on his own, Ranglen had gained knowledge of all these sites.

That alone made the find incredible.

He tried to move the projector-machine and discovered it was free of the carton below, so the need for the metal now must be over. The carton too was freed from the rock. He took the Airafane device inside—he was tired of getting in and out of his spacesuit.

Poised at the center of the map was the new star around which Annulus was being built. The projector thus read the Clip's location.

Ranglen looked for the site of the nearest ruins. He wanted to fly there as quickly as possible.

The nearest star with a blinking light was Homeworld's sun.

But he didn't know of any ruins on Homeworld.

He wondered if touching the star in the map would cause that area to grow larger.

He stuck in his finger. The screen zoomed in, and the planetary system of Homeworld's star appeared. The magnification stopped at a new level where Ranglen could see the inner planets.

The light blinked on Homeworld.

He wasn't surprised that no one had discovered ruins there yet. Though the planet was colonized decades ago and had a burgeoning independent culture, settlement was not widespread. The terrain of the planet was still unexplored though well mapped from satellite coverage. But since Airafane ruins didn't show up on satellite scans, you had to "be there" to discover them.

The Homeworld image showed continental outlines that were accurate today. Yet the Airafane were long extinct. How did the information in the Clips update to present time? They surely had no knowledge of the future, but there it was.

The machines *did* work miracles.

Still, the picture was accurate only in its geological and oceanographic configuration. There was no sign of plant-life, meteorology, or, more significant, human habitation.

This was crucial information. Could the Airafane technology read the future of continental drift and geological change, but not the presence of intelligent life?

Or, he wondered, maybe it just *chose* not to. You wouldn't want to indicate what you *can't* do by only showing what you *can*.

He touched the image again. The zoom brought him to a spot in what he knew was the Great South Desert.

Ranglen planned.

The next time he touched the chart, the images went back to their original positions. He could make the picture zoom in on any planet with a blinking light just by touching the screen. But the details on those other worlds were not as strong as they were for Homeworld. Was that an indicator that he should go only there instead of anyplace else?

Eventually, after he didn't interact with the map for a while, the image was replaced by the original diagram of the rooms, and these two pictures alternated, back and forth, every 23.47 seconds.

During the 2-day, 3-hour, 47-minute and 7.85-second duration of the "passage" in light-space (he refused to think about the coincidental alignment of numbers), Ranglen, on his spaceship, paced relentlessly back and forth, from the bridge past the cabins to the storerooms and engine room of the after section, then back to the bridge. His inability to eat and sleep returned.

By taking the Clip to its designated site, he'd move to a higher level of illegality.

Keeping the Clip was obviously bad. Opening the crystal was very bad. Operating the Clip to get information from it was *really* bad. But *acting* on that information was indescribably and horrendously bad.

He still could forget all of this, even try to put the crystal together again and convince the authorities he had nothing to do with opening it. He felt a nagging insufferable dread he was entering a trap, being set up to unleash the Apocalypse.

His paranoia was out of control. He wondered if the authorities feared this too when working on Clips. So far all the results of the Airafane devices were benevolent technological gifts. They became history-changers and de-railers of progress, but they still were helpful for civilization.

So far, anyway. Maybe everyone was on the road to destruction already and they just didn't know it.

He reached Homeworld.

He landed at a spaceport and rented an aircar that he filled with supplies. He flew into the Great South Desert. He found a sea of orange dunes under a pink sky, huge mesas of multicolored rock.

He first established a cache kilometers away from where the Clip indicated the ruins. The scale of the map in the Clip projection had become larger as he neared the planet, conveniently highlighting his goal.

He then proceeded in his aircar. He arrived at a ravine that apparently led to where the ruins were located. He emerged from his vehicle feeling tense but resolved, wary with the destination so close.

He saw no trace of anyone else.

As he walked forward, the sands kicked up wisps around him. They made a hiss as the grains rubbed against each other. He admired the exuberant colors of the strata that formed the cliffs. He liked the place. He could easily spend much time here.

He knew he was trying to distract himself.

Then, suddenly, the ruins lay before him, as extravagantly tinted as the surrounding rocks. He stopped to appreciate them but again he knew he was just delaying, postponing the inevitable that was now so close he could never resist it. He looked around again for signs of visitation but still saw nothing.

He entered the complex. Based on the known floor-plan of every set of ruins on every world where they were found, he reached the room the Clip indicated.

It had no features that made it different from other rooms. The kiva was empty, the ground inside it flat and uninteresting.

He chose an area of the wall that appeared smooth enough. The surface was no different from any other part of the structure.

He took the projection machine from his flap-covered pocket and lifted the Clip out of it. They were not bonded now. He held it flat against the stone.

The Clip adhered. He could feel it tighten against the rock, as if magnetic. He removed his hand and the Clip remained there. Presumably he could still pull it from the wall but some connection had been engaged.

He waited. Seconds passed. A full minute. Then an hour.

He had known this could take a while. He brought something to eat but he couldn't stomach it. If he had to wait into the evening, he'd stay in the ruins and try to sleep there, though he knew he'd be awake all night.

The Clip moved. One end flipped up 90 degrees. Then half of the Clip slid into an opening that appeared in the stone. He was sure such an opening had not been there before.

The glowing star map appeared in the air, this time apparently projected from the end of the Clip itself. He didn't need the other little machine anymore. The chart showed the same stars, but *lines* had been added now that connected those stars which had ruin-sites on worlds revolving around them. At the center of the field was not the star with Annulus but Homeworld's sun, shining brighter than the other suns, and all the lines connected to it.

The Clip obviously could read its own spatial coordinates, and in current time.

"Okay, but what the hell are you trying to show me?"

What did the network of lines running between the stoneworks on different worlds represent? Communication? Transport?

Randomly, he touched one of the spokes that led to another star.

The spoke brightened.

Pale bluish light filled the room in which he stood. It came from a wide glowing column that appeared behind him inside the kiva, filling outward to its edge.

The cylinder of soft blue light was tinted slightly violet around its edges. It perfectly defined the circle of the kiva and seemed to emerge from it. The glow rose into the air about two-and-a-half meters and then quickly faded. Since there was no ceiling, and the pink sky was still bright, the glow was barely visible, and yet it stood out against the warm brown of the floor and the multi-colored wall behind it.

No Airafane ruin had ever shown life of any kind. This was unprecedented!

"I shouldn't have done this."

Ranglen felt the responsibility too great, the tension too high, the fear too personal. Then an idea struck him.

He glanced at the star-chart where the line between Homeworld's sun and the other star still glowed. He could tell from the scale it was beyond the reach of current human exploration, the second sun being close to the edge of the map.

He picked up a rock the size of his hand. He threw it into the glowing blue column.

It landed in the middle of the kiva, kicked up dust, sat there.

Nothing happened.

He looked at the Clip, still buried half-way into the wall.

Then a wild inspiration struck him.

He pulled out the Clip. The column of light vanished. Yet the opening in the wall remained.

Then he *turned the Clip over* to its "bottom" side, and re-inserted it.

The blue light returned. And, after a few seconds of waiting, a flare of white light appeared around the stone.

The rock vanished.

His heart almost stopped.

He examined the star-chart. The sun at the end of the line he had touched glowed more brightly now, though briefly, and the line itself faded to the same intensity as the others.

He knew the secret of the fourth Clip!

Teleportation.

He didn't move for a long time.

"No, it's more than that," he finally said. And he added, very softly, just in case anyone was listening…

"It's escape."

Chapter 7: Doorway to Elsewhere

"Hello? Anne?"

Anne Montgomery was an ex-lover and sometime friend living on Homeworld. Motivated by big dreams, she was currently finishing a Master's degree in Alien Materials Procurement and Finance. The relationship between her and Ranglen had been intense but rocky, and it had come to a deafening severing conclusion. It left both of them frustrated but not enough to start again.

A typical Ranglen relationship.

"My, my," she said over his cellpad in sardonic surprise. "It's the great wanderer. How have you been?"

Ranglen hadn't spoken to her for a year, and he couldn't remember if the talk had ended in anger or not. "I'm taking a long trip. I might be gone for some time…a *long* time." He waited for a response.

None came.

"I'm serious," he added.

She made a sound he assumed was a laugh. "So what do you want from me?"

He wasn't sure. He couldn't discuss his decision. Perhaps he just wanted to prove he was still connected to people, even though he was about to leave them. "Maybe just advice. I'm not certain. Do you think what I'm about to do is wise?"

She sighed loudly. "Why do you ask something I know nothing about? This is so typical of you, Mykol. You say nothing for months, I don't hear from you at all, and then you expect immediate close conversation. Even answers to your personal problems. How can I respond when I can't learn anything from you?"

He felt foolish. He remembered he seldom trusted her. She hoped to develop an import business after graduation and she always pumped him for contacts and leads. She once even asked him to invest in her company and become her partner—the *last* thing he wanted, having no business inclination at all and not needing to complicate their relationship more. It made him suspicious of her, feeling their friendship was based

68

on just her attempt to use his experience for commercial gain. He once even accused her of being interested in him for only finance and sex. That didn't go over well.

All these recollections embarrassed him now.

"It would take too long to explain. And I'm not sure where I'm going."

"Then what's the point of your call?"

His reticence was ruining the conversation. He wasn't happy he didn't trust Anne—he really did like her—but the stakes were too high.

"Look," she said. "I know you've never appreciated me digging for information from you, but it's hard for me to help if you give me nothing in return."

"I'm not calling for help. I just…"

"But you're calling for *something*. So, let me speculate.…You're going away. But you do that often, even though you're not the committed loner you like to think you are. You still want to feel needed. Why else did we have a relationship in the first place? You don't like to admit this compromise of your 'gypsy purity,' as you once called it. Yet, at a time like this, you still hope someone will say to you, 'Oh *please*, Mykol, *don't go!* I'll miss you *terribly!*' Because that would make you feel wanted, and thus more human."

He admitted nothing. Yet he found himself agreeing.

"And then—to show how twisted all this is—you ask for such a response from *me*. But I'm the wrong person. And you *know* this. If I said anything like that, which I never would, you'd just reply with, 'Aww, gee, Anne. That's so nice. But, well, you know, I'm sorry, I *have* to leave and be on my way. Thanks so much! It's been great knowing you. But the universe calls me and I must respond.' Or something equally dramatic and stupid."

He had nothing to say. She was probably right.

"Seriously, Mykol, I'm the last person who would say how much I needed you. Because I *don't* need you. You argued that same point long ago, and forcefully, the time you left me."

He cleared his throat. "From what I recall, we left each other. And weren't you the first to raise the idea?"

"You raised it too."

"You said it before I did."

"It doesn't matter! You still don't come to me until something scares you, like this trip. And then you remember, much to your surprise—when it should be no surprise at all—'I'm no better than anyone else. What a shock. I *too* need people.' But, Mykol, you *don't* need anyone. You never have. This is all crap."

He wondered then what he did expect from her. Their conversations usually provided only more reasons for dissatisfaction. She understood him too well, and she was always accurate and much too blunt. "Okay, Anne. I'm sorry. You're probably right. But I appreciate you listening."

A pause. Big silence.

She asked, now with a trace of sympathy, "Did you get what you needed?"

"I think so. Honestly. I did just want someone to listen. Everything's all right."

"Look, if you want to see me, you can stop over. But tomorrow, okay? It's a bit late now."

He hadn't realized the time was nearly midnight. What an idiot! But she had sounded awake when she answered. "I'm fine. It's okay."

"And, just for the record, know that I *will* miss you. I always miss you when you're away. You bring out the honesty in me, and not many people do that. It makes you special."

"I'm not sure that's a compliment."

"Take from it what you will. I'm just saying the truth."

Another silence.

"Well," he said, "I thank you. I'll miss you too. You know I don't talk like this to many people. We *do* have a connection. It's just gets a bit garbled at times."

"I agree." Her sarcasm weakened. "As always, if you encounter something that can be marketed, let me know."

"I'll call again before leaving."

"Fine. But I need to get some sleep now. Have a pleasant night."

"I do believe we had good times together. I want you to know that."

"I love you too, Mykol. Does that help?"

"It always helps."

Another small silence. She said, "Be careful now."

"And take care of *your*self. I love you too."

She seemed pensive for a moment. "In terms of this trip, you're aware, aren't you, that you compensate for too much self-control by being suddenly too impulsive?"

"Sure, I know that."

"Just wanted to be certain. Good night, then."

End of conversation.

Well, he tried. And except for her last ominous lines, he did feel better. He and Anne were not made for each other but that was exactly what brought them together. The attraction was always strange and irregular, and neither of them compromised.

But just for a minute there—for longer than a minute—he felt the old desire again. He doubted he'd call her before he left.

So she thought he was overly impulsive, eh? That wouldn't hold him back. He'd still be the first to use teleportation.

Then he called Hatch Banner, who worked at a spaceship yard and from whom Ranglen got all his interstellar transport needs. Hatch was more paranoid than Ranglen and his stubbornness more difficult to deal with than Anne's. But their shared memories of youth—the two men knew each other as children—sustained them through mutual troubles.

A sour voice grunted, "Yeah?" Hatch could be terse one minute but then endlessly talkative the next.

"Did I wake you?"

"Almost. I was in bed but hadn't fallen asleep yet."

"I'm thinking of a long trip away from Homeworld."

"You need a new spaceship? Let me know what you want and I'll get everything installed."

Hatch was good when it came to spaceships. Ranglen believed he would run his own dockyard and spaceport some day. "No, the last one you got me is fine."

"What else do you need? I'm half asleep here so keep me awake."

Ranglen felt trapped again, unable to describe what he was doing. And Hatch was an Airafane conspiracy theorist. He blamed *everything* on Clips. So whatever Ranglen said, no matter how disguised, would be construed in terms of them anyway. Hatch couldn't forgive people for their obsession with the alien technology—he was furious that a friend of his (Ranglen) had found one. But at the same time, and Ranglen often hounded him about this, Hatch fervently used the benefits of what the Clips provided. All the spaceships he outfitted contained the Airafane FTL and anti-gravity drives. Hatch claimed he only exploited the foolishness of people, but Ranglen knew better. Hatch worshipped Airafane know-how, even when he claimed humanity was being "set up" by it.

Since teleportation would be more liberating than FTL, Ranglen felt guilty. Hatch's spaceships might become obsolete.

But the new technology would make a better legacy for Ranglen than even Annulus. Maybe they'd call it the "Ranglen drive."

"You're never so quiet for this long, Mykol. What's on your mind?"

"I don't need supplies or a new spaceship. I just wanted to let you know I'll be leaving soon. I'll set up a way for you to be contacted if I'm gone too long."

"For god's sake, Mykol, you're such a deserter to the human race."

The line shocked Ranglen, but he reminded himself what Hatch was like. "What do you mean?"

"You've got a scheme going, which is obvious. It's probably another damned Clip. But if you find one more I'm making you swallow it."

"One's enough. I'm not searching for any. But what did you mean by 'deserter'?"

"You're running off on your own, right? You love to do that."

"To a certain extent. But why are you criticizing it? You always said you'd like to do the same."

"Maybe it's because I'm tired and can't sleep. I'm trying to set up a spaceport on Annulus and they're giving me trouble. So I'm not very glad you're running off. Annulus is supposedly *your* world, right? And look what they've done to it. Regulations have cropped up everywhere."

"It never was my world. And you know it makes me angry when you imply that it was."

"It's not my world either. That's the point."

Ranglen had told Hatch of his failed attempts to gain more control over the habitat's future. Hatch reminding him of it was typical, but his comments seemed more barbed than usual. "You know I can't do anything."

"Forget it. Get to the point. You only call me when you need something."

Ranglen sighed. Not only were these calls more difficult than he expected but they now annoyed him—almost reminding him of why he wanted to leave in the first place. He said, keeping the topic vague, "I'm just traveling further than usual. Frankly, I'm a little worried I might not come back."

Hatch, surprisingly, cut to the core of Ranglen's need. "Well, if that's the case, then know that I'll miss you."

"Why...thank you."

"But I'm still certain it involves Clips."

Ranglen groaned but said nothing—which to Hatch, he realized, would be a giveaway.

"And you said you might not be returning?" Hatch said.

"A possibility. I'll get in touch with you when, or if, I do come back."

"Remember, Mykol, Clips weren't made by humans."

"I know that."

"You might not understand what you're setting yourself up for."

Ranglen grew impatient. "Not tonight, Hatch. No conspiracy theories. I just wanted to say good-bye…for now."

"You still need to listen to me."

"I have to go. Take care of yourself."

"*I* can take care, but can you? Look, did you ever wonder whether other Clips were already found, but the finders never told anyone about them? They just kept them to themselves. Maybe they didn't mean to hold on to them, but just for a *while*, so they could dabble in what they discovered, play a little, one-up the authorities. Maybe even see what the Clip has to offer, all on their own, to take advantage of the lucky moment. And we never hear about this happening because they didn't *survive* the experience. We've all heard rumors that governments and corporations have kept Clips secret and exploited them. But what about individuals? Maybe they've indulged themselves too and were sucked away, consumed, 'disappeared'? Maybe they're even still alive, trapped somewhere, helpless, regretful. Or maybe they're just dead."

He voiced Ranglen's exact fears.

But Ranglen stayed calm. He responded with the same argument he gave himself. "I trust the Airafane. They knew the Moyocks would defeat them. The Clips are their heritage, their means of preserving their knowledge. The Clips are gifts, not plots against all future people."

"We don't know what 'people' meant for them, nor what 'heritage' meant, or even 'gifts.' They weren't what *we* are."

Ranglen had no answer.

"So wherever you're going, make sure you can come back."

"I will."

"Good luck, then."

"You're mighty philosophical tonight."

"I'm just pissed. And—one more piece of advice—don't become an alien yourself."

"What's wrong with that?"

"You once said I sometimes act as if I'm the last human alive. I agree with that view. And I don't want to be lonely."

"Gee, Hatch, that's almost touching."

"Not really. Good night, my friend." He broke the connection.

Ranglen signed off and commanded his cellpad to block all calls. From now on he'd trust no one.

He was disturbed by Hatch's comments and yet grateful to him. Same with Anne.

73

He realized then that he hadn't called them in order for them to question his decision, but to reinforce it.

When you have to make a rough choice, you push yourself to where the decision is made *for* you, by outside forces you yourself put into motion.

Thus we manipulate even ourselves.

Things got serious now. He had reached this point through childish curiosity, but play-time was over.

He wrote access-locked instructions to his banker, accountant, and lawyer on what was to be done if he didn't return. His ties with them were strictly formal and he left little room for interpretation. Who knew how long he'd be away or how many worlds he'd see?

He wrote brief statements to both Anne and Hatch that would not be sent for years.

Obsessed with preparation, he assembled "necessities" to take with him: clothes for different weather conditions, waterproof rain gear, lined winter outfits, long-lasting power sources, a small and lightweight shelter, concentrated food, purifier tablets, water, heating and cooling devices, headlamps and flashlights (with red lens covers for investigations at night), spare batteries and spare bulbs, a multi-purpose Swiss Army knife, heavy cord, rope, climbing equipment, a compass and altimeter (if they worked), his cellpad (which largely would be useless with no broadcast networks but its storage unit and processor would run the mapping programs—and it held a lot of books), a light polymer double-action striker pistol (a plasma-laser gun was in production but not perfected yet), extra cartridges, a multi-purpose laser device that could be used as a weapon, sunglasses that filtered UV (with side shields), a lot of sunscreen, lip-balm, a first-aid kit, fire starters (plus matches, with sandpaper on which to strike them), a repair kit, insect repellent (if it worked), an ice ax, a small shovel, signaling devices (but, he thought, who would he signal?), a portable oxygen unit (but since several of the worlds on the star chart he knew had breathable atmospheres, he assumed the other planets would have them too—from what scientists could tell, the Airafane breathed a similar type of terrestrial mix, so he felt reassured, and he could teleport away instantly if the air was deadly).

As he reviewed all this over-preparation he felt he should be laughing, but he didn't even smile.

He wanted to take more.

A spacesuit was too much to carry. It might be a dangerous lack but he had to show trust. He did take a small oxygen tank, breathing equipment and gas masks.

He packed all this into a large cylindrical bag that he'd leave in the ruins when he arrived, and a manageable backpack he'd keep with him always. If the planet turned out to be worthy of longer exploration, he'd expand the backpack and take some of the other materials with him (like the tent).

None of these supplies would last forever. They were just to allow him to get away from his arrival spot for maybe a few days, to investigate before moving on to another planet or returning home.

But he believed he'd encounter sustainable resources. Deep down, he felt—hoped, maybe prayed—he might never return.

He wouldn't look ahead and he wouldn't look back. He'd keep his past sufficiently vague so he couldn't long for it. Nomads need running states of mind. They might own houses but they don't like to live in them.

He placed an old worn notebook into his jacket pocket. He used it for quickly jotted poems. A quaint occupation, nothing serious.

He left for the ruins earlier than expected—to maintain his resolve.

He arrived in the desert late in the afternoon. A storm crossed it, tornadoes moving like dancing snakes before a plodding beast. It moved at right angles to his direction, passed by, was soon not a threat.

He landed at the top of the canyon and unloaded his packs. He fought the impulse to jump into the ruins and leave at that moment, but he wanted to make sure all was prepared, his aircar hidden and sufficiently camouflaged, his supplies well-stored in their two heavy bundles.

Then, after night fell, he lay on the fold-down couch in his vehicle and tried to sleep. He intended to depart, refreshed and ready, early in the morning.

But sleeping was impossible. Like the astronauts who first landed on the moon and found resting prior to their "one small step" to be absurd. After an hour of tossing, he got up.

He ate from the best and most perishable rations he brought with him. He smiled uneasily at the "last supper" mood.

Homeworld's sun finally rose behind the canyon walls, its gold beams shining warmly from a green sky turning pink.

It would be a lovely day.

He washed his utensils and placed them away, still keeping things neat. "Why am I doing this?" He took the keys to the aircar with him—he'd need them when he returned. He donned his pack and hefted his bag.

Finally—he had avoided looking in this direction all morning—he walked up to the ruins, entered them and found the room that now had become so significant.

With a deep breath, he attached the fourth Clip to the spot in the wall where he had held it before.

It adhered, swiveled, slid halfway in, more quickly now than it did the last time. The star chart appeared.

He touched the gleam where he apparently had sent the rock. It was an arbitrary choice. His only preference was to go beyond human exploration.

The line between Homeworld and the other planet glowed brighter. The blue column took form in the kiva.

"Okay," he said to only himself. "A trip of a thousand light-years starts with the simple flipping of a switch."

He donned his oxygen mask and started the pump, just to be safe. (He almost giggled at the thought of "safety.") Then he pulled the Clip from the wall, turned it over and re-inserted it. The column appeared a second time, charged and ready.

He pulled the Clip from the wall. He assumed he would need it for the return. He believed there'd be another set of ruins at the other end of the line.

The column would stay present, glowing and inviting, for just over eighteen seconds after pulling out the Clip. He learned this from repeated experiments. And once an object was placed in the kiva, it would not disappear in its plume of light for six seconds. In both cases, a slight waiting time was allowed, a fail-safe period for corrections or remade decisions.

He didn't dare think of remaking any decisions.

He put the Clip into a sealed pocket of his shirt.

He walked to the kiva and dropped his bag inside it. He stepped down to its earthen floor, still wearing his backpack.

The blue light surrounded him.

He was sealed off now, as if he had left the world already. But he still could see the room around him.

The remaining seconds lasted forever. An impulse flooded him to jump out and stay. But it was easier, at that point, to do nothing.

A burst of light.

The room disappeared.

Chapter 8: The Blight

He fell—

Struck growth on a cushioned slope and tumbled down a hill, his heavy bag rolling behind him.

He came to a stop with his face buried in bright red leaves.

He raised his head, saw an immense landscape before him. Broad, open, free of human life, like high-latitude boreal forest giving way to tundra and distant mountains. The air was chill but not unbearable.

Frightened birds rose up around him, cawing, squealing, with long rainbow plumes on their heads bobbing at him like whiplash antennae. They flew away in anger.

He stood up warily.

Thunder. A vibration in the ground.

He saw upslope a line of huge animals running straight at him—four-legged, green, as big as moose and as lean as elk, with large black shovel-like antlers that swung before them and looked perilous.

He fell to the ground.

Heavy hooves and hairy legs crashed by, kicking up dirt, branches, leaves. The animals swerved around him, never touched him and rumbled past.

They were gone in seconds, leaving dust-clouds and pellets of soil that rained down on him.

He wasn't physically hurt but his nerves were shattered.

He stood up again, more slowly now, looked around to make sure no other beasts were about to rush by or attack him. The creatures who stampeded gathered now beside a river at the bottom of the hill. They were almost sedate with heads bowed as they drank water. They didn't look harmless—they were too big and the antlers immense—but they weren't charging anymore and they seemed interested in only refreshment.

Dazed, trembling, feeling moderately safe, he tried to calm himself and look around.

The sloping field on which he stood was covered with leafy red growth and scattered yellow-green shrubs. Tall trees, conifers, as black-green as fir but more prickly, formed clumps and forests around him. The brightly colored hillside sloped down to the river where a sheaf of fog drifted above it, the water a pastel milky turquoise. The pale color of the caribou-like animals blended into the stream's tint. Beyond the river lay more woods and meadows, then distant snow-covered mountains. The sky above the craggy horizon glowed a slight Homeworld pink, but maybe just from morning light since the zenith brooded indigo-blue.

The clarity was Arctic, the colors distinct.

Now more accustomed to the place, Ranglen felt a call to a majestic freedom.

He checked the programs on his cellpad for this world's physical data. The planet was similar to Homeworld (and thus to Earth). Roughly the same gravitational attraction, a somewhat whiter G4 star, the atmosphere comparable though the CO_2 was less and the oxygen higher, surprising Ranglen given the open vegetation. No lethal pathogens or toxins could be found.

Bravely, or foolishly, he removed his mask and took a deep breath.

A cool woody odor struck him, like mahogany, laced with something sweet—vanilla?

He felt intoxicated, but from his own pleasure and not something in the air. It might have to do with the near-death experience he just survived, but he now seemed full of vigor and excitement.

And drawn into the distance, the grandeur, the immensity. He realized how much he had longed for this, how deeply the loss of Annulus affected him, how weighted he had been by the responsibility of being the only one aware of teleportation.

The cellpad read the magnetic field and Coriolis effects to give the location as high in latitude, so the boreal tree-line sense was accurate. He had visited similar locales on Earth. The sky here was darker, the sunlight sharper, the ground vegetation more dense, but the result was similar. A frosty glitter from snow in the shadows indicated the sun had just risen—like back on Homeworld. The brisk air made him glad for his warm clothes. The distant birds still cried, perhaps annoyed with him.

Nothing threatened now. The earlier stampede was not directed against him personally. The animals were just migrating to the river for their morning drink, and he happened to get in the way. He watched them use their antlers to throw water on themselves and each other, giants being playful.

But the world obviously was no park.

Up-slope he saw an arranged set of stones—the Airafane ruins, the same as on Homeworld but made of dark-grey rock, like the outcrops of strata around him. He had arrived near but not inside them, and one or two meters up in the air from where he fell and rolled downhill.

He picked up the items that had fallen from his bag and approached the ruins.

He saw tracks in the red growth, and small clumps of possible waste droppings, so other animals inhabited the area.

A coyote-like creature appeared before him from behind a shrub. It was as yellow-green as the leaves of the bush, and it stared at Ranglen with a close attention. The black-centered peridot eyes seemed overly curious and alert.

He and the animal pondered each other.

The creature's neck sported a useless lion-like mane. Ranglen wondered if it grew erect when the creature felt threatened.

The hair lay limply now, and the animal soon turned away and prowled off into the trees, not looking back.

Something about it nagged at Ranglen. It seemed too contemplative, evaluative.

He better make sure he could return to Homeworld.

He entered the ruins, their dark metamorphic rock glittering with mica and white veins of quartz. He reached the familiar room with its kiva. He looked about to be certain no one watched him, then pulled the Clip from his sealed pocket. He placed it on the wall and again it attached. Several minutes passed. The Clip lifted to a horizontal position and slid halfway into the rock.

The star chart appeared.

Ranglen sighed heavily in relief.

He found Homeworld's star and placed his finger on it. The line connecting Homeworld and his current planet brightened, and the blue column then glowed behind him. He pulled out the Clip, turned it over and re-inserted it. The column appeared again. He threw in a rock, and in a flash, it disappeared.

He had his way home. He felt much better.

He pocketed the Clip, waited for the column of light to vanish, then left the room and re-emerged into his newfound world.

A giant beast with tusks attacked him.

Enormous paws swung at his chest and knocked him to the ground. He turned his face aside to protect it while sickle talons struck at his coat. He kicked back, surprising the beast into retreating. Ranglen picked up a rock the weight of a brick and threw it at the creature's head, making it stagger. He took this chance to roll quickly, get up and run back into the ruins, then leap behind a wall and pull out his pistol.

The creature followed. The blunt snout with frightening tusks poked out around the edge of the wall—it saw him, howled. The mouth opened like a bottomless cavern and a horrible odor hit Ranglen in the face.

He fired his pistol into the mouth.

The animal lurched, almost fell. Ranglen fired again—again! The noise echoed throughout the ruins.

The animal toppled, struck the earth. It twitched and moaned and finally went still.

Ranglen choked and almost vomited, then stared at the beast.

It was a hideous combination of walrus and bear, the fur long, sleek, dark green, with a comic moustache over the mouth and ears like fluffy cotton muffs. But the paws hung heavy and ungainly, frightening even as it lay, edged with long scimitar talons that looked well used, cracked and stained. Its eyes, still open, shone milky like the river in the valley. From cataracts maybe, or disease? A wet froth rimmed the mouth, making the animal appear sickly, and its howl had been a staccato painful bark rather than a sustained roar. A white stripe ran down its face, outlandishly like a dog's.

Ranglen examined himself for wounds. He was sore from the blows but nothing was broken since his field coat had protected him. But a gash in the back of his right hand oozed blood.

He pulled from his pack a first-aid kit, spread disinfectant on the wound and clamped it shut, laboriously. He was right-handed so this wasn't easy. He then wrapped it in gauze and tape. He took antibiotics to fight off infection, doubting their efficiency as well as any real threat of contagion—alien chemistries were usually too different to be a problem.

The coyote returned, seemed to appear out of nowhere and made no sound. It was like a tiny lion with a narrow wedge-shaped head and thin legs. The polished gemstones of the yellow-green eyes mocked him. They looked vigilant and superior.

Ranglen said to it, "I liked your world but I'm not sure now."

The creature grinned—or rather, showed its teeth—and prowled away.

Ranglen felt it was too much like a visitation.

But such reactions were common on alien worlds. The mind forced its interpretations, gauged events through unreliable terrestrial impressions.

He sensed movement in the brush. Small rodent-like creatures with reptilian hides ran for the fallen walrus-bear and tore at the beast. Their efficient claws made them eager butchers.

Ranglen grabbed his bag with his left hand and withdrew into the forest. He wouldn't camp near a feeding frenzy. He could hear them chomping away behind him and the noise wasn't pleasant. He set up his tent deeper in the trees and stored his items inside. His hand was sore and he should relax it, for he knew it would be weak for several days.

Yet he moved in circles away from the camp, crossing the ankle-high red growth between the larger yellow-green shrubs. The caribou-like animals had left by now. He was certain the milky blue-green stain of the river came from glacial scour, scraped from the bottoms of ice-flows in the mountains and filtered into the streams. He had seen the phenomenon in cold mountain country. On the other side of the water, more forests and fields flowed to the peaks that walled off the distance, but he surmised that further north the trees would give way to complete tundra.

He loved the panorama as much for its familiarity as its alienness. It was like the northern latitudes of Earth, the plants and animals almost recognizable. It wasn't as different as what he hoped, perhaps, but the breadth, sweep, and grandeur of the land were immediately appealing.

He could stay here.

The sun started to dip. The planet must have a short day, or else he arrived early in winter. His instruments couldn't tell him about axial tilt.

He returned upslope to his camp. He'd stay overnight, explore tomorrow and for a few more days, see what he could see. Then he'd move on and seek another world, or maybe even stay here. Either prospect was satisfying.

As he passed the ruins, he heard more creatures digging into the carcass, birds now participating too. Some made squeals as they flew overhead and passed through the branches, reminding him of bats outside one of his childhood homes. Their echoes at night then had appealed to his longings, and he loved that he heard them again now—like a signal sent only to him.

He entered his tent and ate a prepackaged meal, looked at the trees around him. They dipped their needled limbs to the ground, adaptations for deep snowfalls—the flexible trunks would bend in the wind and the tilted boughs could shed snow. They suggested the winters here were rough.

In the west, the sun neared the horizon.

But instead of relaxing, Ranglen stared with restless yearning at the rocky crest of the hill behind him. It formed a ridge that stretched away in either direction, a stone escarpment that must overlook the area further east. A whole new vista might be seen from up there.

Though the sky darkened, the urge to walk to the ridge before he turned in grew strong. It wasn't wise leaving so late, but he justified it by claiming he needed a better understanding of the *entire* landscape to feel secure when he slept. He shouldn't leave half of it still hidden, he claimed.

He grabbed a hand-light and started out.

He followed a trail apparently made by animals up toward the ridge, which resembled a jawline of worn teeth. Rocks swelled up around him and made a formidable barrier, but he maneuvered a narrow saddle through it.

Just when he realized the sun was hitting the horizon behind him and that he might have started out too late, the ground leveled and he crossed the ridge. The boulders opened and a view spread before him.

But it was very different from what he saw till now.

It even felt wrong. After the logic of the "Alaskan" world, this landscape looked twisted, jumbled, abused, yet eerily attractive at the same time.

Swept by the low bars of sunlight still streaming from behind him, it remained shadowy as if *avoiding* the rays, or lying under the smoked glass of a lid. The illumination swept across but did not touch the landforms or make them brighter, as if reluctant to touch them.

Rolling hillocks lay in peculiarly varied colors—yellow, orange, many shades of green—but subdued and grim. Though everything seemed obscure, the color and clarity of the farther mounds didn't fade with distance, which made perspective seem violated, the landscape foreshortened, like a stage-set or table diorama. And lines of impossibly serrated rock crisscrossed the knolls, black hedgerow-like boundaries too fiercely jagged to be natural, as if sharpened to discourage invaders. Geologically they made no sense—such pointed stone would weather quickly.

Nothing he saw fit known standards of land creation, the place like an artist's self-indulgence, with its narrow mesas and dagger-like walls. Vegetation of unknown height grew uniformly across the hummocks, resembling mold or colored shrubs, or even tops of forests, like thick carpets thrown over topography and punctured by the black reefs. Ranglen felt the place too raw, too unfinished, as if some brutal god had sliced up a work that displeased him when it was still half-done.

As the sun sank lower, shadows crept from the black boundaries and seeped into the colored woods, like tarry resin exuded from the earth. The flat horizon became undefined as it faded into the murky sky, its only feature a vaguely large uplifted mound like a smoothed peak. The sky above it looked heavy, too thick to be made of cloud, more like strata of luminescent stone (thick purple, mineral blue, a narrow line of hot crimson) sitting on this depressed and mistreated realm. Everything teased, repelled, beckoned.

"Now *this* is alien," Ranglen muttered. "Enter at your own risk. Look but don't touch."

The horizon changed.

The central hill seemed to grow bigger or at least become more revealed, as if drapes of the plaster sky had moved away. It was still gloomy, nearly as high as it was wide, a coarse outline almost organic, with huge shapes clustered around its base like a nest of limbs, bridges, pipes...*tentacles*.

Horror touched him—for he recognized it!

"Cannibal at the North End of the World," he said.

He once wrote a poem with that title, about a mythological figure from a Native-American culture on Earth. He had pictured the creature as a vast brooding hump-backed giant crouched in the center of a flat landscape, like Dante's monolithic Satan in the middle of Hell's imprisoning ice-field, stern in bitter contemplation of itself.

And here his beast appeared to him as a mountain, surrounded with extremities and fractured landscape. The poem used different details but the emotions were the same, the reactions one would have to a sierra-like formation, construction, life-form, half-risen egg-shaped moon.

He stepped back, wanting to hide among the boulders.

He knew now—he shouldn't have come this late in the day.

He glanced at the rocks that stretched to the north, along the edge of the steep slope that moved into the distance and curved to the right, as if the wall were part of a crater-rim that encircled this "blighted" area.

Something caught his eye.

A light appeared near the top of the cliff. Weak at first, it slowly grew brighter, yellowish but too steady to be a flame. It was artificial and yet primitive, like a strong oil lamp.

Was it left here by a visiting intelligence, like the Airafane ruins had been?

Or was he not alone on this world?

Then he glanced to the south, to the other flank of the rim wall, and saw *another* light, brightening just as the first had done.

And then farther, one more.

This made him turn back to the first light. He looked past it and saw an additional glow switch on. Then another beyond that.

And one more, very dim.

A whole row perched along the cliffs, extended in both directions, curved slightly out into the plain, part of the crater-wall that stretched beneath the horizon. He counted seven lights in all, three to the south, four to the north.

They had not ignited at the same time. The one nearest him started them off, as if passing a signal to the two on each side, then the others awakened in step past them.

Ranglen knew he'd return here tomorrow. He had to learn more.

But before leaving, he stared into the crater again.

A pale natural phosphorescence glowed there, the forest cover like a sheet of cotton over tinted lights. A real mist now also spread across the trees, softening and yet spreading the illumination from beneath.

Emboldened by the wonder and apparent harmlessness of this phenomenon, he looked again at the hill on the horizon.

Mists gathered on the bottom slopes and hid what seemed to be the appendages he saw earlier. But above them he now noticed a series of elliptical horizontal shapes, like intricate decorations on an embroidered cloak.

Then—all at once—

The shapes "opened," revealed reflective, gelatinous pools—each with a central circular orb—that *stared* at him.

Eyes!

Ranglen almost screamed. They had to be illusions—near-round lakes, volcanic craters, artificial domes, luminescent growth.

But every eye *watched* him—shot spikes into his fortitude, his self.

He crept behind the rocks so he couldn't see the mountain—so he couldn't be seen by *it*, so no line-of-sight came piercing after him.

I won't believe this, I won't give in to my imagination. It's just a new world getting to me. I'm struggling with something I can't understand.

He hurried away, almost ran, sped through the rocks and down the slope— too quickly and dangerously in the dark. He didn't want to shine his light—not even with its cloaking red filter that he so carefully had brought for his trip. There was just enough sky-glow for him to see the path but hidden roots could trip him.

He reprimanded himself for giving in to the irrational. *I'm obviously misreading some natural phenomenon.* But his thoughts were desperate and out of control.

When he passed the ruins, the smell of the carcass hung redolent, and little hungry creatures still scurried about.

He reached his tent, scrambled inside, closed and sealed the flap behind him. It was hardly protective, but he needed the sense of shutting out the night.

Nothing that big could be alive, nothing that large could change so quickly.

He pulled the Clip from his pocket and stared at it.

He could leave this world in minutes—abandon his gear, enter the ruins through a back entrance, be gone immediately.

He could.

But he didn't.

Chapter 9: The Illuminated Forest

Sounds awoke him. Clanking, shuffling, like a small group of troops on the move. A thin light seeped into his tent.

He looked outside.

Seven figures walked in a line on the rim of the hill. They appeared human.

Like soldiers in a loose formation, they moved fast and didn't speak, apparently on a mission. They had small backpacks and peaked caps, but he couldn't tell if they wore uniforms since they walked silhouetted against the rising sun. They carried what appeared to be rifles.

The sound of them faded as they marched out of sight behind the rocks.

He knew now, he was not alone on this world.

He grabbed his handgun, water, jacket, and left the tent. He had slept in his clothes so he'd be ready to move quickly.

Keeping low and taking advantage of cover as he approached the ridge, he soon reached the spot from where he had viewed the valley last night.

It was different now.

The sun rose before him and threw light onto a sea of fog, a gold-tinted white blanket that flattened and covered nearly everything. Only the hill on the horizon broke through, its outline more rough today, almost hairy, with the skirt of vapor heavy around it—making it look like a mastodon pushing up through a covering of ice.

But this time, at least, it had no eyes.

Ranglen couldn't see the soldiers. They probably descended into the mist.

But to his left he saw what had to be responsible for the beacon last night—a delicate tower that rose from the ridge, opalescent white with a crystalline top, shaped like a lighthouse but more aesthetic and fragile looking, much too pristine for this rock-strewn environment.

Single-floor buildings sat around it that were constructed of wood. They looked functional and rough, human-produced while the tower seemed alien. He could see people moving about, and he assumed the soldiers had come from there. A well-used trail led from these "barracks" downhill. The shadows had hidden all of this last night.

He heard a scream.

Then another yell, and a shriek that had to be from an animal.

Two people emerged from the fogbank, supporting a third whose face and leg were bloody. They—a man and a woman—helped the wounded man as they led him slowly up the trail to the tower.

Another person rushed down to meet them, a slim woman with a braid of black hair down her back. She had no cap like the others but she wore a similar jacket with different boots and slacks. Given the sameness of outfits but lack of uniforms, the people looked like members of an unofficial home-grown militia.

The woman stopped when she reached the other group and talked with them quickly. She gave apparent encouragement to the victim. But then a disagreement broke out between her and the two who supported him. Ranglen could not make out their words but the two helpers seemed angry and frightened, displeased with the woman and yet needing reassurance from her too.

Then the three continued up the hill, perhaps following the woman's orders or suggestions. She proceeded downward, entered the mist and disappeared.

Another screech from the fog. Then a long silence.

Ranglen pondered what to do.

He crept down the hill by following the path, remained out of sight behind rocks.

When he neared the mist, he hesitated, but only briefly before stepping into it. Tall rocks rose around him, shrouded in murk.

Another scream.

He stopped, listened. Hearing nothing more, he proceeded on.

The slope leveled. The mist formed a lid above him, leaving cleared air beneath it. He entered a forest...

Where the vegetation glowed, in absurdly varied colors.

Against a basic yellow-green background, tree-trunks rose dark blue with creepers of brown encircling them, large violet or yellow mushrooms squatted on the ground, saplings stood with gaudy green-and-purple leaves beside orange or pink flowers, burgundy limbs ran overhead through leafy boughs of bright red or blue. The grass varied from short yellow carpets to taller green waves on slightly higher ground. Even the boulders that swelled up in places were azure, purple, brown, pink—each rock with its own separate tint. And all the vegetation glowed softly, as if its decorative excess had ignited to counter the darkening of the mist above.

Ranglen was astounded. He couldn't understand such intensity of pigment or luminescence, unable to see any evolutionary need. The colors affected his other senses too. The place smelled of wax, vanilla, and crab meat—like, he concluded, a scented crayon factory by the sea.

Noises came from ahead, people talking.

He slipped off the trail and hid in the undergrowth, abundant but easily passed through. He crouched in a clump of fat green leaves with yellow bottoms and white bugle-shaped flowers that had crimson centers. The forest nestled around him like a softly melting stained-glass window.

More arguing and yelling.

He couldn't understand but several phrases teased at recognition. He heard what apparently were names repeated: "Mylia," and "Sabal."

Then, a gunshot!

He crouched, stayed hidden in the leaves.

"*Geh ooh!*"

Ranglen jumped. The command came from beside him.

The braided woman stood only two meters away and had snapped the two words at him. He never heard her approach.

She aimed her short-barreled rifle at his head. It had a small magazine, a wooden stock and no hand-grip, like an ancient WWII carbine.

"*Geh ooh!*" she repeated, pointed the rifle upward.

He stood, raised his hands, showed they were empty.

"Ai oot a oojine!" She pointed at his pistol holster and opened her hand. "*Ai oot! Ai oot!*"

He assumed she meant for him to remove the gun and give it to her, which he did. He still had his multi-purpose laser device and a knife in his pockets, both of which he could use in a fight.

She dropped his pistol into her backpack, said "Yohk a yay!" and waved her gun to her side, indicating he should step into the trail and stand in front of her.

"Yah air yee donnair?"

He felt on the verge of comprehending her words but he didn't quite have it. "I don't understand...."

Her eyes narrowed, as if she recognized what he said. She stepped back. "Sond hare. Dahn moof."

And suddenly he had it: "*Stand here. Don't move.*" It was English, but with such a strong accent he could barely recognize it. He thought back to her first line, "Geh ooh!" Maybe "Get out!" or "Get up!"

She stood before him with authority and confidence, examined him with the same attention he studied her—and her curiosity was more than just that of captor for victim.

She was slender, of medium height, in a combat-fatigue jacket with pockets and clips. Her dark slacks fit her snugly and her high black boots, though functional, were obviously not military issue. She had a handsome face, straight nose, full mouth, prominent cheekbones, and eyes that looked as black as her hair, which was pulled into that long braid but thick enough for curls to fall onto her ears and forehead.

"Essurecsion?" she asked, with almost politeness

Ranglen took a chance and said, "No."

She pointed the rifle down the pathway. "Moof! Aah yay," or "Move! That way." The t's were silent, the w's had become y's.

She obviously meant to lead him to the other people, who still argued among themselves.

He kept his arms away from his body as he walked the trail. She followed behind. He glanced back and saw her maintain an appraising expression. He would have expected more surprise. Who was he, after all? His khakis didn't match her blacks and grays, and his complexion and hair were both lighter. Though she and he were human, of course, he was an obvious newcomer.

The trail now accompanied a stream. Impossibly, it flowed in four parallel bands of milky tints—pink, light blue, pale green, soft orange—flowing beside each other without mixing together. Unlike the glacial scour of the river he saw yesterday, which was explainable, this phenomenon looked unnatural, like a child's work of art.

Something moved in the water.

A large creature glided through the stream, its back breaking the surface but the opaque fluid hiding its detail. It had to be long. It stayed beneath the water as the two of them still walked forward.

"Yait. Ztop."

Ranglen understood. Wait. Stop.

A peculiar scene unfolded before them.

Four fountains in a large pond sprayed water, each in a different pale color, forming the streams that ran parallel beside the path. By the pool but further along the trail stood the "soldiers" he saw descend into the mist earlier, two men and two women in an obvious state of tension, disagreement, and fear. While they argued, they looked warily around themselves, awaiting some hidden threat in the trees.

Beside them lay bodies.

The nearest were a dead man and the carcass of a walrus-bear, both covered with blood. The man, apparently one of the soldiers Ranglen saw earlier, had long rips in his clothes, and limbs that looked twisted and broken. The walrus-bear lay dead from a gunshot. Both killings seemed recent, and Ranglen assumed they were the cause of the shrieks and shots he had heard.

But four other corpses also were present, lying in an orderly symmetric row on a slope of the tall green grass, dressed in similar gray outfits as if for a standardized funeral service.

And the argument among the people grew louder. The dispute carried throughout the forest, causing birds to fly into the mist and unseen animals to stir.

The creature in the water suddenly showed itself. It crossed the pool, crashed through the colored fountains—and rushed directly toward the group.

It was longer than a crocodile but lean like a snake. It moved quickly on its stumpy legs, shaking off the streams of milky fluid and growing bigger as it emerged. Its long tail was encircled in rings of color—not stains from the stream but part of its hide—ending with a plume of wet feathers that spun as it charged, making it look like a motorboat surging through waves.

Its mouth opened, wide.

Everyone in the group and the woman with Ranglen lifted their rifles. But one man must have been waiting for the beast because he beat all of them, blasting immediately at the creature's head.

The skull blew apart in blood and gore.

The people jumped back, tried to avoid the plummeting body. It crashed forward and collapsed at their feet, throwing up a wave as it almost reached the shore. The rainbow tail stretched in long dead loveliness and settled onto the tinted lake.

The man with the rifle shouted in triumph. He dropped his gun and pulled out a knife, ran to the creature and slashed at it—over and over as if in revenge.

The woman beside Ranglen yelled. She abandoned him and rushed to the massacre.

The man who killed the beast, in the colored water up to his waist, shoved the creature over and now sliced at its underside, hacked, ripped, crazed by his anger. The others plunged into the water and tried to stop him.

The woman with the braid also rushed in, pulled frantically at the man's arms.

The killer fought back. Water splashed around them.

It was the perfect time for Ranglen to escape.

But he didn't want to. He had to see what happened. He left the trail and moved into the growth beside it. He hid himself in the bushes but managed to keep a view of what occurred in the pool. He felt concerned for the woman who had captured him.

The fight settled, maybe from exhaustion. The man allowed himself to be led from the water. He sank onto the shore, breathing hard, looked exultant but played out emotionally.

The people said nothing as they emerged from the pool. The dark-haired woman stayed there the longest, beside the creature. She obviously admired it and regretted its death, showed more concern for it than any of the others.

The rest looked stunned, confused, frightened—for good reason, Ranglen thought. A magnificent but slaughtered creature floated in the pool before them. Four dead bodies rested on the grass. A newly killed companion and a dead walrus-bear lay nearby. And a near mad champion of violence (who maybe saved their lives) sat in bitter victory beside them.

Talk ensued, but no more arguing. Ranglen's captor came out of the lake and assumed a leader's role, making suggestions without giving orders. He heard them address her as "Mylia." Three of them, blankly and resignedly, started back along the trail, walking past Ranglen's hiding spot and toward the exit out of the forest.

He watched them closely as they passed, struck by how similar they appeared—relatively young, physically fit, darker in skin tone than Ranglen but curiously bland in expression and movement, though he felt that could be the result of the events he just witnessed. They didn't talk.

The serpent-destroyer followed on his own, isolated now from the rest of the group. For all his recent anger, he did not act differently from the others.

The woman with the braid stayed behind, saddened and concerned. She stared at the creature in the lake. The death must have resulted from an explosive shell in the man's rifle.

Her regret made her seem more genuine than the others.

The pastel water, now mudded and ugly, mixed with the blood and bodily slime. Much of the carcass had sunk away but he could see the tail with its vivid bands of color. He also noticed a ring of green feathers, long and lustrous even when wet, lying in a circle around the creature's neck. Like a mane.

Ranglen thought of the coyote he had seen.

Mylia—so he thought of her now—examined the four gray-cloaked bodies. They had been disturbed, with clothing ripped and skin exposed, as if mauled. Had the walrus-bear done that? Did the group discover it attacking the corpses? Had they shot it when it came after them and killed the other person lying there, the recent one with the twisted body?

Mylia looked deep in thought.

Ranglen understood—since arriving on this world he had seen a mountain he thought was alive, two exotic creatures murdered, one man killed, a person wounded, and four dead bodies left to be assaulted.

Mylia started along the trail.

The dead were left behind, nothing done with the bodies at all.

When she neared his hiding spot, she turned and pointed her rifle at him—*precisely* at him.

No hiding from her, he thought.

"Oo umming?" she said.

They deleted initial consonants too.

He stepped out from the bushes and looked at her almost sympathetically.

But from her expression and the movement of her eyes, he could tell that someone walked up behind him. He turned to see who it was—

A sudden blow struck the side of his head.

He fell.

He wasn't unconscious, just dazed, and not for long. The side of his face lay half buried in dirt where he had dropped onto the trail. His head rang and pain throbbed behind his left ear.

He heard Mylia arguing, more loudly than she had with the others. Whoever this newcomer was, he was more on her level in authority. Words like "stranger" and "visitor" stood out, the local equivalents to "foolish," "unnecessary." He assumed she disagreed with his being struck. But she also mentioned "killing," "anger," "confusion," "unprecedented," and he assumed she described what had happened by the lake.

Then silence. She must have left.

Footsteps moved on the ground near his head. He pretended to be unconscious.

"You can get up now," a male voice said. "I didn't hit you that hard."

The voice had no accent. He could follow the words perfectly.

He turned his head and opened his eyes.

A pale man stared down at him, stooping lower so both of them could get a better look at each other. His eyes were narrow, harder than Mylia's, their darkness contrasting with his lighter skin. The round face had a short beard with no moustache, and his focused attention gave him a stern sense of control. His mouth looked chiseled.

Ranglen spoke first, "Why did you hit me?"

"I wanted to get rid of Mylia and be alone with you. Quickest way to do it."

"Go to hell."

The man laughed. "Finding its direction from here would be difficult."

Ranglen sat up and brushed dirt from his side with his bandaged hand. "Who are you?"

"I'm called Sabal. I run the local light station, which I assume you know nothing about."

Ranglen slowly nodded.

"That's what I thought."

Ranglen scolded himself. He accidentally had revealed his own ignorance.

"Come on." Sabal offered his hand. "Mylia won't be back and I've got a lot to tell you. You've come at a very bad time."

Ranglen allowed the man to help him upright until he stood carefully on his own feet. Dizziness struck him and his head ached.

"Steady there," Sabal said. "Let's walk a bit to loosen you up. And then we'll sit. I know a place. And I want to stay here in the woods while we talk. No one will bother us." Sabal led him further down the trail by the lake, past the five human bodies and the two dead animals.

He didn't even look at them.

"Why don't you speak like the others?" Ranglen asked.

"I do. I just remember the way I *used* to speak and I can still talk that way if I have to. Don't worry, you'll pick up the accent fast. I'll use it more as we talk, just so you'll learn it as we go along."

"Why are you being so helpful—right after hitting me?"

"That was a warning. You might not be welcome here. And…well, there's a bigger reason." The man glanced at Ranglen. "You and I *share* something. I've been through what you are about to encounter. And since no one prepared me for it, I thought I at least should do that for you."

Ranglen was suspicious. "What can we share?"

"More than you know. Like, first, I can see that you're not from around here."

Ranglen grew more cautious still.

"And," Sabal added with a sinister grin, "*Neither am I.*"

93

Chapter 10: Alchera

Sabal led him to an off-shoot path that came to a clearing, surrounded by the flamboyant trees. The forest made Ranglen feel he was in a warehouse of products that came in different colors, or the backlot of a factory where huge transparent containers were stored paints and dyes.

A pool of water in the center of the clearing, though also colored, was mundane in comparison and quite explainable. A geological hot spring, its concentric rings of color were explained by algae adapting to the different temperatures and depth: on the outside a thin band of dark red-brown, a wider circle of yellow-orange, then as the pool got deeper, a rich green that darkened into blue-green at the center. The water was clear but seemed to rise from a bottomless hole. A delicate steam drifted from the surface, with taints of rotten eggs and sulfur.

He wondered if the whole area he had seen from the top of the cliffs might be a caldera, the collapsed summit of an old volcano that now formed a large bowl. The hot pool in front of them supported that notion.

They sat on a convenient bench-like rock—pale blue in color, geologically *un*believable.

Sabal asked his name, but when Ranglen gave it to him he didn't seem to recognize it. The man said only, "We're both outsiders here. *All* of us are, but you and I came later than the others. They arrived in a colony ship over a hundred years ago. I came more recently. My ship failed and I escaped in a lifeboat. Then the craft broke up in the atmosphere and I had to bail out. I lived on my own before the people here found me."

Ranglen felt a sudden irrational disappointment. He thought he had traveled beyond human influence. "You were flying outside the Confederation, alone?"

"I was caught up in the craze exploring for Clips. It was easy then, and cheap. How did *you* get here?"

"The same way." Ranglen lied. "But I never made it to my lifeboat. I jumped out sooner. And I haven't been here long."

Sabal looked at him with dry mockery, as if admitting disbelief in *both* their stories. "Maybe it's not a coincidence that each of us wrecked, even years apart. I've wondered if the planet has some strange influence on spacecraft. The ship that brought the colonists crashed too. So you'll find the people not too skeptical of your being stranded here. They're not distrustful, usually."

Ranglen remembered how bland they seemed to him. "What are they like, and why did they come here?"

"They came right after the first two Clips were discovered, funded by international organizations who wanted to provide outlets for Earth's population. Many ships left at that time but little was heard from them. They either were lost or the colonists didn't want any more people once they settled, so they kept to themselves. The expedition here managed well enough but it didn't prosper. Not much of the cargo survived. They don't keep records or maintain knowledge of their history, so it's hard to learn about the early years. They're peculiar that way, which might make them seem naïve, but they have strong resilience." His words suggested he had pondered their nature for a long time but that he still didn't understand it.

"They came from all over Earth," he continued, "but especially India, Australia and Western Canada, with a lot of mixture even before they arrived. I'm guessing a little, since they focus more on the present than the past. They sometimes deny their roots are off-planet and even mythologize them. They haven't progressed beyond the little technology they kept—some flying transport, power systems, medicine, techniques for working raw materials. But their economic structure is archaic. They have some light industry and metallurgy, but they mostly farm. I can't tell if a 'back to basics' movement spawned them, but it seems likely. They don't want a future—they want the present to *extend* into the future."

"A defense mechanism?"

"Maybe. They've been plagued with strange events since they've come here. And instead of studying them and trying to stop them, they accept—even celebrate them—as unexplainable mysteries. It's how they cope. They don't question deeply or look for alternative interpretations. They establish routines and then perpetuate them, 'functioning' more than 'living.' It makes them seem plain, too similar to each other—with exceptions, of course, like Mylia. If they had the chance to leave this world, I doubt they'd go."

Sabal paused, as if wanting to stress a point. "They're not soldiers but they act that way, not making or taking orders but following unsaid assumptions. No one directs them but they act in concert. Their government is based on called-to-order mutual agreements, dealing with problems as they come up. They're more reactive than proactive. And they don't argue much unless a crisis comes. They're not passionate, or else their feelings are just slow to stir. Leaders know they can only go so far in pushing them."

"They seemed rather passionate to me," Ranglen said, uneasy with Sabal's sweeping overviews. "I heard a lot of arguing and saw a brutal killing of an animal."

Sabal scoffed. "That's because they have some real issues right now. Big ones, in fact. It's the reason why I'm sitting here talking to you. I wouldn't do this normally. But I came here right away when that wounded man was brought up to the tower. I'm glad I did—I intercepted you before Mylia brought you back, which could have been a problem. You see, all their issues have to do with *this* place." He swung his hand to indicate their surroundings.

"These woods? This crater?"

"All of it. After the people arrived from Earth, they developed small settlements across the planet—they call the world *Alchera*, by the way, from Australian Aboriginal mythology. They managed well enough. But then strange events occurred. People were killed. Reports of bizarre and impossible life-forms. And they all seemed to originate from this area, which was already known to be peculiar. It's a volcanic caldera but it also shows evidence of being struck by a meteor. They call it 'the Blight,' though some Alcherans say the term is too derogatory, especially Mylia. The weather's different in here with a strange nightly fog. Have you seen it?"

Ranglen nodded.

"And the geology's peculiar. Like that central mound—which might be the uplift of a complex meteor crater, or an extinct volcano that followed the collapse of the caldera. And the mound also seems to change shape, or appear differently to different people."

Ranglen kept his face neutral.

But he didn't fool Sabal. "You know what I'm talking about, don't you?"

"Hard to say."

"Yes, it's difficult describing what happens here. There are too many inconsistencies and different interpretations. We don't know if the mound's *appearance* changes, or if it *actually* changes. Normally it's just a mist-shrouded mountain, but then someone will say it's a monstrous creature—a mammoth, an octopus, a serpent, a spider, 'Vishnu, the Preserver and Destroyer.' The mound, of course, is too big to be alive. But too many people see different things. I think it's all just optical illusion from clouds and sunlight. But the abnormal happens here."

Everything around Ranglen suddenly became ominous—the overhanging mist, the multi-colored trees, the little noises of animals and birds, the dead lack of wind, the sweetish, waxy, fishlike aroma that warred with the rotten taint from the pool. "Has the mountain been explored?"

"We've tried, but people came back drastically changed—delirious, hysterical. One went into a coma and never recovered. Some didn't return at all. The survivors say it's filled with caves you only get lost in, that it's like…"

"A labyrinth."

Sabal looked uncomfortable for once, and not surprised at Ranglen finishing his sentence. "The people here have an odd self-interest in maintaining the secrecy of the place. They don't want it fully explained."

Ranglen wondered if Sabal had tried to explore the mound himself—and failed.

"This will sound crazy," Sabal said, in a conspiratorial tone, "but the people here feel that each night the mountain absorbs the Blight entirely, that all the living objects beneath the mist, all these colored trees and animals, are sucked into the central mound and then reformed into *new* objects, that everything is reborn for the next morning—that you wouldn't be able to find what you encountered the previous day, that you might not even remember what you did encounter." He pointed to the steaming pool before them: "*This* will probably last till tomorrow—it's a real part of the basic geology. But all this vegetation and life, the animals, the birds, even some of the wilder topography like the jagged reefs that run through the forests, could change overnight. And it *does*. I've seen differences from day to day. That's why it looks so unlikely, so unreal."

Sabal's words confirmed Ranglen's impressions—that the place resembled raw material, that it was still being created and had not yet reached closure or finality. "Have you left instruments beneath the mist overnight, recorders or sensors to see what happens?"

"Long ago we did, when the people still had such instruments, but they disappeared too, apparently 'absorbed.'"

Sabal went quiet then, as if hesitating before something important.

Ranglen couldn't wait. "What about those towers I saw last night? You said you're in charge of one? What are they?"

"We call them light stations or 'monitors.' They've been here since the colonists arrived. Some believe an alien race landed on the planet and encountered the same issues with the Blight, so they left watchtowers to look over the caldera. But others think they are made by the Blight itself and are always maintained by it. They don't really do anything except advertise their location with their glows, marking a direction out for anyone trapped in the Blight. But they also provide shelters, especially for the people who come here to drop off the bodies of loved ones."

"Bodies?"

"They put them into the Blight to be reabsorbed. It's the perfect burial ground. A loved one gets donated to the making of new life. The Alcherans think it's a wonderful gesture. They've made these towers into guard stations and depositories, watching over the sea of mist—or the House of the Dead, it's sometimes called. By me, anyway. Things get very strange down here, and for anyone chased by some new devil created by the Blight the lights are encouraging."

Suddenly Ranglen knew exactly what was coming.

"No one survives being caught here at night," Sabal continued. "The person vanishes before the next morning, as if absorbed too, to be used in making more forms of life. But the Alcherans also believe—and here's where their self-preservation sneaks in—that if recently deceased people are brought here and left beneath the mist, the dead bodies will be *restored to life,* and reappear elsewhere on the planet, maybe even on the other side of the world, but without their memories. This has never been proven, and to me it's obvious wish-fulfillment. But some vague circumstantial evidence does exist. You don't find many old or young people. Births and natural deaths do occur but not many. Instead you get a lot of *un*natural deaths caused by native animals—or new creatures from the Blight. The number of the colonists has slowly grown but never as fast as it should, as if natural births are being replaced by this alien form of regeneration, replacement, or resurrection. This is an obvious reason why the Alcherans don't want to probe too deeply into the truth of it all. Ignorance really is a form of bliss. Or, a form of *life,* a form that miraculously seems to recur."

Ranglen felt very uncomfortable with the idea.

"I confess that since I've arrived here, I've tried to become like the Alcherans—simple, accepting, 'close to the earth,' a poor castaway confronted with the possible gift of immortality. I'm demeaning and patronizing them, but I can't give up my rationality, the prove-it-to-me disbelief I brought with me and still believe in—something I'm sure you have too, being from elsewhere and not some resurrected life from here. I can tell you're not a resurrection, incidentally, just by the way you speak. I've managed to fit in. Alcherans look up to me. But I'm not really one of them. And now…there's this crisis that no one was prepared for. Now—"

Ranglen broke in and declared, "Now the bodies are no longer being absorbed and brought back to life. They're staying dead."

Sabal looked at him with obvious approval. "Exactly! Just yesterday it all began. They normally take the bodies down into the forest right before sunset, leave them here, maybe even build a makeshift shrine for them. Nothing lasts the night so you don't want a full-blown church or memorial. But then suddenly, yesterday morning—they found the bodies still here. They tried again last night, and this time the bodies were mauled by animals. Nothing had been absorbed. That's what the group you saw earlier discovered. Mylia told me what they found, and what happened—why they argued, and why they killed. So...the greatest miracle you can imagine—rebirth!—suddenly stops. The Alcherans, obviously, are a little disturbed."

Ranglen understood too well. He saw how bad his position could be.

"This issue of resurrection is contentious for them. It's the one area where they show difference of opinion. They're really not combative, though violence is a big part of their world. Dangers come out of the Blight constantly, but they indulge in no violence between themselves. Their social relations are less important than their connection to the Blight. They're more focused on *it* than on each other. And the Blight's transformations have become part of their mythology, not so much a religion as a series of shared narratives, an attempt to justify its unpredictable dynamics—a place that produces both monsters and miracles.

"And because it's so much a part of their lives, this sudden stopping of the resurrections is serious. The bottom has fallen out of their world-view. It changes *everything*. I've never been a supporter of the Blight and I've talked against it often. I once even proposed bombing it. And though I've lived here for years I'm still considered an outsider. So they're angry with me now, and it'll get worse. Mylia believes in the Blight more than anyone, preaching its benefits *besides* the resurrections, its new creations as great wonders and positive additions to the world. People never argued against her before, but they're doing so now. They see her trust as immature and dangerous, so she's suspect too. That's why I didn't want her taking you back. They might despise you from just the association. And they already feel..."

He faced Ranglen then. "You see, you're in the *most* danger, not just because you're the newest outsider, but because this crisis occurred at the *same time you arrived here*. You shipwrecked on this planet at just the wrong moment. They'll obviously think these changes are connected to you. For all their mild habits, some very deep emotions are stirring inside them and they're bound to break out. You're very lucky it was Mylia who found you first instead of any of the others. Because, seeing immediately you're not one of us, they might have done to you what they did to the creature in the lake, and it would have been you who got butchered instead."

Ranglen shuddered. It all made sense now—the arguments he heard against Mylia, the unleashed vengeance in killing the beast, the unattended bodies, the amount of death in just the few days he had been here.

"And you're stuck here now," Sabal said. "You're a part of this place just like I am. If you want to survive, you'll have to become one of us. Mylia's already seen you. *I've* seen you, and others will too as soon as you walk out of here—which you'll have to do before sundown unless you intend to be transformed. I wouldn't want to be you. You brought too much coincidence with you, too much bad timing."

It sunk in then—he was in the place where all the transformations supposedly occurred. "What time of day is it?"

"Not that late. Not yet. Why? You getting scared? Don't you want to see if the place really works?"

"No! Of course not."

"Come on, Ranglen. Aren't you feeling lucky? Don't you want to take your chance on being resurrected, rebuilt? But then, you might come out as an animal instead. Which still could be interesting."

"Stop it! Let's get out of here."

"You don't want to try? People *have*, you know. Some insisted on staying here after dark because they wanted to see if resurrection really happened, prove it to themselves. So they came into the forest and sat here overnight. Maybe right on this rock here. And—you know what?—it *well* might have worked. Because…we never saw them again."

"That's enough."

"They could be out there now, running through the trees. Or maybe they *are* the trees."

Ranglen stood up.

"Hey. Wait. I'm sorry about that. Mylia accuses me of being cruel, that I push confrontations and play dangerous games. She's right. But it's just my way of maintaining objectivity. I *have* tried to be like the Alcherans, but they annoy me after a while. And if I can't control reality then maybe I can manipulate people instead."

"What the hell are you getting at?"

"Oh, Mykol, don't you see? Do you think I sat here and told you all this out of generosity and friendship, giving you background information on the nature of this planet for the convenience of your adventuring? This wasn't a handy briefing or download. It was a *test*, an *interrogation*. I kept you here for as long as I did because I want to know—just what the hell are you doing here? You're no resurrection, what others might think or even hope. That's why I said they won't question you much.

But I think you landed here by choice and didn't wreck. Because…I *know* who you really are."

Ranglen stared back at him in confusion and rage.

"I was still around when the third Clip was discovered, found by someone named 'Mykol Ranglen.' Your reputation is present even here. You should have used a secret identity. Or you should have been more open with me. Either way, I don't trust you. Such a well-known person turning up here is just too unlikely. And when you came, right before Mylia ran into you, all hell broke loose, and 'life' changed here for the worse. How do you explain that?"

Ranglen couldn't answer. He didn't know. "There's no connection. I just… crashed here."

Sabal stood up and said with scorn. "All right then, fellow 'traveler in space.' You can keep to yourself if you want. But know this, Ranglen, if the Alcherans blame me for what's occurring now, or if they blame Mylia, then I certainly will blame *you*. If both of us have to be stuck on this planet, I'm not letting you take away my advantages. It hasn't been easy for me, and if they need a scapegoat yet once again, they're getting you."

Sabal walked off into the corridor of leaves. "Find your own way out of here. Mylia will be waiting for you up at the light station if you make it. She'll help to keep the Alcherans away from you. And—don't forget—you have to leave this forest before sundown, which, I'm afraid, isn't *that* far away."

The leaves closed quickly behind him, and Ranglen couldn't see him anymore.

Chapter 11: Hokhokw and Crooked Beak

He quickly pursued Sabal but the man couldn't be found.

Ranglen left the offshoot path but missed the major trail, frightening himself as he wandered through the coruscating leaves. But he finally did manage to reach the main track and he hurried along it. He passed the lake, the corpses, the death. He thought the light from the overcast sky had faded slightly but he wasn't sure. Then he wondered if he wouldn't be able to tell because the luminescence of the vegetation might compensate for the gathering darkness.

Such contradicting thoughts only scared him.

The ground eventually rose. The lid of mist enveloped him as he moved uphill. The trees disappeared and he was surrounded by rocks once more. He then broke into the open air as the rags of fog drifted away from him.

The sun neared the edge of the western wall but plenty of time remained before night. Ranglen stopped to breathe with relief.

Why had Sabal tormented him? Why had he explained so much and then left him hanging, even accusing him of bringing disaster?

The mountain behind him came into view, still resting in its skirt of obscuring haze but glowing with the sinking light. The top shone bright red. The color had to be part of the mountain itself since the ivory-gold sunlight would not create that particular shade. It resembled an open wound, as if the peak had been cut off with a sword and then blood oozed out.

He wondered if he should just leave the planet. He was fascinated by it but too many events conspired against him. If he kept himself hidden and walked up the hill, he could get out of the crater, return to the ruins and then teleport away.

But he couldn't help feeling responsible. Would this happen on every world he visited? Did the teleportation cause local complex incidents after arrival? Why did he feel bound to the place already, as if recognizing parts of it? The mountain, the forest—they awoke something in him.

He could see the tower better now. It still reminded him of a lighthouse but it was slimmer, cleaner, more pristine than the ocean-abused rusty structures he remembered. The sides were patterned with sea-shell marbleized tints, the circular catwalk supported by braces that looked as delicate as filigree lace. The gallery chamber, the cylinder of glass that must hold the lamp, was grooved with rings, as if the entire lantern room formed a Fresnel lens itself. And above that the dome or cupola capping the tower was also made of glass with circular patterns. Four narrow white struts held a small globe at the apex.

Such delicate beauty—especially since it rose from the dull barracks-like structures that were made from logs or wooden panels, crude housing surrounded by a clutter of crates and packing.

The tower made him want to stay. Could he solve its mystery, learn yet more of the illuminated forest and the Blight?

The longing, the longing—which he knew so well!

Then he saw movement. A bird up in the air. It flew past him back toward the mountain.

And there, at the top of the mound, he saw three dark specks revolve around the exposed redness. They swung and dipped and rose and dived. If birds, they had to be very large to be seen from this distance.

They swung out further, made great circles above the area between the peak and the tower.

The scene nagged at him, reminded him of something.

At first the creatures just flew over the mist of the crater, but then they came closer to the cliffs, their dark feathers gleaming in the light. Two of them swung lower while the third stayed high—as if spying the landscape for the two below.

One bird flew overhead and Ranglen got a closer look at it. The wings were large and black, the tail long with feathers that extended into what looked like spears. The beak was sharp and very narrow, also black, with red lines running along the rims where the jaws came together. White patterns rose from the beak and encircled the eyes.

As he watched it closely he was hit with a sudden and dizzying dread, a recognition.

He looked for the other bird swooping about. Yes, it's beak was yellow, thicker, *crooked*, as if the bill had been slammed to one side by a savage punch, leaving a heavy, blunt, ram-like snout.

He knew the names of the two birds. Hokhokw and Crooked Beak.

And he knew their task—to break open skulls and eat brains.

He looked to the third flyer, the higher one, and assumed it was Raven, the spy, who surveyed the scene below and stayed out of the fighting. It normally didn't participate but when it did, it plucked out eyes.

They were companions to the Cannibal at the North End of the World—all subjects of that poem he once wrote.

Ranglen now understood what Sabal meant. How do you keep your rationality, your logic, in the face of this?

One of the birds—Hokhokw—dived for the barracks by the tower. It came to a stop and hovered above a wooden deck that spread outside the entrance to the largest of the buildings. People gathered there to watch the birds, in a careful and defensive circle.

The huge wings beat like sails in a wind.

And the stiletto beak, like the spike of an ice pick, jabbed down at the people—aimed for their heads.

Ranglen ran up the hill toward the building. He couldn't leave the Alcherans to face this alone. His knowledge of the danger made him somehow accountable, too much a part of it.

The figures on the deck scurried to keep out of the bird's way, but the beak thrust down relentlessly. Someone's shoulder ripped open. A head burst.

Ranglen rushed to join them, leapt onto the deck. He didn't have his pistol since he gave it to Mylia and his laser device would be too weak, but he grabbed a club—as many of the others did—and tried to swing it at the creature, reach up and strike the beak away or hit the bird's wrinkled claws.

The prong of the red-and-black beak lashed down at the people who backed against the wall. The bird's eyes shown yellow with sinister black centers inside them. On the crest of the head a line of plumes like black swords swung and dipped.

He saw Sabal and Mylia run onto the deck and join the melee, using rifles to shoot at the beast. He recognized the soldiers he had seen in the forest. He saw a tall black-bronze woman with rust hair who stood out from the crowd. She fought fiercely.

Mylia noticed Ranglen and threw to him the pistol she had taken, surprising him with her trust.

The rifle fire drove the creature back, but it didn't have a lasting effect. The bird was wounded—red spots splattered its wings—but its attacks didn't lessen.

Then the other assailant, Crooked Beak, joined the fight. Its bright yellow but blunted beak was so large it could ram more than one person at a time. It pummeled people, knocked them down with its battering weapon, crushed them.

Ranglen hurried to the side of the deck where a low wall lined the edge. Mylia ran there too to get out of the crowd and lay a better angle on the attackers, shooting with her rifle that soon ran out of bullets. She then swung it like a club.

The purplish-gray wing of Crooked Beak struck both of them and they tumbled over the parapet.

The volcanic ash cushioned their fall but the grit and powder blew up around them, burning their eyes and stuffing their throats. Mylia scurried back to her feet and climbed onto the platform. She seemed more angry than hurt, annoyed with being kicked out of the fight. Ranglen followed.

By now, the two beasts backed off a little. They still hovered and tried to stab, but they no longer flew directly into the crowd or tried to land on the platform. Slowly they withdrew, twenty meters, thirty—

Finally they banked away. Gunfire followed but to no effect. The screeching grew less loud.

They glided out across the Blight and lowered in altitude until grazing the mist, then they flew higher and were touched by the final rays of the sun, as if to absorb the power of the light. They plunged down again into the soupy thickness, disappearing, but then emerged still farther away.

The attack must have lasted only minutes but people lay dead or wounded. Some moaned and still tried to move. One person's head had been smashed, blood spreading in a fan away from it. Another face had been torn open, the skull broken into.

Torches were lit and stretchers brought forth. People didn't stumble about in shock. They efficiently examined the wounded and carted them away to what must be a medical ward. The dead were sealed in translucent plastic bags and taken inside for temporary storage.

Ranglen helped, did what he could. He needed to, to compensate for his knowledge of the creatures, his undefined connection with them.

The people didn't seem critical of him but they weren't welcoming either, neither questioning nor refusing him. Maybe everyone was just too busy. Or, in the face of destruction, they all became equal.

But he still tried to stay near Mylia. Even though she once tried to capture him, she didn't seem to mind him now, almost welcomed him. "Ear Eykol, oo can elp." Or "Here, Mykol, you can help." Sabal must have spoken to her and explained his situation, gave her his name. He certainly felt better being with her than with Sabal.

Arguments broke out among the Alcherans, disagreements on what to do with the bodies. Listening to these, Ranglen was amazed at how well he could understand their speech now. Sabal's training must have been good, and Ranglen could fill in meanings if he had too.

In the midst of the debate, he said to Mylia, speaking with her accent, "Would the bodies normally be taken into the forest? Left there to be absorbed and resurrected?"

She nodded, understanding him now too. "But since the ones we saw down there weren't taken and were mauled instead, no one knows what to do."

"Can't they be buried or cremated, or returned to their home village?"

"That's not our custom. And they have to decide fast. The sun's almost down, and since people died here at the station, we always do a small ceremony before they're taken into the Blight."

The sun was dropping behind the crater wall.

Debate continued. Mylia participated, as well as the tall woman with lustrous bronze-black skin Ranglen had seen fighting the birds. Though everyone else dressed alike and looked similar, her appearance was exotic—baggy leggings, sleeveless vest, bare arms, and a thick sheaf of cinnamon hair.

Eventually a decision was made. The tall woman—Mylia called her Barinda—walked over and said to them, "They've decided to compromise on disposing the bodies. Two will be taken down into the Blight, one returned to his home village, and the last one buried."

"Are you giving the ceremony?" Mylia said.

"Yes. They asked me. Sorry. They felt it best."

Ranglen assumed Mylia normally performed this ritual, but since she was out of favor—according to Sabal—they asked Barinda instead.

The tall woman glanced at Ranglen. "You're the newcomer?"

"Did Sabal tell you about me?"

She laughed, and walked away.

Ranglen looked at Mylia, who explained, "She and Sabal don't talk to each other."

Before he could ask why, Barinda stepped up onto the parapet bordering the deck. The light in the sky was sinking fast, and dramatic clouds built behind her. She looked imposing.

Everyone quieted and listened closely.

"We live in the morning of Creation," she said, "in the light of galactic dawn. We continue the Dream that was started then. We are made from it, and we are makers of it. We are the monitors of the Blight. We contain this realm, to channel its fruitfulness and its creations."

She paused to give a sufficient aura to the words, to let them be absorbed. "Because the Blight does not change, *we* do not change, and we don't lose life when one of us dies. Even when we do die, in whatever shape we were born, the Dream goes on, the Dream of the world and the Dream of ourselves. We continue to create it. We continue to Dream it. Thus it re-makes us. Whether we return to Creation's womb or are buried in the earth, whether we rise again in a new form or vanish for years, we are never separate from the Dream. We return to it, renewed by it. We walk in a world of continuous Creation."

Ranglen was fascinated. He added the capitalization in his mind, feeling it was required. And he heard the influence of Australian Aboriginal myths, which some Airafanologists claimed helped to understand the similarity of the ruins across distant worlds, that the folklore implied a material/immaterial connection that sustained the likeness.

Barinda continued. "The Sky People fell and hollowed out the land, made the central mountain, the valley and the plain. The Rainbow Snake encircled the valley and became its walls. The place was meant to transform and yet exist forever. We are the children of that Snake and agents of the Spider. But the stranger who came from outside brought Time and imposed regularity, death, endings, on the flexible earth. His worst fears were used against him. He was destroyed, but the Dream is now hidden, though it continues to Dream. No difference exists between the people of today and the people of the past. We draw and live from a larger breath of life. The Sky People exist in people's minds and the Dream makes them real."

Maybe "hollowed out the land" referred to the meteor. But who was the Spider, and the stranger who brought Time? Since the latter was an outsider, Ranglen was not surprised the Alcherans didn't like Sabal or himself.

"The Rainbow Serpent flies in the night, burrows through the ground. And like it we are Rainbow people. We are community, we make connections. We once were only Rain people, turned in and alone, knowing only ourselves, dismal and gray. But the Sky People changed us. And we, Sky People ourselves, are now of this place, this stir of matter and fluid creation, this mix of shaping and new generation. Our lives are paths that travel the landscape, our tears are lakes, our cries are wind. We fuse with this world, reform it, become it. We do not die. With no certainty, we yet continue. Nothing is changed. *All* is changed."

No wonder Mylia had been so angry at the man who killed the multi-colored serpent in the pool. Maybe it wasn't *the* "Rainbow Snake," but the associations would have been inevitable. The Sky People sounded like alien space travelers, but Ranglen knew the name was common throughout many mythologies and did not indicate ancient (or even recent) visitations. And human lives described like trails crossing landscapes resembled Songlines, also known from Earth.

Ranglen was intrigued. He admired any culture that argued ties to its surrounding landscape. And some things he had never heard before. Rain people? Rainbow people?

"Though this world has no gods, it is a cathedral. And we are its Keepers—keepers of oneness, connection, creation, and the unending Dream. We are Keepers of the Blight."

Barinda finished. The ceremony concluded. The two bodies slotted for the forest were quickly taken down into the mist by people carrying stretchers. Mylia asked if she could go with them but Sabal said no.

One of the dead was the man who had killed the rainbow lizard—he must have hidden the explosive bullet for years since they had to be rare by now. Another victim was the one who had argued with Mylia on her way down the hill.

Ranglen asked her, "Has Sabal ever given this speech?"

"He's an outsider. Though people accept him they still remember who he is. Usually I give it, but people don't want me talking now. Barinda's in charge of another light station, and since she was visiting here, she gave it."

Ranglen stared out into the Blight. The central mound was nestled in gloom, the clouds behind it thickening and heavy. The red glow at the top was subdued. The birds had not been seen for a while.

He felt conflicted. "Knowing" the murderous creatures deeply unsettled him.

And Sabal walked over and said to him then, low and close to his ear, "The light stations often get attacked by creatures that come out of the Blight. But never this violently. Something different is happening now. And these kinds of birds were never seen before. You know them, don't you?"

Ranglen said nothing.

"Of course they're yours," Sabal insisted.

"They're only myths, stories from the past. I know their names and how they behave. But they're not *mine*."

"Don't tell anyone what you do know. The people will hate you if they find out."

He didn't trust Sabal, but in this case he felt the man might be right. He could understand the Alcherans blaming him.

As Sabal turned to go, Ranglen said, maybe just to show that he too could be devious, "I know how you came to this planet, incidentally. It wasn't by any spaceship."

But Sabal again surprised him. "Of course you know. I assumed you did."

In the silence that followed, Sabal left.

Ranglen then did something he regretted.

He looked at the mound.

It displayed the elliptical shapes it had shown to him last night. They were shadowy yet touched with the last glow from the sky.

This time they weren't eyes.

They were open mouths.

With teeth.

Chapter 12: Mylia's Tale

The second corpse was placed in a coffin to await a caravan that would take it to the village where the person had been born. Barinda told Ranglen that returning the body could take weeks. "Some caravans travel the length of a continent."

He imagined a line of vehicles and walkers strung across a snowy wilderness. The picture appealed to him. He wanted to go too.

Then Mylia took him into the largest building and found him a room they used for travelers. The "barracks" had many of them. "People travel a lot here," she said. "That's why we seldom return to the place where we were born. We trek all over and call the whole world our home. 'Households' are really extended space, not one spot within a landscape."

Ranglen liked the idea.

If people believed in resurrections, then the notion of being "born" could get complicated. Which "birth" would be valid? No wonder the place of origin was unimportant.

After he saw his room, Mylia then took him to the mess hall for food. There, the people of the station ate in quiet shock after the bird attack, but they seemed to weather the event stoically. They kept to themselves while Mylia and Ranglen sat together.

She spoke of the Alcherans with pride, as if wanting to explain why they were withdrawn. "We're survivors first. We don't complain."

"How do they feel about me?"

"They talk about you, but they won't do anything to you, even though there has been some recent violence. You saw an example of it down in the lake. They're used to strangers from different parts of the world, even possible resurrections. Still, they connect you to Sabal, meaning you're an off-world latecomer."

Though the people didn't stare at him, when Ranglen caught a look it was penetrating and suspicious. "Does that bother them?" he asked.

"Normally, it wouldn't. But they're scared now. They're not prepared for the people being killed and maybe not returning."

"But are you certain people came back before?"

She admitted they had no census records, statistics of birth, figures on population growth, so there was no proof one way or the other.

Ranglen wondered if this intended lack of evidence was their way of not facing the truth, of preferring the storied narrative instead, as Sabal implied. Still, he was tempted to believe her. Nearly all the people he saw had the same average age, dark complexion, body structure. So maybe a gradual normalization was occurring (with exceptions, like Barinda and Mylia). Could resurrections do that? Did the Blight homogenize the people each time they were "restored"—which in some ways could hurry their evolution?

The idea was intriguing, but, like Sabal, he couldn't help seeing it as wish-fulfillment. And the vagueness of the notion (people appearing on the other side of the planet after losing their memories) seemed an unconscious attempt to avoid disputing its implausibility.

Ranglen explained to Mylia how he arrived on the planet and entered the forest, but he used the same story he told Sabal. She didn't question it, which proved the claim that people would not be curious. But she also admitted that Sabal had spread Ranglen's story already, which made Ranglen wonder if Sabal was trying to make him more acceptable to the people there.

Or setting him up as a sacrificial victim.

Either motive worried him.

Barinda came in and sat with them briefly. Others turned their heads and noticed her, then quickly looked away, either in respect or mild fear. She obviously didn't fit any standardized norm here.

Mylia asked, "Did you walk from your station?"

"I left yesterday morning. It took a while to get here, but I'd never ask a favor from Sabal, you know."

Mylia said to Ranglen that Sabal limited the use of aircars and ground vehicles. The machines had to be preserved, and the people agreed.

Barinda added, "Sabal sent messages to all the stations telling them what had happened, the bodies not absorbed. I figured I'd respond myself."

Mylia said a few radios still worked.

Ranglen asked Barinda, "Are you in charge at your tower in the same way Sabal is here?"

"No one's in charge at any of the towers. Every monitor has an 'overseer' or 'main keeper.' That's me, as Sabal is here. But it's not a position of authority. It's more like 'designated trouble-shooter.'" She said to him then, with a bit of accusation, "What's

Sabal trying to do with you? He's a manipulator, you know. He always tries to get something out of you. So what does he have that he can use against you, or what do *you* have that he wants?"

"I don't know," he said honestly.

Barinda tilted her head. "Best be aware. Mylia's too optimistic so don't always listen to her."

Mylia wanted to argue but Sabal walked in. He sat at their table without acknowledging them. He spoke to only Mylia and Ranglen. "I have a job for you two."

They looked at Barinda but she made no gesture.

"We need to know what's happening at the other light stations. I want you to take an aircar and make a circle of the entire Blight, hitting several towers. We need information. We can't plan until we learn more about what's happening. Maybe it's just local, but no one likes the number of deaths that are occurring. And if resurrections aren't valid anymore, then we need to act. But we don't know yet what action to take. You two are ideal for this. Mylia, you're familiar with the Blight and with what we believe in, so you'll recognize changes. And Ranglen, you're an outsider, so you can bring objectivity and rationality."

Ranglen protested. "I might not have the same kind of 'rationality' you have."

"You're close enough. And we need the balanced perspective between you two. Everyone else is too frightened. And, let's face it, maybe it's a good time for you two to get away from here in case matters get worse, like if we have more attacks. You'll still need to keep your eyes open. And your minds too."

Mylia said, "We'll stop at Barinda's station first and take her back with us, so she doesn't have to walk."

Sabal gave no answer but didn't disagree. Barinda nodded.

"When should we leave?" Mylia asked.

"Tomorrow morning."

She glanced at Ranglen, who hesitated only briefly before he assented.

"Good," Sabal said. "I already have an aircar for you, and I'll get it supplied so you don't have to do it."

"Is that necessary?" Mylia asked. "I can supply it."

Ranglen wondered if she believed Sabal was keeping her isolated from others at the station in order to protect her. But he hadn't noticed much antagonism against her in the mess.

"I'm worried," Sabal said. "Incidents like these, when a whole culture's beliefs are threatened, can bring down any civilization. I've seen it elsewhere. No one can say what might happen, so it's best not to provide ideas, or *people,* that can be blamed."

An ominous silence fell over them.

Barinda challenged. "You still can't accept us, can you, Sabal? You've been here for years, yet you still patronize. You go to Mylia to find what we are, and to Ranglen for what you call 'rationality,' but you just treat the rest of us like undeveloped children. You *choose* not to understand what we are. That makes you more ignorant than any of us."

Sabal ignored her and spoke only to Mylia and Ranglen. "Bring me answers. We need them."

He stood up to leave, seemed hesitant to add anything in front of Barinda. But he said anyway, "And remember, both of you…*come back!*…Don't disappear on me. Don't disappear on *us*."

He didn't wait for a response, and he left.

"He's scared," said Mylia.

"Only for himself and not for us," said Barinda.

They looked to Ranglen, as if awaiting his deciding opinion. But he compromised. "I'm not sure he's doing this just for himself, but he *is* worried."

Barinda stood. "I'll see you both tomorrow, early."

Ranglen and Mylia left too. As they walked along the corridor, Ranglen said, "What happened between her and Sabal?"

Mylia considered, reluctant to say. "Let's go someplace private…like the top of the light-tower. I'm sure you want to see it anyway."

Ranglen agreed.

From the front of the building, the tower looked beautiful, glowing softly and rising to the clean white light at the top, shining now in darkness. He was glad to see the sides close-up, seemingly made of opalescent shell but probably a processed metal or stone. They walked inside and climbed translucent spiral steps—"122 of them," Mylia said proudly. They clanked like iron but clearly were not made of it.

They reached a hatchway and stepped into the light chamber, where an amazingly familiar, and beautiful, Fresnel lens sat fixed on a pedestal. Less than a meter tall it was like a slim barrel with a widened center and tapered top, made of glass prisms above and beneath the curved middle, filled with a column of blazing light that awoke in its prisms splinter-like rainbows. The bowed center amplified the glow and the angled layers reflected radiation into a beacon, that surely could be seen across much of the Blight.

Ranglen knew the optical details, and he thus was shocked to find the same understanding in this alien structure, obviously applied for aesthetic reasons too (the glass of the outside canopy was beveled and prismatic also, though more for decorative than practical reasons). The laws of physics allowing for the concentration of light would be the same on any world, but it still was surprising to find similar notions here, leading to what could easily pass for a third-to-fourth order standard lens on Earth. The frame holding the prisms even looked like brass.

They walked outside onto the balcony, where the white bannister seemed as thin as stalks of wheat, but the material was solid with no trace of wear. The dome at the top had many circles that shrunk in size to the peak, where a small globe with a lantern blinked white, red, and green.

The Blight lay before them, dark now and thick with mist, covering the forest and most of the central mound. A few vague glows could be seen from the growth beneath the fog, but just barely. He looked for hints of the flying creatures but saw nothing.

The light behind them was almost overpowering, so they moved before a screen that blocked the glow from aiming westward over the forests.

He asked Mylia, "Has anyone ever said they 'knew' the animals that came out of the Blight, recognized them from before they appeared?"

"Yes, we've seen things that remind us of Earth, though we have no direct memories of the world. We've gone through several generations, so connections aren't close. But we still have pictures. The creations act independently though."

He asked nothing more about them, afraid of the answers. "Barinda and Sabal— what's their story?"

She took a deep breath, letting him know the story would be involved. "Barinda once had a close friend named Orani. She claimed Orani was her younger sister but she didn't look anything like her. She was shorter, lighter, with black hair that she tied in a pony tail. When Sabal arrived, he and she became close, until, obviously, they fell in love. Barinda was protective, Sabal critical and stand-offish, but everyone saw Orani as a softening and positive influence on him. He seemed more a 'joiner.' Everyone assumed this would be Sabal's final acceptance into Alcheran civilization."

She paused. "But then…Orani was killed. By something from the Blight."

Ranglen suddenly understood. "Is that the reason he's so against it?"

"He always had been against it, but this made it worse."

"A creature killed her?"

"No. A *plant*. A huge egg-shaped tuber-like thing that sat on roots which lifted it from the ground. It was taller than a person and covered with knife-long thorns, as hard as spikes. When Orani walked near it, the thorns shot out and killed her. We often expect violence from the animals, but this seemed new, perverse, even more out-of-the-ordinary. Barinda blamed Sabal."

"Why?"

"The plant appeared right after he came, and it disappeared following the killing and was never seen again, as if that were its sole purpose."

"But that's crazy."

"No one had seen such a plant or encountered that kind of killing before. It was too coincidental. We have a lot of deaths here from the Blight but they're random, and we've come to believe, and accept, that they're countered by the resurrections. We have few 'crimes of passion,' so this seemed almost premeditated. Indeed, you could say that our strongest belief *in* the resurrections came after the incident. Maybe we were desperate and needed to believe in them. And since Sabal was so much a *dis*believer, acceptance seemed almost a way to counter the whole incident."

"How did he react?"

"He was devastated. But soon he grew angry—angry at the Blight, and especially at himself. He claimed he *was* to blame for Orani's death—that the plant was 'his' and that he knew where it came from. He was hysterical. I tried to stop him. I believed he just wanted to punish himself. But his claiming responsibility convinced Barinda. Since she suspected something from the start, his attitude seemed to justify hers."

Ranglen kept still.

"A big fight occurred between them over what to do with the body. Barinda wanted to take it under the mist in the hope of resurrection, but Sabal insisted she should be buried. They fought over it—*literally* fought. We were appalled at what they said and did. He snuck into the storage room and stole the corpse, carried it away right in his arms, and not in any plastic body bag."

Ranglen tried to picture Sabal doing this. It was incongruous, and yet believable at the same time. "Did he bury her?"

"He tried. He took her up to the ridge and started to dig. But by then people discovered the theft. A group gathered around Barinda and they trailed him. I saw it all. He didn't hide his tracks so they found him easily. Barinda and he fought again but this time it was worse—they almost killed each other. We tried to interfere but we got pushed aside. He hit her with his shovel and knocked her into the hole he had dug. She pulled out her hand-gun and shot at him—she always has it with her. She missed him and he shoveled dirt on top of her. Finally we managed to jump between them and pull them apart. Sabal screamed. Everyone backed away from him. But he didn't go after Barinda anymore. He became quiet.

"Then, slowly, but with fierce determination, he picked up Orani's body again and walked downhill, toward the forest and the mist. Barinda did nothing to stop him now, she was too hurt and couldn't follow. But no one else tried to stop him either. They walked along with him, helping him when she became too heavy for him—he's not very strong, but nothing could stop or get in his way that night. He walked into the mist and we followed, transfixed. Yet it was late in the day. People were frightened to be there at that time. Yet no one turned back.

"He walked through the forest, avoided all the places where we normally left bodies. He even passed right beside the plant that killed her—it hadn't disappeared yet—almost *daring* it to stop him. The plant did nothing and he marched on. He was so confident that all of us walked right by it too. This was foolish—those spikes were deadly.

"For over an hour he continued on. The darkness was coming and we all were terrified of being trapped there. Then, suddenly, we realized his destination....the central mound."

Ranglen said nothing.

"People hate the mound. Some of us won't look at it. They claim crazy things about it, that it's evil, insane. But he was adamant. He meant to go all the way that night, right to the center, to everything we feared and dreaded the most. I think he would have dragged Orani by her arms if he couldn't carry her. And it wouldn't matter if it took all night and he got killed and absorbed right along with her. He meant to bring her to the one place we've never understood, that we avoid, that we're too scared of—because we don't *want* to understand it, that we fear we'll go crazy if we get near it. But nothing stopped Sabal that day. He didn't believe in it. He was there to *challenge* it."

She paused. And all the night and silence around them seemed to be listening.

"We reached the slope at the edge of the mound where the forest thinned. He placed Orani onto a shelf of moss—gently, lovingly. He looked exhausted, half dead himself, but I think he would have carried her until he collapsed. He stared at her face but she did not look serene, not beautiful, not even human. Just empty, absent, futile...dead.

"Then he stared up into the fog, toward the mound itself. None of us moved. We were all too frightened.

"And he said...slowly and emphatically...'Come and get her, you Airafane *bitch!*'

"Then he turned away and walked back toward the light station, his pace as deliberate, and his face as unreadable, as when he came. We walked with him but most of us rushed ahead. Night had nearly fallen and he moved no faster. We were

115

horrified we'd be caught in the mist during the darkness—that we'd be melted down and then remade. But he was relentless, and some of us did not walk any faster, because he radiated such rock-like confidence.

"We did make it. A slight glow was still in the sky when we emerged, though the forest had grown brighter with its luminescence. Some people even claimed it had never shone so bright and colorful, that it burned that night, that each leaf was on fire. I don't know. I was too preoccupied. The tower's beacon looked very attractive."

She stopped.

Ranglen had to ask, "And afterward?"

"He never spoke of her or the incident again. He became what he is now—cynical, critical, sometimes cruel. And Barinda never spoke to him after that. I was glad she had been too hurt to walk with us. Who knows what would have happened between them."

"Was the body absorbed?"

"It was gone when we walked to the spot the next day, so we assumed it was. Sabal didn't come with us."

"Was she seen again?"

"We think so. Like all the resurrections, nothing's ever certain. Memories are lost. At least one person appeared who resembled her, acted like her. But Sabal would have nothing to do with her. He had no faith at all. I felt sorry for him. He grew distant. I frankly hoped, when you came, that you and he might relate since you're both outsiders. But it doesn't seem to be happening. Instead, we get this crisis. Maybe it's because I hoped too much."

"When he left the body, why did he say 'Airafane' to the mound?"

"I once asked him that. He said he was distraught, angry at everything, and that to him the Airafane were the embodiment of all that humans have no control over, that he didn't mean it literally. But, deep down, many of us feel the Blight *is* the result of the Airafane. The place is obviously unnatural, so who else could have caused it? And Sabal once claimed our mythology has Airafane elements in it, though he also said no one is certain what they believed. And Airafane ruins exist here, right over the ridge. We have nothing to do with them but maybe their closeness is significant to the Blight."

Ranglen wanted no one to get interested in the ruins, so he didn't follow up on her mention of them. "What did Barinda do afterward?"

"She left the light station Sabal was part of and went to another, eventually becoming its Keeper. They never talked again, though I don't think they really dislike each other. They just happened to share too much pain and anger, and they needed to separate themselves in order to deal with it. She was gone for a whole year walking the planet. That's common, you know, after someone dies."

"Are the resurrections the reason for your wandering life-style? People in pursuit of past loved ones?"

"I don't think so. We'd be walkers anyway. It's the nature of the landscape. But I see what you mean."

Ranglen felt compassion for both Sabal and Barinda, but also for Alcherans in general. He wanted to give them all the warning he now told Mylia. "One shouldn't expect miracles from the Blight."

"No one does, but they seem to have happened."

"There's no predictability, no order, no roadmaps."

"We take nothing on faith. We're just open to possibilities. We see creation in the Blight every night, and that's overwhelming enough. If resurrection is possible, then somewhere, somehow, it must occur. If the Blight didn't exist, none of us would accept such a fantasy. But it *does* exist."

"Why do so many of you stay by this crater? Why don't you all just leave it?"

"It's become our job. Everyone performs monitor duty at some time, becomes a guardian of the light. They prevent dangerous and new predators from getting out, police the area for drastic changes, and they carry the deceased down into the forest to be deposited there."

"That's a habit. It's not a reason."

She spread her hands, as if acknowledging she could not explain it. "By being here we live on the edge of reality, right on the verge of creation itself. We see it happening. We can *touch* it. We go further than anyone else can go. I might be able to show you, but I can't tell you. And even if I showed you I'm not sure we'd be seeing the same thing. And…wait, here's an example…

"After the event with Orani's death, I came up to this balcony where we're standing right now. The night was serene, perfect, clear. The forest was exposed and glowing, the mound big and clearly outlined. I was thinking of Orani. Maybe I was trying to will her back into existence. And then, suddenly, a huge flat ring rose up around the central hill, and a cloud formed a globular shape inside it, so that together it resembled the planet Saturn with its ring system." She stopped, as if nervous about being believed.

"Go on."

"It had to be an illusion, of course. It was way too big for a physical manifestation. And on that ring, coming from its left side, an old Earth motorcar, like what you'd imagine a 'Model T' to look like, drove around the ring as if it were a road. A person drove inside the car, a woman, with a small child beside her. They waved at me. They were far out in the Blight but I could see them. They continued on around the other side, circling the ring, and the two people waved at me each time they passed. Then clouds moved in and hid my view. I couldn't tell if either one of them was Orani. But the scene had to be significant in some way. It moved me, touched me.…"

She looked at him closely. "*That's* what the Blight gives to us."

Ranglen didn't know how to respond. They stood there silent for a long while.

Then Sabal surprisingly arrived, stepping through the door from the light chamber and saying to both of them, "There's been an incident at Barinda's light station. It came in by radio. A killing, maybe not related to the Blight. She spoke to them and there's nothing she can do from here, so she asked if you could move up your departure time."

"Sure," Mylia said. "We can go right now."

"No. She wants things to settle a bit. Maybe in three or four hours, though. That way you can get a little sleep."

Both she and Ranglen nodded.

Mylia asked Sabal, "You told her yourself? Directly?"

"Yes," he admitted.

"Well…good for you."

He said nothing, and left.

They descended the tower and entered the barracks, proceeded on to their individual rooms, not saying much to each other, both of them maybe played out by the story.

Ranglen tried to sleep but found it near impossible. And during the brief time he did, he was disturbed by dreams.

In one of them, the coyote he saw with its lion mane came to him, grinned its demonic tooth-filled mouth and *spoke* to him. He could hear what it said (it used Barinda's voice) and even see what it said, for the words had structure:

You are destruction,
Your defenses grow lean,
Your secret's almost known,
You are not what you seem.

The coyote moved about his room, explored with a sure arrogance and grace. Then it settled on a mound—on *the* mound, in front of an immense sky and stars. It grew larger, and it said:

Their stories are small.
Deep Story *you'll* find,
A suspended revelation,
Told in Galaxy Time.

The words grew bigger. They swelled over him and swallowed him. When he felt he was drowning, he suddenly awoke.

He slept no more that night.

Chapter 13: In the Country of You

Long before sun-up they met in the hangar beside the working aircar. The vehicle was used for only important missions.

Sabal wished them "good luck." He and Barinda glanced at each other but said nothing. Mylia took the controls. The aircar taxied through the portal of the hangar and took off into the night.

The light of the station fell behind. The world around them grew dark and mysterious, the glows in the aircar small, subdued.

They followed the ridge of the crater rim, a dark saw-blade of twisted rock that ran beneath them. To the left, night forests cloaked the landscape amid banks of snow. To the right, the crater lay like a smooth glassy sheet because of the mist, the central peak dark against a nearly-as-black sky.

Ranglen noted the aircar interior's torn upholstery and scratched panels.

"There aren't many of these left," Mylia said. "Sabal's right to preserve them."

"Why do Alcherans neglect their technology?"

"Don't judge us, Mykol. We don't need an industrial base. We lost the chance of it when our spaceship crashed. We have food production, clothes, shelter, power, even weapons. That's enough. And we don't need cities. Some of us are like gypsies living always in caravans."

Barinda added, "In the long run, the Blight could provide us everything. We already tap power from the light stations."

"Maybe you depend on the Blight too much."

"We never *depend* on it," Mylia countered. "It's a big part of our lives, but we feel it was meant for us, created for us. Watching over it has become our role. By confining it we maintain it. We've adapted to it and it's adapted to us. We welcome its creations—even monstrous attacking birds."

Ranglen didn't smile.

They passed two stations, strong gleams from toy-like towers in a vast dark, signs of reliant if innocent occupation.

Then they rounded bulky peaks and saw Barinda's lighthouse in the distance.

Part of its barracks were on fire, sending a pall of sparkling smoke into the sky.

"Quick! Land there!" Barinda guided them to a platform-deck like that at Sabal's station. The burning building was small and off to the side, a storehouse apparently. People surrounded it and were putting out the fire with pumped water. It seemed under control and wouldn't spread.

A woman ran out to the aircar. She had the Alcheran look, Ranglen noted—dark skin, dark eyes and hair, relative youth. Barinda called her Disha. She said that the fire started after an argument over a murder. The killing apparently had not been done by any creature from the Blight, so it must have resulted from the uncertainty, frustration, and anger over the resurrections stopping.

Barinda said to Mylia and Ranglen, "It's hard to believe, and it'll only get worse. Resurrections cease and we immediately start killing each other—just when human life becomes most valuable. It makes no sense."

"They're distraught," Disha argued. "They don't know what they're dealing with."

"Then they're fools. For once I agree with Sabal. Killing's not the way to negotiate a life-threatening crisis. We've gotten too smug. Take away our assumptions and we lose control." But she tried to settle down and regroup for her duties. "Thanks for bringing me," she said to Mylia. "You've got your 'mission.' Go. Find answers."

"Do you need anything?"

"No." She waved her hand at the people of the station, who looked frightened now since they no longer were occupied with controlling the fire. But their bleak expressions of loss and fear were countered with determination. "*They* need help. Not me."

Mylia and Ranglen re-entered the aircar and left.

He asked her once they had lifted away, "So, why *are* they killing each other?"

"Barinda once said to me that life on Alchera has become too cheap, that because of the resurrections, and being able to dump corpses into the Blight and assuming they'll return, everything became too expectable and safe. So maybe now, the people don't know how to deal with life being precious again. And by still treating it cheaply—through killing—they're trying to re-establish the old status quo."

"That's twisted reasoning."

"They live in unique situations, and in a very unlikely world."

"You still believe in them, don't you?"

"Yes. They'll learn. But I believe in the Blight too. We don't need resurrections to take advantage of it."

"I don't understand."

"I'll show you later. But I have to call in now. Get the radio from the back. The one in the dashboard doesn't work."

The back seat was loaded with supplies—Barinda had been cramped sitting back there. Food, blankets, maps (GPS satellites didn't survive the wreck of the colony ship), hand weapons, rifles, even a small shelter in case they crashed. And a radio that worked.

Mylia called Sabal and told him what they encountered. They didn't talk long.

"He told us to keep going but to avoid the central mound."

Ranglen didn't ask why. He didn't want to know.

The sky lightened and morning came. They could see their surroundings now.

In the caldera, the whitish slopes angled down, stained with trails of yellow, orange, and red-brown—rhyolite traces, Ranglen assumed. The floor of the crater stretched away to the central peak, which from here seemed just a mild rise, free of detail. The mist lingered, but Ranglen had been told that the colored forest did not extend this far north.

The further they flew, the more the obscurity in the flatlands faded. The plains became a barren gray-white, soda crust marked with pools of boiling water, geysers from underground heat. Volcanism. The round pools were ringed with red on the outside, then yellow, and dark blue-green in the centers, like the pool Sabal and he had sat beside—or like Annulus, Ranglen realized. Others shone milky or soft violet, turquoise, golden-brown, like hauntingly beautiful opals and agates, as if a perfect world of color dwelled beneath the scabbed ground, showing up through the circular gaps.

"The eyes of the earth," Ranglen said.

"I like your name better than Sabal's. He said they looked like running sores."

"He's been here too?"

"Yes, but he doesn't travel much."

They passed several towers and then circled one that had only a few small structures around it. The delicate mother-of-pearl pylon shone like the last standing piece of a castle in a severely gothic, threatening landscape. All highly Romantic.

They landed, and a man came out to greet them, older than most Alcherans. The small number of elderly could be proof of resurrections—or of the very dangerous lives lived here.

Mylia asked about recent changes, and the man spoke with an ironic sourness. "A different kind of death has occurred. More violent, not what we're used to, and we didn't get to see what caused it. One soldier claimed that big birds perched on the reefs and tried to attack him. But no one else saw them. And the body of someone brought here from outside wasn't absorbed two nights ago. A creature ate part of it instead. We haven't decided what to do. We assumed the lack of absorption was temporary, but nothing happened on the next night either."

"You're not alone. Your radio doesn't work?"

"No. And we've never encountered this before."

"The birds are real. We've seen them ourselves. We'll fly on to other stations to see if their experience is the same."

Ranglen said nothing. The mention of huge birds, of course, disturbed him.

In flight again, he said, "I still feel the Blight is too much a part of your life."

"We're at our best when we interact with it. It's odd to say, but we're most *alive*. Beyond the caldera, in the rest of the world, we're only farmers, mechanics, merchants. Important but dull. Here we can be Heroes, part of the Dreaming. Where a new world is born every night."

"I haven't seen much difference day to day."

"You haven't looked."

Ranglen worried. The Alcherans were becoming addicts of wonder.

Throughout the morning they visited more stations, heard the same stories of unexplained killings, unforeseen violence, un-absorbed bodies, maulings, fears.

The barracks became more rundown, not maintained well.

Mylia said, "They don't get many visits here, from either us or creatures from the Blight. Some parts of the caldera generate more 'events' than others. Sabal's area is most active, probably because of the closeness of the mound, or because the landscape beneath the mist is more intricate there, with the knolls, reefs, and colored forest. In other places the caldera's rougher, the crater floor stark and bleak, the mist absent. Even the towers are further apart, and not as many of them housed with guards. We don't have enough people for each one."

"Is the population in decline?"

"No, but we don't think it's increasing either. Our economy is not dependent on growth. We prefer it that way."

"A steady-state culture?"

"Maybe, yes."

As they flew on, the stations now looked decayed, crumbling, deserted. "Like remains of a war."

"We have no war here."

"But you have a lot of death."

She didn't respond.

The wall on the northern edge of the caldera was less defined. Snow-covered mountains from the north came down and buffered the outside of the crater rim, seemed to pile up against it in waves. "People avoid this area," Mylia said. "Too many rumors."

"Rumors of what?"

She didn't answer.

Ranglen suddenly pointed. "Wait! Down there. I see movement!"

"I knew you would. I was hoping—"

"Did you bring me here just to see this?"

From the rim wall that was nearly lost in the mountains from the north, glaciers ran in opposite directions, south into the crater and north into the inlet of an apparent sea.

In a high saddle of snow between the peaks, a line of figures walked north like refugees.

"They're leaving the Blight," Ranglen said.

"Going out into the world," corrected Mylia.

She swooped downward to give him a better look at the migration. The figures, dark against the ice, walked stiffly, as if stakes were tied to their limbs. But they also caught the sunlight that occasionally broke from between the clouds—and they glowed with mirror-like gleams, as if sealed in reflective carapaces that were almost crystal.

"We need to land," Mylia said. "I want you to see this."

"But what are they?"

"It's why I believe in the Blight. Remember I said I could *show* you but not tell you."

"Is this why you didn't question Sabal asking us to take this trip? I had wondered— you seemed too eager."

She smiled at him, her face glowing.

Far ahead they could see a bay clotted with icebergs, that broke off the glacier when it reached the water. They followed the river-of-ice to the coastline where everything was buried in snow. The water of the bay looked savagely cold. Clouds hung heavy on the jagged mountains. Falling snowflakes came in sheets.

They threw on coats and jumped out, ran upslope to the edge of the glacier and lay behind a ridge of ice. There, they watched.

The figures that came were like animated jewels, walking crystalline life-forms, human-like in shape. The arms, torsos, heads, legs were all made of gem-like material, faceted aquamarine, clear as glass and cut and polished. The eyes were like rubies and the finger-tips diamond. Yet the objects were alive—gemstones that moved.

"Impossible!" Ranglen said. "They look hard as quartz."

"Maybe the facets are pieces or plates, attached to a flexible undersurface."

"Nothing transparent like that can live."

"But I've seen these before, Mykol. And before that I even dreamt them."

He was reminded of his own impressions coming to life. He grew excited, but scared too. "They're leaving the Blight."

"Maybe all life on the planet has come from here. These are just the newest additions."

"But no one would believe you. They might not even *want* this."

"Yet it's wonderful. Where else can you find so much new life, coming forth, over and over?"

He couldn't answer her. He understood her enthusiasm and he almost agreed. But still…"Let's go, before we're seen."

By now the aircar was covered with snow. They swept it off, Ranglen impatient, Mylia laughing, saying she felt nothing of the cold. They entered the car and let the heater dry their clothes. Mylia wiped vapor from the window and watched the walking jewels on the ice. Ranglen could tell she didn't want to go. But she revved the engine and took to the air. She flew over the figures, too exuberant to remain hidden from them.

She said, in an almost childish fervor, "When they cry, do you think the tears form little glass beads, which fall to the ground and tinkle as they hit? Could you collect them, like little blue marbles, put them in a bowl and keep them with you as reminders of sorrow? You said you're a writer, Mykol. Write me something called 'Crystal Man's Tears.'"

He felt his reason slipping. He was becoming too infected by her excitement. Sabal's command to stay rational was failing.

He didn't care.

She spoke from a depth she must seldom show. "I want to break free, Mykol. I want all this to spread from here. I want to bring the Dreaming to the entire world."

"Did you ever report these creatures to anyone?"

"No! This is ours! I won't let Sabal trap and dissect them."

"You've already been here, haven't you? What else have you seen? What's *already* come out of the Blight?"

"I don't know, but I'm sure it's happened. And…wait—we're entering the wildest part of the caldera. We'll see more."

They followed the broken wall east and then south. The central mound lay farther away and they encountered no more light stations. Mylia said they clustered on the side of the crater nearest the mound, the western part, as if whoever built them believed the greatest threats from the Blight came from there.

"We don't know the real reason for the towers," she said. "Maybe the Blight's creations were meant to follow the lights but then stop at the crater's rim. So the towers could be beacons instead of warnings."

"We now know the creations can be independent and leave the area. We saw that. But maybe just where canyons cut through the cliffs." He wondered about the walrus-bear he had fought, the coyote with the lion's mane, maybe all the animals he had seen.

"The Split Place, the Bitter Water place, Meghalaya, the Mountain Canal."

"More legends?"

"Stories, notions, names that come to me. The Blight, with what it does, charges the whole world with meaning, makes the earth animate. It's what I want to do. I want lines radiating out from here, even from the mound, caravan paths or pilgrimage tracks laid out across the whole planet, to reach 'holy' places, special spots, sacred mountains, important villages, the crash site of the spaceship, the—"

"The site exists? You can go there?"

"Yes, I've seen it. We couldn't fly there now. It's too far, and the ship is wrecked. But the place, the event, it's meaningful for us, and I want the whole planet to become a network of important places, of deep meaning."

His mind whirled.

"It doesn't matter where we've come from and what we are," she said. "We're not leaving here. We've become as much products of the Blight as we are of Earth. So why should we always restrict this place? We need to connect it to the rest of the world. You don't *find* a sacred landscape. You *make* it, build it."

Though attracted to her ideas he knew how illogical they could be. But he also knew how logic didn't exist when meeting the alien, when becoming part of a different existence. Her dream was in some ways the same as his—opening to the new, melding into a different world, *becoming* an alien landscape.

She said, "We have the chance to participate in creation ourselves, to evolve the planet. I see all of us on those pathways spreading out from here and encircling the world, walking them in ritual exploration, finding ourselves, becoming reanimated, a developmental resurrection that makes us more than what we are."

"Is this you or the Blight talking?"

"We're the *same*, Mykol! You know this. I've seen how you look at the central mound, at the forest, the mist. You see things. You see yourself. They're not separate phenomena for you."

"But I want them separate. I don't want to create them, I don't want to feel so responsible for them."

"But you already do. You came to this planet. That's not an accident."

"I chose—" he stopped. He had almost admitted to how he arrived.

"Of course we all crashed here," she added. "I'm not claiming we were 'drawn,' that it's part of some silly predetermination. But it's what we *do* with the accident that counts. How we use it. How we find advantage and progress. You say we're too dependent on the Blight, but that's why we have to spread away from it, to create our own world, to make it into something unique to ourselves."

"I—"

"Look! Look down there!"

The crater wall had become ugly and brutal. Even the flatland was jumbled now, wrinkled, fractured, steaming with pits spewing gas. All looked misshapen beneath the darkening sky. Landscape noir.

"I want to land here," she said.

"It's volcanic. The surface could be just a thin crust that we'd break through."

"I'll look for solid rock and test it first. I saw something here once and I want to see it again, to show you."

She hovered the aircar low to the earth before touching down, testing for a solid base, but the test was perfunctory and he didn't think adequate.

She didn't care. She jumped out quickly and Ranglen followed—losing his hesitation, enthralled.

A pillar of flame crept up out of a crater, stood upright and slouched away.

It left a trail of fire behind it. The narrow figure, as tall as a bonfire but as slim as a torch, moved across the ground with melting feet, with sleeves of flame that draped from its arms. It reached another crater and dived into it.

"You see!" she called to him. "It's made of fire."

More yellow-orange creatures emerged, flung out plumes, ran from one pit to another, traced flames tinted with burning minerals in the soil—blue, green.

Did these colors make patterns? Symbols? Codes?

The beings would stop and "stare" at the two, like curious children, with bright limbs and crests of red, with white eyes that flickered in the heat. No bodies could be seen because they were too sheathed in fire—or *made* of it, as Mylia had said.

Burning flags waved from their lips.

Then they slid away, leaving bridges of flame between them that formed designs. Ranglen was grateful they made no sense.

Nearby eruptions—that didn't spew life—flung out burning cinders, sulfur, choking gas.

"We have to go," he said.

"But—"

"We *must*. You've made your point. I'm as excited as you are."

They hurried inside the craft and lifted away.

"Creation is never finished," she said. "We supply the shapes in our myths and memories. The Blight forms them. Manifestations. Because of our thoughts, matter comes alive."

Ranglen was drowning in Mylia's words—or drowning in Mylia.

She banked and circled another broken area. "That river down there. See it? It's like a rainbow."

It reminded him of the stream they had found in the forest with its parallel bands, but these were more vivid and varied, running brightly through the spectrum. It looked like a serpent crawling over the landscape—and at one end of it a flame-creature made a fiery eye.

"We don't view or walk over a landscape, we negotiate it, interact with it and give it form. I've seen this river in my mind and now here it is. It's not a fantasy. The colors come from chemicals in the hot springs, from different algae that live in hot water. But to me it's the Rainbow Serpent—that calls forth the light-towers, that builds them from seashell, opal, and quartz. I've seen all this."

A blast of wind shook them. Heavy clouds moved in the sky.

"Is night coming already?" Ranglen asked. "We shouldn't be in the Blight after dark."

"There's no mist here yet. We don't have to worry. I'll head south."

But they forgot that this new straighter route would take them near the central mound. It grew before them.

Fear welled up inside Ranglen.

The hill was all too clear now, too precise. It was surrounded by stone arches, or tentacles, like a hulking body entangled in the landscape, imprisoned, tortured. Slumped crevasses led to it like a spider's web. Ranglen knew that a meteor and a caldera together would make a mess of geology—igneous flows, shock metamorphosis, banded rhyolite, fragmented rock, boiling vents, impact melt, all buckled into monstrous folds—but no such explanations helped. Nothing in his science protected him now.

It wasn't the *thing* but the impression it made, the feelings it left. It seemed like a vile object from space, a spiteful god trapped on a planet it now despised. Or some massively engineered machine readying for apocalyptic battle, trying to right itself and break free. A half-sculpted Michelangelo "captive" imprisoned in stone but longing to howl, take to the air, attack, kill.

All pictures from his ultra high-strung nerves.

"Don't go near it," he said.

"But this is our chance to take a close look. We don't have to land. What are you seeing?"

"Never mind what I see! You don't want to know."

"I see a rainbow snake coiled into a crown and sitting on its top. If we go nearer we can—"

"No! Go south. And fly through the crater wall when we get there."

"But the chance we have—"

"*Trust me!* You don't want this!"

In its cracks and hollows, its eyes were opening, its wet mouths with sharpened teeth. It tried to stand and walk toward him.

"Get us out of here!"

She speeded the aircar and flew directly south. He didn't look back. In the coldness of the cabin he sweated and writhed.

"Are you all right?"

"Just keep going."

The clouds dispersed and night fell. He noticed stars. The aurora flickered in wide curtains of undulating green with a fringe of red or violet beneath. It reflected on the snowfields, this area not volcanic enough to melt what was frozen and the snow that lay.

"I love the aurora," Mylia said. "Can we land and watch it?"

"After we're out of the crater."

"We've almost completed a full circle around the Blight."

Ranglen said nothing.

"The sky won't be clear for long. I think it'll snow again soon." She was trying to divert him.

"I'm sorry I shouted. I thought I might be sick. It made me…"

"I felt it too but not as bad. The people who tried to explore the mound said they encountered terrible things."

"It just surprised me. I should've been prepared."

"I flew too close. This trip has made me too excited. I've never talked to anyone about any of these things."

"I'm glad you flew close. I learned something. Are we out of the crater now?"

"Yes. We just crossed over the wall. The light stations should be coming up again."

"Go ahead and land, before we get to them. Let's walk a bit and relax. I want to get outside."

They touched down by a frozen lake. She emerged from the vehicle and put on a long coat, turned up the collar. Ranglen followed her.

She walked to the snow-covered shoreline, looked across the cold solid lake, absorbed by its isolation, its starkness. The bare limbs of the small trees were crusted with ice. They resembled frozen shriveled claws, white cracks in black marble.

Ranglen slowly walked up beside her, watching her. Clouds filled most of the sky but open portions hinted of the aurora, celestial, green. Snow fell but not thickly. They stood in the middle of a vast silence.

She said, "I'm so alone in defending the Blight. But I felt certain you'd understand."

"I do understand."

"I feel we're both in another country."

"The country of you."

She glanced at him playfully, seriously. She tilted her head and peered into the sky. Flakes of snow landed in her hair, on her lashes, her lips.

He stood in front of her. With one fingertip he touched her cheek, drew it slowly down her face.

His finger trembled.

He stopped at the edge of her mouth and slid it along her lower lip. The end of her tongue reached out and touched him, followed his finger.

He raised his other hand and held her face.

He kissed her.

The kiss became long, intense, deep.

The aircar was chill but they felt warm, cramped together. Snowflakes struck against the glass.

She said, "I'm scared that people think I'm deluded, obsessed."

"You're just more focused, more clear."

"I love that you think that of me."

"You scare them a little. They're not as eager about the world as you are."

"I want to accept everything, explore everywhere. While standing by the lake, I longed to hug the snowy boughs."

"I thought I just wanted solitude and aloneness, so I could go where I wanted to. But you've changed that. I'm lucky I came here."

"I don't believe in luck. You came because you needed to—and because I needed to find you. I didn't realize how much I was waiting for this."

"Mylia, you create your own myths and stories. You don't need to follow any that you don't make yourself."

"I don't care about the past or the future. I don't care about starting points or destinations. I care about…the road."

"'Our longing is blind, but our longing has wings.'"

"You wrote that, didn't you?"

"Long ago."

The radio signaled an incoming call.

Ranglen could hear Sabal's voice. It asked Mylia, *"Are you on your way back?"*

"More or less. What's happening?"

"Much of the same but the Blight's become extreme. You better return now."

"Has anyone been killed?"

"One, from an argument. But things seem to be stirring more in the crater now. Just come back."

"We haven't been to all the northern stations, and we never reached the southern ones at all."

"I don't think you'll find anything different. From what you radioed, it sounds the same at most of the places. It might be worse here though."

"We're on our way."

She and Ranglen grew quiet after that. Their special mood didn't evaporate but responsibility now took over.

She flew further south so they wouldn't be tempted to check more stations. They passed over the sweeps of forest and tundra beneath the stars. The clouds had broken up and the snow stopped. Then she swung west and finally north.

Time passed, but it didn't exist. They felt they lived outside it, but even though wary of sudden guilt. So much happened elsewhere and yet here they were, amazingly happy. They held hands while looking into the night, their fingers alive in each other's grip. "Soft-handed love," he called it, a subtle intoxication of touch. The aircar filled with their knowledge of each other.

The aurora returned. She noticed him staring at the ice streams that lay below, that glimmered with the reflected light.

"What do you see out there?" she said.

"You," he said.

Close to dawn, when they reached the station, they encountered the reason for Sabal's concern.

The Blight looked disturbed, the mist like an ocean moving in waves and swirling with plumes that thrust themselves upward. The jagged reefs resembled mountain chains assailed by low creeping storms. The mound, rising above the cauldron, emitted a corona of dirty light-beams, like a tyrannical ring-leader in a circus of tempests.

The little stations on the peaks appeared besieged.

Mylia maneuvered the craft downward and landed on the deck beside the hangar. They walked to the parapet, gazed into the distance.

Something happened to Ranglen. He saw things, out in the mist—

Galleons of weed-encrusted wood peopled with pale-lit screaming ghosts. Dinosaurs grappling with giant squid amid shooting beads of luminescent foam. Drowned spaceships tossing on their sides as planets emerged, cities crashed, moons took to the sky or swam, witch-fires laced the flotsam boil and shined through eyes of corpse-gaunt pirates. Whole universes sprang into existence, quantum fluctuations between consciousness and death.

"Mykol, are you all right?"

He keeled over.

"Mykol! Mykol!"

His eyes snapped open and he looked around. "I'm fine, I'm okay."

"You were passing out."

"It's all right. I got dizzy but I'm fine now. We have to talk to Sabal."

"We'll go to him now."

"Good. Let's go. Now. *Now.*"

They left the deck and hurried inside.

They both knew their special journey was over.

Chapter 14: The Hoxcar

They talked in Sabal's office and described what they saw (the stations, not the creatures they encountered, and nothing about Ranglen almost collapsing). Sabal had few questions in return, as if not surprised by what they said.

Then he told Mylia, "I want you to go to the mess hall and get reacquainted with everyone, without Mykol. I think they're ready to accept you again. Except for some outbursts, they seem to have settled. I'll keep Mykol here for a bit. I'm sure they're *not* ready for him yet."

Mylia hesitated but Ranglen told her to go. She obviously was still worried about his behavior on the deck but he reassured her he'd be fine.

She left.

Sabal said immediately, "You have something to tell me and you didn't want Mylia around when you did."

Ranglen nodded. "I know what's causing the Blight, the creatures, the light towers—everything you've encountered."

Sabal leaned forward.

"It's a Clip. I'm certain. And it's located in the central mound."

Sable looked suspicious. "*How* do you know?"

"Because I know what it's like to get close to one. I felt it when Mylia and I flew near the mound. It has to be buried there, and I'm sure it's responsible for the entire phenomenon of the Blight, the reworking of the landscape, the resurrections. It's the only power exotic enough to bring this about."

He let Sabal assume that all Clips felt that way, though it wasn't true, only this one. But he also didn't mention that the nest of roots beneath the mound reminded him of the Airafane labyrinth in his asteroid. Another connection.

"Why would a Clip do all this?"

"I don't know. That's the problem. But Clips do whatever they want. We're not meant to understand them, remember? That would diminish them—but I'm certain you've thought of all this before."

Sabal glanced away. "Of course I wondered. But I was never sure. Why do you think I wanted you to go with Mylia in the first place? I needed your reaction. It wasn't to bring the two of you together."

Ranglen felt both embarrassed and insulted.

"Don't be stupid," Sabal said. "Clearly something happened between the two of you. You're both trying too hard to be casual. But know that it's dangerous—foreign outsider and native idealist. Not a good mixture, especially now."

Ranglen wouldn't talk about it.

"Get back to the Clip," Sabal insisted. "Why is it behaving this way and not like the other Clips?"

"I'm not sure. And that bothers me."

"Maybe it's broken, malfunctioning."

"Or mutated beyond its original purpose. Maybe it's entered some higher realm and got lost in its delusion of grandeur. I don't know. We think they're logical with their 'instructions included,' but nothing's certain."

"How did it get there?"

"I assume it came up through the original volcano that formed the caldera, rising from the mantle like the other Clips." But, he didn't say, not like the one he found on his asteroid.

"Maybe the meteor damaged it when it struck," Sabal said, "changed its programming. The stasis field is supposed to be indestructible but if the meteor disrupted it somehow, then the Clip would be left unprotected, maybe vulnerable to change."

"We're just guessing."

"And we don't know what the Blight will throw at us next."

"*No*, Sabal," Ranglen said firmly. "I think we do know. Or at least we'll recognize it when it comes."

Sabal squinted as he stared back at him.

"Don't try to pretend you don't know what I mean. You understand exactly where all those things in the Blight originate and what determines them. The Alcherans know too but they don't like to think about it."

Sabal's face became hard.

"The Clip reads our minds, uses *our* thoughts for its creations. It takes pictures from our brains and makes them real—every night! All these bizarre manifestations, they come from us. We provide the image and the Clip brings it to 'life.'"

Sabal still didn't speak.

"Everyone knows this but they won't admit it, won't accept the consequences. Think of all the things that appeared since I've come here—they're from me, from *my* imagination. The killer birds, the Cannibal mound, a vision I had just now when we got back—they're line-for-line from my poems and stories." He said nothing of what he and Mylia encountered, the jewel creatures, the flame beings, the Rainbow Serpent, all of which he assumed were *her* creations. But he wouldn't share those with Sabal.

"These aren't just events from our pasts," he went on, "traumas or repressions. The Clip raids both our daydreams and night-dreams, takes them from us and plays with them, neither attracting us nor using them against us. Maybe the Clip *is* corrupted. Maybe it lost its purpose but not its power. Maybe it devolved into some foolish prankish childhood. We just don't know."

Sabal finally answered. "All right, I understand what you mean. I've thought the same. But it can't be random. No Clip is random. It might not be following *our* physics but it's still physics nonetheless, *Airafane* physics. I thought at first the Blight was providing some weird psychological help, that by objectifying our thoughts it might be offering a practical therapy and that this was its purpose. But it's too arbitrary. The objects made are already familiar, not hidden neuroses. They'd be darker if they were."

In Ranglen's opinion they were dark enough.

"They're more like parts of some huge archive," Sabal continued, "an unorganized library of human imaginings, collected and stored. But instead of being useful they resemble timid first drafts—unintelligent animals instead of people, mythical monsters instead of real ones."

"Maybe our expectations complete them. We probably see different versions of the same thing. Or the Clip trains us to become more creative while it populates the world with ever-improving objects from our fancy. Maybe the minds of the colonists were tapped to bring life to a barren planet. They say their memories of Earth are bad—maybe all their recollections were stolen. Maybe nothing was here when they arrived and the Clip covered the planet with their thoughts. That's why the culture is such a mixture of the ancient and new—foot travel and aircars, mythology and guns. No wonder they talk so much of the Dreaming. It's what they're living."

Sabal added, "They're as much created by the Blight as they're overseers of it. But the manifestations are not dreams, they're not hallucinations or holograms. They're *real*, if not permanent. The mist must be a kind of building material, like the nanotechnology the other Clips use. But you can't take samples of it. We've tried. It dissipates and you get nothing."

"It's what Mylia is trying to tap, in her own way, through stories and myths, letting the Blight spread across the planet. And it's inevitable that it *will* spread. The Alcherans have become more dependent on it, and such dependency will only grow. The economy functions because—I'll bet—the Blight provides more and more of what they need."

Sabal admitted this. "There are still farms and a few factories but they make less each year. Food can be found beneath the mist, even building material. The light stations create their own power. The people here haven't taken advantage of everything that's been offered to them. That's what Mylia wants to do."

"And they'll need to eventually. But Mylia wants it done out of choice, not as a last resort."

"And the resurrections still haven't returned."

Which brought Ranglen to a halt. He was acutely aware of this fact, that they stopped immediately after he arrived.

He stayed quiet for a bit, while Sabal let him concentrate, as if recognizing he pondered something important.

Then Ranglen declared, "I can stop all this. I can bring it to an end."

Sabal looked unconvinced.

"The whole Blight and all it does must depend on the Clip. Everything here has to result from it. But I can *find* it and take it away, remove it completely off the planet."

"How?"

"You have to take my word that I do know a way."

Ranglen could tell that Sabal was suspicious but the idea obviously appealed to him. "We've been to the mound and it's not easy to explore—physically, emotionally. You might die before you find it."

"I can give you pin-point accuracy, perform a kind of surgical incision to the exact location. Never mind how, just believe me." He was thinking of his shard and its proven ability to locate a Clip.

But the shard was back on Homeworld. He'd have to return there in order to retrieve it.

Sabal countered, "If you get rid of the Clip, then you destroy the Alcherans' dependencies, their function, their 'job.' They won't like that. And what about the resurrections? They'd definitely be gone then, with no chance of returning."

"They might be gone already. And, frankly, the Alcherans are better off without them. Their loss is what they think they're struggling with, but it's more their independence that's frightening them. If they want to remain human, they need to become free of the Blight, and that means freedom from resurrections. Births still occur, don't they? Once they realize they're on their own, they can live again."

"But it's their choice, not yours or mine."

"Yet I can give them the chance to make such a choice. I want to reveal to them what they've hidden, that their world is false. I want to answer their fears. I know it might be impossible, but I'm now caught up in Mylia's energy and optimism. Her liberating visions are no dreams. But they're not what the Alcherans are living now. This is something *I* can do."

"It sounds wrong, Mykol. It sounds like the outsider justifying his personal—and selfish—reasons for changing people's lives. You want Mylia, so you try to remake her entire world."

"But it still can be their decision. I want to give them the means to *make* the decision. They don't have that now. I realize they might not be happy with the reality of the choice. But they have to learn it can be done, *needs* to be done—so they can be free and become themselves."

Sabal considered. "What about Mylia? You'd be taking away what she wants to give to the world."

"But this could allow her to be *able* to give it, to open up the rest of the planet and not be so focused on the Blight. She told me herself—you don't find a sacred landscape, you make it. As long as the Blight exists, the Alcherans will focus on only it, and not their own potential and worth. Mylia wants the best for them, but that's not limited to only the products that come from this crater. She believes in the Alcherans and this world—and that's *more* than only the Blight."

But then Sabal looked withdrawn, as if pondering a darker thought. "There's something else, Mykol. Something I haven't told you."

Ranglen stared at him.

"You came here expecting a great escape, right? Leaving your old world for a new one that would be filled with adventure, excitement, freedom, even love. I know the story. I lived it myself."

Ever since the bird attacks, Ranglen assumed Sabal knew how he arrived here, by teleportation—the same way, he believed, that Sabal did. All of this had been left unsaid, but it hung between them. "In some ways, yes."

"But you have to remember, the Blight doesn't give you just what you want...but also what you *fear*. This world can be your realm of escape, but it can also be a trap. And know, this is especially pertinent to you and me."

"What are you getting at?"

"We tend to hurt what we love the most."

Ranglen remembered the story of Sabal's lover, how she was killed by something in the Blight.

Ranglen went cold.

When that killing happened, Sabal was the outsider. Ranglen was in that position now.

"Mylia told me the story," he said. "The plant that killed her…was that *your* manifestation?"

Sabal took a while to answer. "I saw the plant on a world I visited. So I'm the only one who would have known of it."

Ranglen also remembered from the story that Sabal had yelled to the mound, *Take her, you Airafane bitch!*

The Airafane, the makers of the teleport system.

But Ranglen still insisted, "I can find the Clip—I'm certain. I can get rid of it before anything happens."

"I'm not persuaded."

"Sabal, the *Clip* is to blame for her death. Not you or me. Once I find it, you can do whatever you want with it. We can move it to where it can't harm anyone."

"Weren't we saying that's the Alcherans' decision?"

"They don't know about the Clip yet. I'll give them the truth."

"You're deciding other people's lives when you do. And you still don't know them. Barinda's right about that."

"You don't believe in the Blight either. You said you once wanted to bomb it."

"That was for vengeance, and I had my own reasons. They're different from yours."

"But at least let me *try*. I'll find that Clip for you, for everyone. I just need to leave here and be gone for a while."

"Will you come back?"

"Of course I'll come back! Obviously, for *Mylia!*"

"It's a longer trip than what you think." And he spoke this as if he shared a secret that Ranglen already understood.

Sabal quickly added, "Wait until tonight at least. I want to see what comes out of the Blight. And I think you should see it too. The place was 'disturbed' the last time I looked. Maybe you'll understand it better than me."

Ranglen remembered his own recent hallucination. "Maybe that's not a good idea."

"You can see Mylia before you leave. You two deserve the time together. If you walk the barracks, just keep to yourself. Then leave after tonight."

Ranglen did want to see Mylia, but he was afraid if he stayed too long with her then he'd never go.

He agreed to remain one more night.

The people in the mess hall were still not friendly but they seemed polite. Ranglen encountered none of the anger or threats that Sabal hinted of. The Alcherans accepted Mylia again, so he wanted to be careful and not stay around her.

But he couldn't keep away. There was much discussion among all the people about the events in the Blight, and throughout the morning when he encountered her they felt embarrassed. Their easy attraction seemed almost offensive in the midst of so many troubles. When others were around them they became awkward, self-conscious. They didn't know how to be intimate and yet formally public at the same time. They were almost too aware of each other. What had been so simple and inevitable on their trip now was complex, burdened by other people's stares. Making the right move and saying the right word all became difficult.

They wanted to touch each other, but only their eyes were free to do so.

Finally, in the afternoon, they met in Ranglen's room, more isolated than hers, and they stayed there for hours. At first they felt conflicted, but even with all the tension around them they couldn't deny what they felt for each other. This gift of time was too precious, this chance to establish their claims on each other.

They made love. They declared their love.

Yet when she left in the afternoon, she checked the corridor so no one saw her.

Ranglen, eager for the night to come, watched the sun drag its light across the caldera. For no obvious reason the mound looked forbidding. And it felt close, though it lacked detail against the sky.

As darkness fell, Ranglen, Mylia, and Sabal stood outside by the wall of the deck, waiting to see what the Blight would produce.

Objects materialized out of the mist.

They looked like a fleet of ancient sailing ships with black canvas, gliding through the fog as if it were an ocean that levitated the galleons. They didn't follow any wind direction, the sails positioned for visual effect and not propulsion. Wet seaweed clung to the hulls. Shrouded figures with glowing eyes lined the decks. They wailed and screamed.

Ranglen was appalled. The same hallucination he experienced that morning had been brought to life.

Sabal shouted, "What the hell's all this?"

Ranglen muttered. He should have left sooner.

Mylia asked him what was wrong.

"It's a vision from a poem I wrote. But it's now real!"

In a broad line the ships neared the shore, stretched into the distance like a choreographed theatrical performance.

And the ships caught fire.

Flames leapt upward like released demons, igniting the rigging and the parchment sails, engulfing them and soaring higher. The fires spread as if flammables had soaked the decks.

"Fire ships," Ranglen said. "An old sea-battle technique."

Thinking of Sabal's earlier fears, he warned Mylia, "You should leave now. If violence happens or anyone's hurt, get inside immediately and hide yourself."

"I'm not leaving."

"You could be killed."

The mists broke apart like waves of water, and dinosaurs rose up behind the ships.

Ranglen felt out of control. The world could throw *anything* at him now.

People were too fascinated and frightened to turn away. Ranglen yelled for everyone to run.

Then a single object moved deliberately from the chaos below, seeming to come into existence as Ranglen stared at it. Shaped like a long narrow blimp with a sharpened prow and decorated sides, it floated in a straight line up the hill. It was layered with balconies, prongs, staffs, flimsy communication dishes, long antennae, strung ropes, collapsed metal insectile arms. The features looked excessive, baroque, decadent, made to impress, startle and affront. It was like a beetle with folded wings or a junkyard pressed into the shape of a dirigible, painted with scarlet and bronze swirls beside black-and-red stripes.

Ranglen recognized it. He had created it. It was an imaginary vehicle from one of his stories. "A hox-car," he whispered.

"What?" Sabal snapped.

It continued up the slope relentlessly—aimed for the tower, whose beacon ignited.

People now scurried between the rocks, into the barracks, out of its way.

But in all the confusion, Ranglen lost Mylia. Sick terror overwhelmed him.

The hox-car neared and couldn't be stopped. The sharp prow moved directly for the lighthouse.

While Ranglen scrambled in search of Mylia, the vessel struck—halfway up the side of the pylon.

The cupola crashed, the finery shattered, the opalescent fragments tumbled down, pieces of the lantern chamber spread across the top of the hox-car like a thousand broken goblets of glass. The vessel slid over the smashed ruins, grinding the stub of the foundation and scattering it out into the rocks.

The craft then glided over the rim of the crater, vanishing from sight behind the ridge. It screamed a howl of twisted metal and crushed wood as it fell into the trees, finally coming to a defeated halt. One could hear small explosions. Plumes of smoke and flame shot up, laced with wreckage that soared into the air and fell.

Ranglen saw Mylia. A piece of falling debris hit the ground, bounced, struck her. She collapsed.

He rushed to her

She held her left thigh as she squirmed in pain. "It hit my leg!"

He called for help. People rushed around tending to anyone who had been hurt. They hurried over and then called for a stretcher.

She insisted on trying to stand on her own but they wouldn't let her. They carried her to the medical rooms. Ranglen followed. Other victims were brought in too. A few injuries looked severe but most had only minor wounds.

The room was crowded. A nurse chased Ranglen outside so more patients could be wheeled in. Then, after a while, a strained doctor came to him and said, "It's a thigh contusion, intermuscular bruising in the quadriceps. She'll have a lot of swelling, and pain. She's resting now. We put ice on the leg. Luckily it's not a fracture—the femur's one of the toughest bones in the body. She'll need to be careful but otherwise she'll be fine. She said to tell you not to stay with her, to get out and help others."

That sounded like her.

Ranglen felt better, but he knew he'd return later to see her—before he left to stop all this.

He hurried back to the wrecked tower and helped with any more wounded and clean-up. Like before, the Alcherans accepted him during a crisis. But he was there because he felt responsible.

He saw Sabal but he said nothing to him.

When things seemed in order, he returned to the sick bay and found Mylia in a bed in the hall. The medical rooms were still busy. She was asleep, likely sedated. Her bandaged leg was elevated to keep the knee bent. The pack had been removed. She looked peaceful, even content.

But he felt pain while watching her. The universe could hurt her in so many ways.

He said to her as she slept, quietly so no one else could hear. "I have to leave for a while. Just a few days. I know a way to end all this, to stop any more threats from the Blight—threats to you. I *will* stop them."

He held her hand and kissed her. He hoped she might be aware of him. But he had to go now, before he was tempted to stay and never leave at all. It was better she wasn't awake. She could persuade him—or insist on coming with him, which he expected she would do even in her condition.

He took a long look at her to remember her. The braid of her hair lay across the pillow.

He quickly left.

He didn't see Sabal and didn't want to, afraid the man might try to stop him from going.

Though the tower had fallen, few of the other buildings were hurt. The wreckage of the hox-car still burned over the ridge. And behind him, columns of smoke rose from where the fire-ships had crashed.

He had no trouble accepting what happened—no matter how unreal and outlandish it seemed. This showed the extent to which he had accommodated the events of the Blight. He now was a part of them. All that happened seemed dreadfully appropriate.

But he'd make sure they'd never happen again

He avoided the people around the burning hox-car. He couldn't remember how he came up with that name. In his story, the huge bloated vehicles carried victims from dead cities and dumped them in what he called the Sunken Plains. All on a world named Little Redemption.

The Alcherans found no one on board the wreck, no bodies, no life. He felt they hadn't expected to.

He stopped at his small camp in the trees. It showed no signs of having been discovered. He took a direct route from there to the ruins.

For all the time he had been on this world, and except for Mylia's brief mention, no one had showed any interest in the stonework. The Alcherans were obsessed with only the Blight.

The skeleton of the walrus-bear had been picked clean.

He took a last view of the landscape around him, the hox-car burning behind the trees.

He *would* come back. He had found his escape.

He reached the kiva and pulled out his Clip.

"Going somewhere?"

Sabal sat in the corner of the room, hidden in shadow with his arms resting on his raised knees.

Ranglen forced his shock to settle, accepting that he shouldn't be surprised. "So," he said, "we really *do* know how each of us got here."

"I knew from the moment I saw you. That's why I struck you—it wasn't planned, it was out of recognition."

"And I never believed your lifeboat story. But I wanted to believe it. I wanted you to come here by a different way than I did."

"I might as well have. I've committed myself. I *can't* go back. I got rid of my Clip, the one that's needed for the teleporting to work. I decided early on to stay here—while *you* go running home at the first sign of distress."

"I told you I'm returning. The Alcherans face too much danger. What if the next person the Blight taps is insane, or a killer. We just had pirate ships. What if we get an army, atom bombs? Who knows what someone's imagination will hatch?"

"I can't believe you're leaving when Mylia's still hurt."

"I don't want to. But it's better she doesn't know."

Sabal sneered.

"You said you got rid of your own Clip. What did you do with it?"

"I didn't throw it away. I *destroyed* it."

"That's impossible."

"You have your little secret. I have mine. Nice distribution of skills, don't you think? You find Clips, and I kill them."

Ranglen tried to read Sabal's expression. "I'm leaving now. You can't stop me."

"And I won't. Get what you need. It *is* time to control the Blight. But, like I said, be sure to come back."

"I promised I will."

"You might find the transition more difficult than you think."

"Stop playing with me. What do you mean?"

"I'm not certain. I'm just naturally suspicious. You've noticed that quality in me, haven't you?"

"I still have to go."

"Don't forget you owe us. Everything's a mess here since you arrived. You destroyed the tower, and almost killed Mylia."

"*I* didn't do that. And I *will* change things."

"I hope that's true."

Sabal stood up and began walking from the room. Ranglen stopped him. "Watch over her, will you? Give her some idea why I left. I hate doing this without my telling her."

Sabal nodded, said nothing more. Then he was gone.

Ranglen, fearing the loss of his resolve, quickly placed the Clip into its invisible slot, and as soon as the star-chart came up, he set the coordinates for Homeworld.

After reinserting the Clip, and when the blue column appeared a second time, he stepped into the kiva.

And vanished.

Chapter 15: Doubts

And came down on Homeworld.

He rolled, kicked up sand, stopped against a rock. All was still except for the dust-cloud drifting away.

Three small moons gleamed in the night. A green "ghost" trailed from a dune. He was back.

He stood up and pulled out his cellpad to verify his location, but of course the battery had gone dead. He stepped around the rocks and saw the Airafane ruins in the moonlight.

Nothing had changed. No one was here.

He hurried to his camp. He plugged his cellpad into a portable charger then pulled out a spare and checked the date.

The same time had passed here as on Alchera.

So it wasn't like near-FTL travel where time underwent dilation and contraction. He was surprised. Though light-speeds weren't involved, such vast distance should make similar time-tracks impossible. Maybe how teleportation worked was by locking all the ruins into a galaxy-wide entangled simultaneity. And maybe that was why they never changed, because they existed at the same time forever and that's why you could travel from one to the other—with literally no separation between them in either space or time.

Who could say? Modern physics had become a muddle since Clips were discovered. The Airafane brewed their own realities and served out miracles, but humans could only watch. And use.

Ranglen didn't care. He wanted to get back to Alchera and keep his promise. The authorities had taken Annulus from him, but they wouldn't take this. He had his own world now.

He needed the shard from the Clip he found, and he had to return to his asteroid to get it. It had been the only place where he felt it would be safe.

He closed up his tent, loaded supplies, uncovered his aircar and flew it across the desert. Dawn came, just like back on Alchera by now.

He reached the settlement from where he had left, and then took a public flight to the capital. He talked to his lawyers, rewrote his will, established conditions for becoming legally dead—very complicated now with FTL's flexible time streams.

If he never returned, all his wealth would go to Annulus, to charities (especially for homeless children and vagrants), and to funds that would create a Society for an Independent Annulus. He still wanted that world to be left alone, and to be recognized as its founder and creator. Maybe it was only a dream of grandeur, or of buying recognition through his money, but he had to do something, even if not planned very thoroughly.

Since he already had said good-bye to his friends and then returned after just a few days, he felt no one would take him seriously if he called them again. Anne would laugh, Hatch scowl. So he spoke to neither of them.

He lifted ship as soon as he could and reached his asteroid. There, he pulled the shard from his safe. He held up the piece of so-called "fluorite" and looked through it with delighted nostalgia.

So easily a Clip could be found—such Airafane magic!

He chastised himself for not bringing it with him when he teleported to Alchera. But who could've known he would need it.

He flew back to Homeworld and put the last touches on closing down his life— eager now to leave it all behind, to start over, to return to his new and separate calling.

But then the Federal Investigators from Earth showed up at his door.

Three of them, of indefinite gender and imprecise race. Not quite clones but clearly a standard. Only one of them talked. "It's come to our attention you're planning a life change."

"I'm taking a long trip, if that's what you mean."

"You've modified your will, reorganized your bank accounts, set up trusts. Your lawyers have been overly busy. It looks like you don't intend to return."

"That's not true." He lied. "But if I did, is there a problem?"

"You discovered the third Clip, Mr. Ranglen."

"So?"

"We keep watch over those with direct connections to Clips. It's in everyone's interest. You're too special to be left alone, and Earth would object if you're thinking of leaving the Confederation. You've talked of that in your writings."

"But then you'd also know—from my writings—that I often make solitary expeditions into space. I'm preparing for one now. I just expect it will last longer than most."

"You haven't had your destination or route cleared yet."

"I've never had to do that."

"Then you've evaded some tight restrictions."

"I've left from Homeworld and not Earth, and I'm leaving from Homeworld now. You Federal Investigators are from Earth, so you have no jurisdiction here."

"But we soon will. We eventually intend to annex this planet."

Which shocked Ranglen—both the fact, and the blunt admission of it. He knew nothing of such a move and had heard no rumors. "Homeworld broke from Earth long ago. The people won't allow you to infiltrate again."

"We already have. We knew enough about you, didn't we?"

This also astonished him. "But you don't know enough. You apparently aren't aware of the agreements I've made with Earth, Homeworld, and the Confederation. I recommend you check them before you do something your superiors won't like—and I guarantee you they won't."

"*We'll* worry about that, Mr. Ranglen. Meanwhile, you need to come with us."

"This is absurd. You have no power of arrest here. You'd never get a warrant."

"We don't need one." The two who kept quiet behind the speaker moved quickly and grabbed his arms, crossed them behind his back tightly. He tried to struggle but they sealed his wrists together.

The speaker agent said, "We're taking you to a secure location. Homeworld knows nothing about us being here. There's no chance of them helping you."

Ranglen claimed his rights and demanded to communicate with his lawyers.

The agents said nothing and dragged him away.

They took him to what he assumed was a building in the capital, but he wasn't sure. He could see nothing along the way and the vehicle had been soundproofed. The entrance procedure to the building was complicated, and by then they had drugged him. They kept him there in a locked room, which was comfortable but stark and lifeless.

They searched him and took away his cellpad. But the shard, which he had sewn into the lining of his shoe, they didn't catch. Ranglen was surprised. They should have taken all his clothes and examined them, thread by thread. They apparently were waiting for "higher-ups" before any formal interrogation.

He was frantic to conclude the procedures and get away. With this new antagonism between Earth and Homeworld he was afraid matters could change too quickly—the politics sour, his ruins discovered, his asteroid found, and his great secret for tracking new Clips unearthed and stolen. He was frightened someone would suddenly decide, for political or even economic reasons, that the safest thing to do was just to kill him. So he needed to get back as fast as he could.

They kept him three weeks.

He went out of his mind.

Finally, the agents returned, obviously disgruntled but trying not to show it. They blindfolded him and took him back to his hotel room, not as politely or as securely this time. The two thuggish agents left. The one who remained said, "You're very lucky, Mr. Ranglen. Apparently you *do* have some agreements with our government."

"It took you that long to find out?"

"Our branch officers wanted to make an impression. We learned we had to release you several days after we took you, but we decided to keep you longer, just so you'd remember us well. We hope you enjoyed the stay."

"Go to hell."

"It's very likely you'll see us again. We intend to overrun Homeworld soon."

"I discover a Clip—a miracle benefit for all humanity—and you treat me like an outlaw."

"Other civilizations exist out there, and I'm sure they want Clips as much as we do. Since you found one, you might find another. That's why we watch you. And if anyone else gets the Clip instead of us, then you *certainly* will see me again. And I won't be held back from 'enlightening' you. My two enforcers are great at retribution."

He left.

Ranglen refused to think of the incident. He was more in agony from the time lost than the confinement. He moved quickly now, though he feared everything might be useless.

He left the city through a labyrinth of networks, private and public transportation, in the air and on the ground. Automated surveillance certainly would pick him up, but Earth's agents, even for all their arrogance, could not track him, not on a world where they had no authority.

Still, he rented five DRVs through camouflaged accounts and had them parked in different areas near the desert. He picked one randomly, made more quick purchases, and by a twisted route defined by his spastic paranoia he reached his aircar on the outskirts of the desert. He flew that car, again not directly, to another DRV, and drove it further into the dunes.

He knew he was obsessed, but he felt justified.

His one big advantage was that the ruins did not show up on satellite or aerial tracking, nor did the material around them (like a camp or vehicles). The Airafane guaranteed privacy to visitors—though no one knew how.

When he neared the massif where the ruins were located, he thought he saw a dust plume from another DRV, leaving the gulley that led up to his camp.

But he wasn't certain.

It worried him.

He sent his jeep on automated guidance back to his cache. He didn't want to leave it near the ruins after he departed. He stopped at his camp to pick up the things he had left behind.

He found the tracks of another jeep, apparently the one he had just seen. And he discovered boot-prints throughout the area around the ruins that were smaller than his. The person in the other DRV obviously had been here.

He looked through his equipment, but he didn't see evidence that anyone searched it. His camp was not in disarray.

But someone had been there.

And he noticed a fact even more disturbing. He could find a number of his own boot-prints throughout the camp, left from before he teleported off Homeworld. But they weren't *really* his boot-prints, even though they were in places where he remembered walking. They were the same size, but they didn't have the stylized imprint in the center that came from the brand of boots he always wore. There was no insignia at all. This made him notice that the tread was slightly different too.

But if his own boot-prints weren't his, then whose were they?

A sweaty chill ran through his limbs.

Finally, after weeks of delay, after disturbing events that were hard to believe, after discovering a conspiracy of Terrestrial agents moving against Homeworld (which never could work—the Confederation would join the fight to stop them), and after being imprisoned at a time when Clips supposedly *increased* individual freedoms instead of restricting them (what the hell was happening to post-Clip culture?), he wanted only to leave. Especially since, if an interstellar war occurred, his private Annulus would become even more lost.

He knew for certain—he would not return.

He looked around at the desert. He wanted to remember it. He loved this landscape.

A particular rock formation appeared different from what he remembered.

This was too much. Apprehension flowed through him. He now needed out of there as fast as possible.

He hurried into the ruins and found the chamber with the kiva. He piled his belongings into the sunken pit. He looked through the openings to the plateau and muttered to himself, trying to be humorous, "It's all a Dream."

He inserted the Clip, marked the star-chart. The blue light appeared. He removed the Clip, turned it over, reinserted it.

When the column returned, he jumped into the kiva amid all his gear.

Something moved outside—

A burst of light.

The room vanished.

Chapter 16: Lost World

And fell onto Alchera—

He rolled down the slope and lay in the grass, saw the trees, mountains, river, felt the cool air. Nothing had changed.

Swept with relief, he shuddered at how frightened he had become, how much the trip back to Homeworld unsettled him, to the point of seeing someone before he left, maybe the person who made the other footprints.

Yet anyone who tried to follow him would need a Clip and have to know how to use it. He felt—finally, tentatively—safe.

He hurried up to the ridge of familiar rocks. Knowing he'd been away so long he felt he shouldn't tempt fate by being too eager, but he couldn't help himself. He needed Mylia.

He rushed between the boulders and looked into the Blight.

Fear struck him.

The forest, the black reefs, the distant mound—those were the same. But the crater floor was filled with wreckage, with huge twisted shapes of metal that lay everywhere, as if a fleet of flying machines had fallen and crashed into the trees. He recognized many of them as combat vehicles from Earth's past—WWII fighter craft, atomic-age stratospheric bombers, early biplanes, supersonic jets, submarines both diesel and nuclear, long bent frames of zeppelins, nineteenth-century men-of-war, early dreadnoughts, military helicopters, torpedos, drones.

Nothing was recent. No spaceships, no aircars. Had someone's historical recollections been mined? But the Alcherans claimed they didn't remember their past. And why was everything destroyed? Ruined craft lay on top of each other and tilted up the sides of the reefs, surrounding even the central mound in an apron of discarded scrap. A smell of burning hung over the view—charred fabric, seared metal, oil, gasoline. And no creeping mist lurked out there, no blanket of restoration or change. Only smoke in tall columns, barren and thin, hardly regenerative.

What could have happened?

He looked to the left and again was shocked—the white tower still stood! The barracks around it lay in disarray instead, with walls torn open and roofs fallen in. Debris from the destruction in the crater spread all the way up the slopes, apparently the cause for the barracks' collapse. But the light-tower stood flawless and bright, exactly as he had seen it the first time he came.

Then he reasoned—if the Blight created the towers in the first place, the mist might have moved uphill after the hox-car destroyed it and then restored it to what it had been. And though he recalled now that he hadn't seen the wreckage of the hox-car as he came up the slope, the Alcherans logically would have cleared it away. Both conclusions seemed plausible.

Down in the crater he saw movement. People scurried in and out of makeshift habitations tucked against the edge of the forest. The people apparently had left the barracks and moved down to the base of the cliffs beside the trees. Maybe they had given up on the resurrections, on any kind of Blight activity. There wasn't enough mist to remake anything now anyway. But they still must be scared of it so they avoided building inside the Blight itself.

Yet all this didn't matter. He had to find Mylia.

He hurried downhill, not sure whether to stay hidden or not. Everything had changed here, but for better or worse he didn't yet know.

Two scruffily dressed Alcherans moved out from the rocks and held their rifles on him, making him stop. The guns still looked makeshift but more dangerous—with extendable metal butts, crude pistol grips, larger magazines.

"We know who you are," they said, "Sabal's waiting for you." They told him to follow.

Ranglen went along, baffled, concerned.

They came to a quickly erected shanty halfway down the slope, hidden in a natural shelter surrounded by boulders. Sabal sat inside, still behind a desk—or a portable table, and much smaller than his original. He looked dirty and unkempt, his clothes ragged, like a fugitive.

He glanced up at Ranglen. "Well, finally. Where the hell have you been?"

"What's happened here?"

Sabal gave an ugly humorless smile. "Quite a lot. After you left, more things came from the Blight, most of them destructive. Then all this floating machinery arrived and fell out of the sky at the same time (it's mostly fake—hollow, like stage-props). The barracks were destroyed and I was wounded. But while I recuperated, Barinda took over, and she hasn't given up control since. She moved people down beside the Blight. The mist never returned so nothing's been changed. They're not scared of the place anymore. I thought it was too dangerous and I tried to oppose her, but she has more people than I do now. We're two armed camps. She's the queen of selfish authority and I'm the lone resistance fighter."

"But what are you fighting about?"

"What's near and dear to the hearts of all Alcherans—burial rights. We agreed to take corpses, and we've had a lot of them, to one cemetery lying at the base of the mound. There's no more common belief in resurrection but it still lurks in everyone's minds, a hope they can't dismiss, so they all wanted it there. My people— not Barinda's—cleared a pathway to that cemetery through all the wreckage, which wasn't easy. But then she claimed control over the caravans going there, and she often restricts us from participating and including our victims. So we fight. I lead the disaffected. All my hatred for her has returned."

Ranglen's frustration peaked. "You have so few people yet you're killing each other! Even Barinda spoke against that. It's nonsense."

"She's worse than we are. And you're not the one to talk, Mykol. You..." He stopped himself.

"What do you mean?"

Sabal stared at him with a touch of pity. He kept quiet.

"Is Mylia all right?"

Sabal's eyes didn't change.

Ranglen understood. He took a deep breath. Then he said, "She's not alive, is she?"

Sabal tried to look sympathetic. "I'm sorry, Mykol...."

Ranglen said nothing for a long time. Then only, "What happened?"

"I don't know the whole story. Barinda does. She has her body and is taking it to the mound. All I know is that Mylia didn't fully recover from the wound she got when the hox-car came. She seemed to be doing well and she left the medical ward on her own. But then she was found dead, on the night when all the wreckage fell onto the Blight. Apparently from a blood clot that started in her leg and then traveled to her lungs, at least that's what I heard. Barinda found her."

Ranglen looked down. He realized he had prepared himself for this, intentionally if not knowingly, during his confinement on Homeworld, where he feared her death so often, so deeply.

He would not allow himself to be devastated now. That would come later. "I want to see her body."

"Barinda has it. And you'll have to get to Barinda on your own. She'd kill any of us if we got near her, but she might let *you* in. She's about to lead a caravan to the cemetery, and Mylia I assume will be included. Barinda's down beside the Blight now, just inside the entrance to the trail. But we're planning to attack her soon. She didn't let us put any of our own dead into the caravan. So we can't help you. You're on your own."

Ranglen didn't care. He turned to leave.

"Wait. There's more."

"Will it make any difference?"

"You left here with the intention of getting something, to find something. You seem to have forgotten."

"It's not important now. I just want to see her."

"Not important for *you* or not important for *us*?"

"Sabal, this isn't the time to talk about it."

"You're not free of responsibility for what happened to Mylia."

"The *Blight* killed her. Not me. We've argued this before and I won't listen to it now."

"The object that struck her came from you."

"You can blame yourself for Orani if you want. But you didn't choose what happened to her. Neither did I. I didn't create my hox-car and you didn't make your killer plant."

"You're over-simplifying. Both of us *did* choose to use a Clip to come here, and look how we've both been treated for it. We lost what we wanted. That's much too convenient and obvious for me. You can't deny it."

"We're not to blame for our manifestations."

"Oh, come on, Mykol. Listen for once. What happened makes a perverse kind of sense. We acquire a dream and then we lose it. It's not a result of some god's cosmic morality—it's not intelligent and certainly not noble. It's just the nature of the Airafane universe. Conservation of *affect* instead of energy. Maybe the Airafane had their own kind of 'cold equations'—they're just more subjective, and a lot more painful, than ours."

Ranglen couldn't handle this now. He had to think of his own sorrow and not a whirlpool surge of accusation.

But Sabal continued. "You can't come here without consequences. Barinda and I had a balance before. Things happened between us but nothing like this. Then you come and everything changes. You and Mylia take your little love trip and the Blight turns inside out. We get a flock of war machines and no one knows why. But *I* know why. I *know* where they came from. I'll bet if you get agitated now, jets will rise up from the wreckage and strafe both me and Barinda, and anyone else who suddenly displeases you."

"They're not mine, Sabal! I wasn't even here!"

"You don't get to just walk away and—"

"Drop it! Now!"

Sabal stopped. He looked at his table, said almost indifferently, "If you want to see her before she's taken away, you better get down there. We won't be moving on Barinda for a while, but we're not waiting forever either."

"How much time do I have?"

"Several hours. She knows we're coming but not when. We can hit her anywhere along the trail into the Blight."

Ranglen moved toward the exit.

Sabal said, "Leave your backpack and firearm here. They won't let you get close to her if they see them. And one of my soldiers will show you to the caravan."

As Ranglen left these on the floor, Sabal returned to his work and did not say good bye. Ranglen didn't know if he'd see him again. He didn't want to. This was no longer the world he wanted to save.

It didn't have Mylia.

And no one beside Sabal appeared to care about the Blight or the Clip that produced it. They were too caught up in their petty in-fighting.

Ranglen had lost one world recently. Now another.

One of the soldiers who captured him earlier led him down the crater wall. He seemed younger than most, though not "youthful." He also seemed eager, but Ranglen couldn't understand why.

He stared at the wreckage in the Blight as they approached it, all of it absurd. The wings of a Cold-War B-52, the hull of a Napoleonic ship-of-the-line, the rear lattice framework of a twentieth-century "whirlybird," the battered fuselage of a Korean-War sabrejet. But they all must have some dreadful significance behind them—the Blight usually acted they way.

And he wondered, since he recognized the objects, whether his own mind could have produced them? Was Sabal right?

But all these thoughts—trivial and meaningless—were only attempts to delay his thinking about Mylia.

He neared the bottom of the slope and saw an opening torn out of the forest to provide a pathway to the central mound. In that opening stood a row of collapsible carts with sealed plastic bags on top of them.

"There are the bodies," the soldier said to him. "You're on your own now. Barinda's people will stop you when you get near them, but they should let you talk to her if you ask. You're still known, so they might hesitate just long enough." Then he quickly left.

Ranglen stared at the line of carts. A caravan of the dead.

He had to confront Mylia's fate now. He walked into the open toward the carts.

People saw him and, suspicious, gathered around him, but they seemed fascinated by him too, maybe remembered him. He marched on and came to the first body bag. As he reached for it he was grabbed from behind, but he shook off the grip and quickly unsealed the bag before him, looked at the face. It was not Mylia.

The Alcherans now encircled him and held his arms. Ranglen tried to pull away from them but failed. He was determined to open as many bags as he could.

"Stop it! Let him go!"

Barinda walked up, with more followers close behind her. Ranglen paid attention to them now. They looked more like soldiers than Sabal's group, in matching outfits—military jackets, baggy slacks, high-laced thick boots. Even Barinda was dressed the same way, and she held a pistol which she, politely, aimed downward.

Her stare at Ranglen was probing and long. Her first question was, "Are you a resurrection?"

"No. Of course not. I've just been gone a while."

Her eyes narrowed.

Ranglen didn't bother to explain. "I know Mylia's not alive. But I need to see her."

Barinda still just stared at him.

Angry, he turned from her, parted the clamps of another bag. Still not Mylia.

"Why are you doing this?" Barinda asked.

He opened one more bag. This face, male, looked familiar. But it was not who he wanted.

"Stop it, Mykol," she insisted. "Aren't you curious about how she died?"

He opened another.

Then he found her.

Barinda waved the other people away. They had stood about like her personal armed guard and easily could have stopped him, but she now dismissed them.

She moved closer to Ranglen and stood beside him. He stared at Mylia.

He was surprised, and yet almost relieved, that her face showed no hint of what she had been, of her warm energy and keen attention. She didn't look asleep, just empty. What lay here was clearly her, but it was still just a shell, an approximation, a bad copy by an inferior artist. It had nothing to do with his memory of her.

Barinda said, "When your hox-car struck her it did more damage than everyone thought."

"It was not my hox-car."

"At first she seemed fine. Her leg became strong enough for her to walk with crutches, and she left the medical rooms on her own. Some people claimed you returned secretly and took her away. That was also the night when all the machines flew out of the Blight and filled the sky. People had never seen anything like it."

Barinda waited for a reaction from him but none came.

"I searched for her. I finally found her up along the rim overlooking the Blight. When I reached her she was still alive, but just barely. She was coughing and holding her chest. Then she couldn't breathe at all. There was nothing we could do. And when she did die—maybe at that exact moment—all the ships fell to the ground, wrecking the forest. The debris destroyed the barracks by the light station too. But none of it touched her. A blood clot had moved from her leg to her lungs. 'Deep vein thrombosis,' they called it, pulmonary embolism. So it was the wound from the hox-car that did it."

Ranglen still gave no response.

"People said all the ships in the sky were related to her death, since they fell at the same time."

Ranglen grew alert, suddenly asked, "Was anyone else with her when she died?"

Barinda watched him with deep concern.

"Well?"

"Yes," she finally admitted.

"Who was it?"

She pointed to the body beside Mylia's, the one Ranglen had looked at before.

He examined the male face again.

The features were familiar because they were his.

The man was himself.

Nausea rose up inside him. His whole world seemed to fall and crash.

"When Mylia disappeared," Barinda said, "people claimed they had seen you with her. I thought I saw you too, so I searched for both of you. You were alone with her up on the ridge. I tried to pull her away from you but you and I fought. That's when the machines appeared over the Blight."

Ranglen grew unsteady, felt he might fall.

"You created them, Mykol. All those war planes had to be your manifestations. Maybe you just wanted to kill me, or kill *everyone* because she was dying. But when she did die, at the moment when you realized she was dead, that's when all the machines tumbled down to the ground and wrecked, in that one instant."

Ranglen staggered back in disbelief.

"The connection's too obvious. I'm not sure if you even noticed it at the time. You were too distraught. You still came just after *me*, tried to fight me and hurt me. I had to shoot you with my gun. I killed you. I thought then you almost wanted me to—that you had suffered enough."

Ranglen could barely hear her now. The blood rushed in his brain too loud. "That wasn't *me*, Barinda."

"It's why I asked if you were a resurrection."

"That's impossible! The body's *here!* How could I have been 'transformed'? I—"

A terrible realization struck him.

With both hands he ripped open the length of the bag that held "his" body.

Barinda yelled at him.

The corpse inside was still clothed, even still wearing boots. Ranglen lifted them and examined the tread.

They had no insignia, not like his own boots. They must have made the unidentified prints he had seen at his camp on Homeworld. Not the small ones of his unknown visitor, but those that were the same size as his—those that created his original footprints.

Barinda's soldiers moved in around him and waited tensely, alarmed at Ranglen's behavior.

Then he shocked all of them. He *kicked over* the cart that held his body.

The bag fell to the ground. The corpse fell out and tumbled on the earth. Ranglen kicked at that too, yelling, "*You bastard!*"

The soldiers grabbed him. Ranglen tried to push them away, but they quickly stopped him and held him still.

Barinda stood before him and stared into his face.

Ranglen asked her, in a near-wailing voice, "Did Sabal know about this?"

"He didn't tell you?"

Gunfire erupted from the trees near them.

A bullet struck a soldier holding Ranglen. The others let go of him and shot back with their rifles, Barinda with her pistol. They leapt behind available cover.

Ranglen kneeled beside Barinda, grabbed her jacket and pulled her ear close to his mouth. He yelled to be heard over the noise of the shooting. "You said the hox-car struck her—but it *didn't!* It hit the light-tower instead!"

"No!" she yelled back. "It went straight for her. It was *aimed* at her and fractured her leg." Even while he held her, she shot at movement in the brush around her.

Ranglen shouted, "The tower *fell!* Her leg wasn't broken!"

"No, Mykol, no!"

Bullets flew around them. One struck beside Ranglen's foot, threw dirt onto him. He released Barinda and she hurried away from the line of carts, staying low to avoid the gunfire.

Ranglen stood up. He didn't care about the guns or that Sabal lied about the time of their attack. He ran toward the slope leading up to the ridge. Bullets zinged by. One struck his arm and almost knocked him over. He staggered but kept going. He never looked back. He tried to hold his shoulder but he felt himself bleeding.

He rushed madly to the top of the hill, where he had to slow himself to regain his breath. When he stopped, he could still hear gunshots from below.

Fools. Go ahead and kill each other. I don't care.

He found two holes in the sleeve of his jacket. The bullet must have passed through his arm—from a pistol apparently, not the big rifles, which would have been worse. He felt pain but not as much as expected. He slipped his hand inside his coat and it came away bloody.

He still didn't care. He wondered if the central mound now laughed at him—at everyone—with all its mouths howling at once. He didn't look to see.

But he did glance at the light-tower and found it still untouched.

Barinda had said it never fell. No mist restored it. The hox-car had gone for Mylia instead. Aimed straight at her.

Murdered her.

Sabal is right. The Airafane equations are colder than ours.

He stumbled through the rocks and into the trees, down to the ruins—that never changed, the one solidity in his crushed universe. But they too came with slippery physics, quantum nonsense, entangled farce.

He was much too tired now and getting weaker. But he couldn't stop. He tripped often, scraped his face and neck against rocks. The pain in his arm grew worse.

He scrambled into the kiva room and tried to insert the Clip. But his hand shook, his body quaked. He had to grasp the Clip with both hands and hold himself firm and still.

He heard more gunfire. It sounded closer.

Finally—*finally*—he got the Clip inserted into the wall. He brought up the star chart, turned the Clip over, made the blue column appear again.

He collapsed into the kiva.

The flash of white light was almost a benediction.

The room vanished.

And came down on Homeworld...

And the hood of Riley's jeep.

Part III: Elsewhere

Chapter 17: Inferno

And landed on Alchera.

Riley and Mykol rolled down a hill of leafy grass, slowed to a stop, stared at each other—she with fear, he with anger.

"What the hell did you do?"

She tried to look innocent but knew she failed. "You had your way out. I wanted mine."

"This is no escape."

"Then why did *you* come?"

"I have something I need to do."

"But that's not the reason you first came, right?"

He stood up, looked away from her and tried to focus. "I shouldn't have told you anything."

She stood up too. "You're not the only one with dreams."

"*You think I don't know that?*" He said this so fiercely she staggered back, frightened.

She examined the landscape: snowy mountains, pale river, forests of conifers, cold breeze, yellow-green ground cover that spread everywhere.

Ranglen looked bewildered. "Where's the red growth? It lay all over."

"Something's changed?"

"The vegetation's not the same."

"You've been away for a while. Wouldn't things be different?"

"Not that much. They—Wait, this is *good*! She might be—yes, this is just what I want."

Riley tried not to interfere. She had pushed him too much already.

"You should go back immediately," he said, "before you're stuck here."

"You mean we *can* go back?"

"I've done it before."

"Then why worry? I'll go when you go."

"This could be your only chance."

"Are you trying to scare me?"

"*Yes*, goddammit, you *should* be scared! I don't know what's beyond that ridge. It could be *anything!*" He indicated the rocks at the top of the hill down which they had rolled.

"You can yell all you want, Mykol. But I know you lied to me, that you intended to leave me before I drove you anywhere in the desert. I figured you'd escape through the ruins, so I needed to see what was going on."

"But you didn't have to follow me."

"Everything you said meant my work was now pointless, that I was wasting my time. You took it away from me. You had *your* great adventure, but you left me nothing."

He glared at her.

"Am I so wrong for wanting more?" she said. "Didn't *you* crave something, that led you to come here? You acted on it, so why can't I? Jumping into that pit was *my* chance to escape."

He looked ready to scream. "You have no idea what you've done."

"We're not on Homeworld anymore, right?"

"We're on a planet called Alchera. But it could be a nightmare."

"Didn't you once throw away everything to come here?"

"Nothing worked out. I made things worse."

"Yet now you're back."

He waved his arms, shook his head in despair.

She continued. "I don't expect anything from you, Mykol. But I want the chance that you once took. That's why I came. I'll do whatever you say, but I'm *not* going back. Not yet. I want this too much."

He gathered the things he brought, said nothing.

"I won't be abandoned," she declared. "Not again."

"I don't have the energy to fight you now."

"But you understand me."

"You won't be happy here."

"I feel better for having done something—anything."

"I should have tied *you* up before leaving."

She tried to smile. "You'd never do that. You're too polite."

"Don't joke about this, Riley. You'll regret your choice."

But she could tell he was relenting. Relief grew in her.

He strode up the hill. "And we might be here for the rest of our lives."

She hurried after him. "So it *is* teleportation?"

"Yes. We're light-years away from Homeworld."

She couldn't be frightened by him—she felt too eager, excited. Alive!

Ranglen forgot to take his bundles into the ruins so, impatient, he ran back and hid them away as best he could.

Riley helped, but the archaeologist in her awoke. She examined the structure and saw it was exactly like the one she knew except for the different composition, the rock grayer and darker.

Ranglen snapped, "We're not here to explore!" and he moved up the hill again. "We might have to leave this place in seconds."

She followed him. "So you've been here before."

"Twice. But everything wasn't the same. That's what I'm hoping is the case now."

"So that…?"

"So we don't find what I did the last time. So that someone I know is still alive."

"But I thought—"

He walked with firmer deliberation and did not stop to talk.

The hopelessness she had seen in him for so long had now vanished. She watched him with fascination—with fear too—envying him, wishing him luck.

People ran over the ridge and down toward them.

To Riley, they resembled soldiers, in black uniforms, tall boots and military-like caps, but they had no weapons. And they apparently ran from something dangerous. They rushed past Ranglen, glancing toward him with recognition and surprise.

He shouted at them, "Ere uh-oo gyne?"

A woman yelled back but without Ranglen's heavy accent. "We don't agree with them. They're about to start but we don't want to see it."

"Start what?" He spoke correctly now, adjusting for the woman.

"The Blight! The Blight!" They ran on without stopping.

"But where are you going?"

"Away from the crater. We won't watch." They ran downslope toward the river which wouldn't be wide enough to stop them.

Ranglen raced up the hill and scurried through the rocks that lined the ridge, Riley close behind him.

The hill fell abruptly on the other side, not a cliff but still steep, spotted with outcrops and worn trails. At the bottom, a sheet of mist spread to a flat horizon, where one near-symmetric hill poked upward—on which, for a moment, she thought she saw a coiled serpent, with plumes around its neck. But the impression went away.

The mist, open in places, exposed a forest with exotic trees of multi-colored foliage—blue, red, yellow-green, burgundy—and serrated lines of black rock that made patterns in the vapor.

People worked at the bottom of the cliffs. They organized supplies that paralleled the tree-line, spreading away to either side. All the materials looked like preparation for an invasion—carts, wagons, bales, machines, stacks of canisters, everything elaborately gathered and arranged, showing much planning and controlled labor. Similar resources lay distributed in piles that spread into the distance by the edge of the mist.

The people dressed alike in the same military outfits she saw, but no one carried guns.

"What is all this?"

Ranglen didn't answer.

"I assume it's not what you expected?"

"The place is similar but it didn't have all this organization."

Behind Mykol, Riley was surprised by a white tower of astounding delicacy. It resembled a slim Art Nouveau lighthouse, with running swirls covering its sides, pale green or opalescent and glittering in the sunlight. The balcony at the top was supported by curved supports of glass, and the transparent cupola gleamed with prismatic rings. A small winged figure, stylized into abstraction, sat on the top.

Riley loved it.

"That's different too," Ranglen said. "It wasn't so pretty, and one version I saw was destroyed."

An explosion erupted below. A ball of flame, a loud crack, a trail of smoke that billowed upward. People shouted and ran about, quickly tried to put out the fire.

Riley said, "That wasn't supposed to happen, I'll bet." The people acted confused, and the fire broke the neat symmetry in the line of materials. "The minute we get here an accident occurs."

Ranglen looked grim. He hurried down the slope before them, not bothering to conceal himself.

She called after, "Will we be all right down there?"

He didn't stop.

Go find her, Mykol! Then she followed.

They reached the crowd at the bottom of the cliffs. No one paid attention to them even though they were dressed differently from the others, and a few people seemed to know Ranglen. But too many were hurt from the explosion and the fires needed to be extinguished. Riley tried to help while Ranglen talked to a man with a short dark beard. They argued.

Ranglen suddenly shouted, "Mylia!"

He left the man and rushed to a young woman with a long black braid of hair. Unlike the others, she wore a red jacket.

They stared at each other with obvious recognition.

Riley moved closer to hear better. She was certain this was the woman Ranglen had come for.

But she didn't look at him the way he looked at her.

"Why did you come back?" she said. "You couldn't stop us before, so why try now?"

"Stop you from what?"

"From destroying the Blight. We'll get every bit of it this time. We're burning it down."

He looked confused. "This was *your* idea?"

"Of course. It always was. And everyone supports me now. Only you and Sabal wanted to stop me before."

People moved up behind the woman, noticing her anger and showing support for her, ready to help if Ranglen caused trouble.

The woman, "Mylia," saw them and said to Ranglen, "They'll stop you if you try anything. They know you never understood me and what we need to do." She gestured to the supplies beside them.

"What is that stuff?" he asked.

"Flammables, distilled from tree resin and coal oil. We've been making it for years. We hid it from you. We're spreading the canisters throughout the Blight and setting them off today. We would have done it a month ago if you and Sabal hadn't stopped us. You might have convinced Barinda with your thoughts but you won't stop me now. You gave us our chance after you left."

Riley could understand Ranglen's attraction to her. The woman had a magnetism and energy of command, a decisiveness that was powerful. But because of those qualities Riley didn't like her. She shut out Ranglen too quickly and often.

He argued, "You always wanted to *save* the Blight. You believed in it."

"I never did, and I don't know what you're talking about. You're not holding me back this time. Just leave us alone."

"Mylia—"

"No!" She backed away as he reached for her. The other soldiers moved in around her and shielded her.

The man with the beard ran up behind Ranglen. "Leave it, Mykol. Come with me and I'll explain."

Ranglen didn't move. Mylia walked away.

Riley marched up to him and she and the other man pulled him back.

The man with the beard led them to a tent where they could keep out of people's way and out of sight. The organized activity all along the trees started up again, apparently on a schedule that approached a climax.

The man moved behind a small table while Riley and Ranglen sat on portable chairs before it. He introduced himself to her as "Sabal." He had severe dark eyes and short black hair. He was handsome, agile, and firmly built, but he didn't arouse much trust in her—he kept looking at her too closely, seemed overly interested in her.

"We can't stay here long," he said. "They'll be shooting off the canisters and we already had one accident. I warned them that people would get hurt."

Ranglen said bitterly, "She's not Mylia."

"Oh yes she is, Mykol. She's just not the Mylia that *you* met. You came to Alchera twice and you saw a Mylia each time. But, most likely, they were not all the same."

"I was not *here*."

"That's my point. You were somewhere else. And you still saw different Mylias—and different versions of me. You must have realized all this by now."

Ranglen said nothing but he didn't disagree. He looked like he didn't want to talk at all.

Riley broke in. "Would someone explain?"

"You're a friend of Ranglen's?" Sabal asked.

"I…guess."

"Then why did he let you come? He dropped you into the middle of something very complicated."

"It was my choice, not his."

"Then it was a bad choice. I don't know what he told you but I think he understands now."

"Understands *what?*"

Sabal looked at the brooding Ranglen, then back to Riley. "Teleportation doesn't work. At least, it doesn't work in our universe. You can only travel *between* universes."

She didn't understand.

"Instantaneous movement—teleportation—across space is impossible. But you *can* make a 'lateral' transfer between two different universes. You don't cross space at all then, you just emerge at a different spot in a wholly separate but similar existence."

"Does that make a difference?"

"A destination can be set before the translation, but you need special transfer points. Those are the ruins. Since the Airafane built them throughout one universe they automatically exist in other universes too, so you can travel from one to the other. There's no 'movement' at all between them. So it's *almost* teleportation but not quite, for when you look at the two worlds closely—or if you teleport often—you'll see that they're different, that their histories have undergone different tracks."

He paused to let this notion sink in.

"And you don't know in which universe you'll emerge. You can pick the location where you'll arrive *within* the universe, through means that the Airafane supplied, but not the exact universe itself."

Riley pondered, finally asked, "If there's no control, why did they have teleportation at all?"

"That question *haunts* me. It's why I never went back to my own world after I teleported here." He looked at Ranglen. "I don't know what I told you before, Mykol—or, rather, what my *other* selves said, and they *were* other selves, in the same way that I encountered different Ranglens—but that's the reason for me in *this* world. I wouldn't take the chance of where I'd end up."

Riley said, "Could the system be flawed?"

"If so, then all of us are in big trouble. The future of human civilization is now dependent on Airafane technology. We've assumed it's perfect. If not, we have problems."

Ranglen stirred in his chair, spoke without looking at either of them. "The Clips that control the teleportation, the one you saw me insert, are relatively easy to find. That too is strange."

"I found one also," Sabal said. "They're not buried in geological strata. They almost lie in plain sight, nowhere as hidden. There has to be a reason. The Airafane always seemed to know what they were doing. It's the only way they kept their perfect control."

Riley thought to herself, trying to grasp the complications of the idea. She said, "The Airafane would exist across all the universes. But maybe they existed in *exactly the same way* across them, consistent from universe to universe, unlike everyone else— transcendent, above the changes, and that's how they became all-powerful."

"I've wondered about that too," Sabal said, "that the ruins work as teleportation stations because they really are alike, in a simultaneous state of entanglement with all the other ruins throughout the universes. The concept is astounding."

Riley felt weak—the great mystery of her "professional" life solved in a moment of casual conversation.

But Ranglen showed impatience. He stood up. "I can't bear this, Sabal. I have to talk to Mylia. I can't watch her do what she's doing and not try to stop her."

"She's not your Mylia here. And this whole place is about to explode."

"I didn't come all this way not to try."

"They won't listen to you. *She* won't listen to you. She damned near shot at you—or your 'other' you—when you left the last time, so she won't change her mind now."

He didn't answer. He hurried outside.

Riley wanted to follow him but she knew she shouldn't. Yet she didn't feel comfortable with Sabal either. She asked, "What was the other Mykol like?"

"There were two here at different times, but the first is the only one I got to know. He was thoughtful, perceptive, maybe overly sensitive. A bit too naïve and idealistic, but a good man. He was attracted to Mylia's intensity. She could have believed *in* the Blight as much as she hated it, wanting to save it as passionately as she wants to destroy it. They disagreed, but the strength in their attitudes pulled them together. It never would have worked between them, and he was right to leave. Maybe, somewhere, the perfect versions of the two of them can flourish together. But not here."

"How big are the differences between the universes?"

"I assume they're slight. But things get tricky. Changes between universes 'alongside' each other should be minor. So, when you teleport, you'd go to either of the ones 'closest' to you, those least different—to the 'left' or 'right' let's say. And we'll call the possible universes L1 and R1. Now assume you go to L1. When you try to teleport back to your original universe, your chance will be 50% of reaching it again, and 50% of going to L2, the next one down the line. If you go to L2, it's still doubtful you'll notice differences, but you will encounter more of them."

Sabal leaned closer to her, warming to his topic. "And if you teleport *again*, from L2, you'll have an equal chance of going back to L1 *or* to L3. And if you wind up in L3, the differences between that and your original world will be larger. Then if you teleport from there, you have a chance of going to L4, and you'd be even further away from your home universe—with a 50% chance of straying yet still further afield. So the more you teleport, the greater the possibility of getting farther from your first world, and the more changes you'll encounter. The landscape, the history, the people who are part of it—all can be different, and considerably so."

Riley grew uneasy. She remembered when Ranglen arrived on Homeworld, that he wanted to know when she first came to the ruins. She must have arrived at a different time than she did in his original world. Or maybe she didn't arrive at all. "How do you know all this?"

"I *don't* know. I deduce, especially after seeing Mykol's experiences. I can tell that your Ranglen encountered something traumatic with his Mylia. It shows all over him. And the Mylia of this world almost was killed the last time a Ranglen was here—all the people here don't like him much. So maybe one version of her *did* die."

"And you teleported here alone? Long before Mykol?"

"Years ago. And the probabilities I just talked about are why I never left."

"Is that the only reason?"

He smiled thinly, as if appreciating her assumption of deception. "Mostly, yes. I don't want the universe pulled out from under me. It's happened before. In some ways, you're bringing it all back."

Surprised, she grew cautious. "Me?"

"You remind me of someone."

She sighed. "I've heard *that* before."

"It's a valid feeling."

"I don't see any reason for it."

"Look, I'm not being forward. I'm just concerned for you. I think you should teleport immediately back to your world. The changes in it shouldn't be noticeable. It still should feel exactly like your home."

"You're claiming I shouldn't stay? But I'm someone who reminds you of somebody else. Don't you want me to stick around?"

"This world isn't good for you because it wasn't good for *her*, the one I'm thinking about. And it's especially not the place for your precious Mykol. Get him out of here."

"But where do you expect us to go? We've just learned the universe—*all* of the universes—are undependable. We might wind up anywhere. Yet he was able to find here the woman he's after."

"She's *not* the same woman! Stop thinking that way!"

"But—"

Another explosion came from outside. Muffled, further away.

They rushed out of the tent. They saw, about a kilometer away, a dirty column of smoke boiling upward beside the line of trees.

"Dammit!" Sabal cried. "They'll wind up killing themselves before they even get started."

People scurried about, tried to stay poised in the midst of yet another accident.

"No wonder people are deserting, running away from the crater." Sabal was furious. "This will be a disaster for the whole planet."

"Let's find Mykol."

"Get him out of here, Riley. You don't want to be a part of this."

She had to agree.

They found him walking in their direction, dejected, bitter. He obviously had not convinced Mylia. "I think she would have listened at another time," he said, "but not now, not with everything ready for what they want to do. I wish I had gotten here sooner. I could have stopped all this, and in a much easier way than burning up their world."

Sabal told him, "You said—the last time—that you went back to get some secret method to destroy the Blight. But when you got here they wouldn't let you use it. You got frustrated then, in the same way. Nothing's changed."

"She won't listen."

"She's not your Mylia."

"Sabal, you said two versions of me came here before. There wasn't a third, was there?"

"No. Just two."

Ranglen said no more, seemed to shut down and close himself up. Riley knew that behavior well.

"You both must leave now," Sabal said.

Though she agreed, Riley was disturbed by Sabal's assumption of certainty. She challenged him. "Why are you so anxious to get us out of here?"

"You'll know soon enough. I'm not exaggerating." He pushed them up the slope. "Debate all you want, but at least get away from all these flammable liquids."

When they reached halfway up the hill, a loud noise erupted from the forest— not an explosion but a fast *whoosh* of air, like the sudden exhaust of a jet engine. A plume of fire in a spreading blossoming trail poured through the trees. As the filthy black smoke lifted, a burning path of flame was exposed, a string of many fires in the woods. The heat of the burning reached them, and smells like turpentine and kerosene filled the air.

Sabal muttered, "They weren't kidding."

"Why are they doing this?" Riley asked.

"Because they can't live with uncertainty anymore. Or with sympathy. The whole area of the Blight has become a test—on how open you can be to the unexplained. And they're failing it."

"I don't understand."

"Neither do they." He pushed at both of them. "Please get out of here. Run to the ruins and return to your homes. This will get very bad. I'm going back to them and I'll try to help them." He ran down the slope, without saying anything more to Riley and Mykol.

Ranglen almost followed, but then another part of the forest spawned a huge evil flower of flame. It too sent a column of smoke into the sky and left only charred burning wood. The two fires alone obscured much of the plain.

"This is madness," he said. "It all could have been avoided."

Another explosion at the base of the hill. The concussion nearly knocked them over, singed their faces. Their eyes burned behind waves of heat.

"It's out of control," Riley said.

"I'm worried what the mound will do in response. It might not *like* being 'burned alive.'"

"The mound? What do you mean? That hill out there?"

"Look the other way."

"*What?*"

"Turn away from me! I'll tell you when to look back."

Scorched branches and cinders fell on them. Riley, baffled, faced away. She wasn't sure but she thought he reached into his jacket or pocket. Then he was quiet until, finally, he said, more to himself, "It's there all right." Then the noise of another explosion was heard, further away, and he said to her, "Okay. You can look now."

Riley didn't have time to think about what just happened. "They must be hoping the fires will all tie together," she said, "form one big surge that'll burn the whole area."

"Which could make a firestorm, sucking in air from all directions and getting even bigger."

"Sabal's right. We have to leave."

He didn't move.

"I know you want to go back, Mykol, but they're playing with disaster. They might kill everyone, and you too."

He stared at the people setting the conflagration.

"She's not your Mylia. You know this. She's someone else that you've never met."

More explosions. A rising wind blew behind them, charging downslope. The fires now could be self-sustaining.

Riley pulled at him. "Let's get over the ridge."

"Wait! Look!" Ranglen pointed to the mound. It was now almost lost in smoke but its top glowed brightly, like a sun piercing through the murk.

"What's happening out there?" Riley thought she saw the serpent again, a light flooding out of its mouth.

They both noticed a change to their left. The tower also had an equally sunlike glow at its top, burning fiercely. The pylon seemed to be consuming itself, melting, dissolving. The wooden buildings around its base caught fire.

Another such glow shone farther down the crater—and another beyond that.

"It's killing the towers," Ranglen said. "The Blight's self-destructing! The Alcherans won't have anything left."

People now ran up the slopes in search of safety. Strong winds drove them back. Fires engulfed them.

"The mound's killing them."

"Mykol! We have to go!"

He finally followed her and they staggered uphill, fighting the growing wind against them.

They reached the ridge and almost had to crawl over it. They slipped downhill on the other side, where the winds were still strong but more bearable. The trees waved, tilted, broke. The grass ran in billows against them. Animals hurried down the hill, galloped away.

They raced toward the ruins as the sky turned black. The noise from behind the ridge was thunderous, like huge engines roaring with power. Flaming debris rained down, then was caught in the winds and dragged over into the burning pit.

They ran straight to the kiva room. The walls protected them somewhat from the winds—and maybe whatever preserved the ruins also guarded them now, at least somewhat, for the moment anyway. Ranglen pulled out his Clip and inserted it, not caring what Riley saw.

But when the star chart appeared and Ranglen looked for Homeworld, Riley stopped him. "No. There's a different way."

He stared back at her.

"Not Homeworld," she said. "Why go back? Both of us have nothing there."

"This isn't the time to argue, Riley." He pointed at the open ceiling where the sky boiled, spilled fire, dropped hot pieces of singed growth.

"Set the controls for *this* world, Alchera, and we'll teleport to a different version of it."

"But…"

"You see what I mean? You came here looking for Mylia—for *a* Mylia, one who was alive. She died on that other world and she probably won't survive this one. But there are more worlds, and she must exist on some of them, must be the Mylia you know. You can still find her."

He then understood. She could see the sudden hope in his eyes.

"Set the coordinates for Alchera, and we'll be taken to *another* Alchera in another universe. If Mylia's not there we can go to one more. Or another after that. Or even more. We've got time. We can do this."

His eyes looked glazed. She thought the idea might be too overwhelming. But she could tell he was tempted.

"You lost Annulus, and I lost my phony profession. Where else can we find an experience like this? Weren't Airafane devices meant to be used?"

More fire crossed the sky.

He said, "I'm accustomed to being alone. This is almost what I first intended. But *you* shouldn't have to come. If I do find her, then…"

"For god's sake, Mykol, I'm an adult. I know I'll be in the way. Don't remind me. But these are big worlds, and there'll be others besides her. I've been alone too. *Enough* alone!"

"We could be killed."

"You told me once you have to trust the Airafane."

Smoke flowed down into the room, choking them.

"We have to decide and leave from here now. If we go back to Homeworld we'll talk ourselves out of it." She couldn't see Ranglen's face because of the smoke. "Come on—let's do it!"

"We'll need my supplies."

"Go with what's here. We can't wait."

He selected Alchera on the star chart. No alarms sounded—so it was not an incorrect or impossible move.

She laughed. "Aren't you glad I came?"

"I really should have used those zip-ties against you."

The sky went white. Something drastic must have happened in the crater. Or to the mound.

"Go! Go!"

She threw things into the pit and jumped in herself. Ranglen reinserted the Clip, pulled it out, leapt in.

The sheath of blue light fell around them.

The room disappeared.

Chapter 18: The Chase

And came down—

    And came down—

    And came down—

    The first world was at war. Vast walking tripods came over the ridge and shot laser rays into the woods. Troops ran toward the river or fought back with bazooka-like weapons. Balls of searing-white plasma erupted on the heads of the walking tanks. Mechanical whips swung from the structures and grabbed at people.

    The machines were Ranglen's, imagined from his readings of H. G. Wells. They must have been escapees from the local Blight.

    Ranglen saw Mylia and Sabal organizing defensive forces.

    Well-aimed ray blasts killed both of them.

    Ranglen and Riley raced back into the ruins. He explained to her about the Clip in the Blight creating objects from people's imaginations. She felt at first his story was just cover for his misery over seeing another Mylia dead.

    The second world was an orange desert with brown rocks beneath a green sky. Super-swift aircars flew overhead. Ranglen thought he saw Mylia inside one of them—before it exploded, crashed, burned.

    Again they left. "She couldn't have been inside," Riley said. "You're just imagining the worst."

    "Sabal claimed I cause this, that my presence is the reason for Mylia being killed."

    "That's nonsense."

    "It happened to him also. He said it had to do with physical laws and paying a debt—that the equations of teleportation require it, that the thing you want most you destroy."

    "That's just a desperate attempt for answers. It reminds me of the 'reasons' for sacrificing innocents to the gods."

    "I *need* an answer. I can't take this."

The third world had huge beetle-like creatures prowling beneath trees, moving on narrow legs that sparked with violet-white electricity. Crab-like heads spouted tentacles that hung from mouths and scraped the ground. They kicked up dust, made high-pitched whines like tempest winds.

Riley said, "They look like the storms on Homeworld seen from above."

"The Clip might be raiding *your* thoughts now."

She felt violated.

"You'll never again be disconnected from what you see. You'll find parts of yourself absorbed into the landscape around you."

She shuddered.

"Be prepared. It's terrible."

The fourth world at first had no people. The Blight was filled with mammals, lizards, enormous birds. Weird combinations of cats and elk, zebras and dogs, giraffes and dinosaurs. Flying snakes chased after fish running on legs. It was a large zoo with no cages or barriers, only snapping fangs, bristling claws, kicking hooves—and no light stations, no protection or guards.

Riley saw reptiles with transparent eye-lids and fan-like tails that propelled themselves through sand.

Ranglen's nightmare of the central mound turning into a monster came true. The hairy bulk rose on a circle of trunk-like legs and crawled forward, the black mass silhouetted against livid clouds. It moved with implacable threat and the animals rushed out of its way. It had one large gelatinous eye.

Mylia appeared on the slope, standing before the creature and shooting at it with a green rifle. Red stains appeared on the glistening dome of the eye. Mylia retreated, ran up the cliff. The monster reached the crater wall. The rubbery arms pulled at the rocks, creating a landslide that buried her. Ranglen wanted to search for her body but the tentacles reached for his legs and the huge mass bore down on him.

Riley pulled him back across the ridge. Like a black moon, the mound rose behind the rocks, its bloody eye seeking them.

They ran into the ruins and left.

On the fifth world the landscape was pleasant, with trees and fields and nothing extraordinary. They walked up to the ridge and looked into the Blight. The crater rim was banded in color as far as they could see: the top of the cliff red, the middle section yellow, the bottom part that touched the plain dark-green and spotted with blue. From the slopes flowed tatters of mist that swirled outward. The mound in the middle was metallic gray with spikes sticking up from it.

"It's Annulus," Ranglen said. "But that's impossible—it's not finished yet. The Clip is showing the future. I have a friend who wants to build a port for spaceships in its center—that's what those spikes are."

"I once read about a rainbow serpent eating its own tail, forming a ring that creates a landscape. From Australian mythology. So this could be my manifestation too. Or maybe you told me about it."

"I don't think the Clip can read our minds before we even get here."

"Maybe each universe doesn't exist until we come to it. We create it by arriving in it. Isn't that a theory of the FTL drive, that we create light-space with each transition?"

"That's just a guess."

"The equations might run separately for each person, restarting cause-and-effect. Any action *becomes* creation."

"You sound like me and Sabal—desperate."

The sixth world had open plains of grass, dark green under a yellow-green sky. People lived in nomad cultures. Their accents were difficult but could be understood. They made annual pilgrimages to the Blight, saying a god lived in the mound who they felt was Preserver, Creator, Destroyer, all at once. In each cosmic day the god created the universe and allowed it to live, but at the end of the day the universe was taken back inside its body as it slept.

"Indian mythology," Ranglen said. "The same story as the mound absorbing everything each night and restoring it in the morning."

But the people said to them the god was wild, that it smeared itself with ash and wore skins of ancient animals, that it had a third eye in the middle of its forehead and that when it first appeared it was immersed in flame.

They called it Sabal.

It once tried to kill the ultimate God of all the universes because that God impregnated its virgin daughter, the Dawn.

She was called Orani.

The daughter long ago immolated herself.

"We're getting lost in myths," Riley said, "losing connections, drawing further away."

"It's all subjective. We have too many associations with each world, and they're distorted."

"You're a writer. Don't artists want to live what they create?"

"Not *this* artist. I once claimed my writings had only three subjects: the obsessed, the pursued, and the space between. I feel like I'm living that scenario now. I don't want to."

"I feel sorry for you, Mykol."

"I feel sorry for *you*. You didn't have to come here. We're both lost."

The seventh world was an archaeologist's dream. Ruins lay everywhere—buried walls, decaying statues, carvings that hinted at mysteries and secrets. Riley went wild. Ranglen found drawings he believed resembled Barinda and Mylia. One petroglyph suggested a map. By following it they found a mummy. Ranglen insisted on opening the wrap. Inside it they found a woman who once had black hair but who was too deteriorated to be identified. Ranglen of course assumed it was Mylia.

Riley thought it might be herself.

The eighth world had open forests and plains, no people. The grass light-blue, the trees pale violet, the sky a vivid amber-gold. They explored. A long lizard passed by them, showing no interest in them. They followed it to a lake in the late afternoon, where the water sparkled with phosphorescence. Just as the amber light faded and the clouds dispersed, at the very moment when night seemed ready to fall, the lizard jumped out of the lake and snapped its feathery tail over its head. The water from the tail scattered into the sky and broke into glowing points. By the time the creature fell back into the lake, the sky was clear—and filled with stars.

"How legends begin," Ranglen said. "A creature who puts the stars in the sky. Mylia would have loved it....*my* Mylia."

On the ninth world the Blight was filled with water. The tower stations were genuine lighthouses, sending beacons across the waves, revolving serenely in the night.

"Did you ever find the explanation for the towers?"

"No. I wish I had. They were beautiful."

The two of them savored the reliant poise and devotion of the beams.

"I once wrote a poem about lighthouse-keepers in love," Ranglen said. "They could never get together, were always separated."

"It's your natural subject, Mykol—the obsessed, the pursued, and the space between. Of course you'd write that."

On the tenth world they emerged immediately above a crowd of people and fell into them. Normally they arrived from each teleportation a varying distance away from the ruins, and always a meter or two in the air, as if to make sure they would not land inside an object. But several people were hurt. Ranglen fell on top of someone who looked like Mylia. The fall broke her neck.

He screamed, hysterical.

Riley pulled him away and back into the ruins, to leave for another universe as quickly as possible.

The eleventh and twelfth worlds they hardly paid attention to. Ranglen was too buried in despair.

The thirteenth world lay covered in snow. A near blizzard fell in darkness. Ranglen wildly searched for Mylia, as if the wintry landscape held promise of her presence. Riley couldn't understand why. Lakes of ice lay scattered between jagged white frozen hillocks. Bare trees stood blasted by the cold. He found an old abandoned aircar that would never fly again. A frozen body covered in snow lay beside it, decayed, unrecognizable.

Ranglen staggered back to the ruins.

Later, after more worlds, he broke down and said, "I'm living a tragedy."

She didn't say aloud, *No, my dear Mykol. You're living a thousand.*

They moved faster now. The places had no people. They stopped counting them.

A world of filigree glass, like more Art Nouveau decorations, covering the landscape in delicate swirls, curves, arabesques, arcs, twists, points of thin crystal and gems, a whole backdrop of light-station architecture. They believed one touch would bring it all down, ringing like a thousand tiny glass bells.

One touch did.

A world of blackish vegetation beneath a roiling red sky.

A world of green crashing icebergs.

A world of ash, fog, gloom.

A world of tornados—Riley thought she was on Homeworld in the midst of a storm.

As they left, she said, "I wonder if we'll remember all this. Can information be shared from one universe to the next? Only so much can be stored in our minds if we encounter more than one reality. There has to be a limit."

"We might *want* to forget. *Have* to forget. Sabal even said the equations require it."

"We're now like the people who search for Clips. Driven, relentless. Everything defined by just the present. All else abandoned."

"No. The Clip-hunters look for objects to remake history. We're searching for history to remake ourselves."

Riley grew more concerned for Mykol.

A world of ghosts, aurora spirits, sand dunes that took to the air, gossamer arms of mists in flight, a luminescent insubstantial dance in a sky that seemed endless, and always dark.

"Did you notice how time is getting peculiar?" she said. "Strained, different. I don't feel hungry or in need of sleep. Everything's condensed."

"Time is changing into space. It's the Airafane way. We're both in undiscovered country. Or the Dreaming."

"It's too different, too unlike everything we know."

"Subjects and objects are interconnected. Where we stop and where the worlds start no longer matter. This is the way life really is. Continuous creation sustaining itself."

Though they made such attempts at simple rationality, what they experienced was disengaged, insubstantial, unanchored. They were drifters in a countryside of flux.

She was fascinated. He tormented.

A labyrinth world. Like Ranglen's asteroid but raised mathematically to higher powers. No treasure was found at the end of the maze. The place had no end, no beginning, no plan—it was all middle. They could safely say it *was* the universe.

"Maybe we're drawn to worlds we understand. Maybe the transitions attract us to them. Maybe there's a sub-basement of unconscious communication or an under-network across all worlds. Maybe the Airafane, and even people like Sabal, can tap into it."

Ranglen shook his head, but she could tell he wondered.

A landscape of checkered squares and dots, symmetrically placed and highly organized, all different colors and flowing into the sky. Ranglen assumed them life-forms of some type.

The worlds became abstract, beyond known physics. Different suns, oddly formed skies, air that took on peculiar substance, ground that was malleable, gravity ambiguous, existence diverse. At times they couldn't see, speak, or breathe. They emerged closer to the kiva in these more extreme places, as if the Airafane were being protective.

And a strange exaltation possessed them, a sense of privilege, of being touched like no one else. They had few secrets between them now, though they couldn't always recall the old stories of themselves from the past—a result of the nature of time they were in. It made them feel like lovers who were too accustomed to each other, as if they once had sex but now couldn't remember it. Sometimes they were unable to recall the words they used in talking about themselves. They remembered only the emotion, a vague but persistent residue of feeling.

"We're in an open state of mind," she said. "Pleasant in its way."

"I've been here before. I called it 'the country of you.'"

"How? When?"

"I think you can guess."

"Maybe I should have said 'who'?"

"Maybe, yes."

They were frank with each other. He was not ashamed to share his love for Mylia, and she talked of her own tangled past though it seemed vague and inconsequential now. They moved beyond restraints and embarrassment, jealousy, envy. They defined all standards by being the only people present. They were the first and last couple. They were like children. Every world was wholly theirs.

Then, finally, they started seeing landscapes they knew, hints of human civilization again.

"We're coming back," Riley said. "We've run the circle. The probabilities are swinging our way."

Again they saw versions of Mylia, Sabal, Barinda.

One world had a highly regimented culture. Barinda ruled it. Mylia was her second-in-command and Sabal the head of her army. Every night they attacked the Blight. All three of them were killed periodically but then they returned to fight again. The resurrections obviously worked here. Barinda tried to enlist Ranglen and Riley in the war effort. Sabal and Mylia flirted with each of them and showed them weapons. They were almost convinced to stay but they ran off suddenly, agreeing it wouldn't work.

In another world a version of Mylia led a religious pilgrimage around the planet. The people she guided said she never stopped to rest and that her converts were dedicated to her for life. She slowed only to acknowledge Mykol, who reminded her of someone she barely remembered, but she quickly moved on and then showed little interest in him. Most of her followers said they'd die for her in worship of her, except for a Barinda look-alike, who only criticized her: "The life's gone out of her. She really should stop this."

Mykol and Riley left, but he said as they departed, "We must be getting close."

The next world physically was almost perfect. But dead bodies lined the crater wall where it touched the Blight, as if every human on the planet had been brought there to be resurrected. Yet there was no mist. The Blight was sterile, barren, dead. Ranglen and Riley walked down the slope and found the corpses of Mylia and Barinda. They didn't find Sabal. They stayed overnight in the nearby woods, hoping that the bodies might be resurrected. But the next morning they saw that nothing happened. The corpses lay motionless. Maybe they had been there for days, even months.

Then one more world—

And it was exactly like Ranglen's original.

The mist, the mound, the red growth, the illuminated forest, the delicate towers (with the nearest one correctly missing), the barracks, the soldiers, Sabal...all the same.

And Mylia dressed as before, wearing her braid, acting as she did.

She even recognized Ranglen. She welcomed him, hugged him. She obviously had been waiting for him. To Riley, she was just the way Ranglen described her.

He talked with her, then pulled Riley aside and said they had reached the end of their quest. "This world *can't* be exactly the same but it feels right, and this Mylia is the one I knew. Her leg wound came from the falling tower, just like before, and it's now all healed. She's long past the time when she could still be hurt from it."

Sabal walked up to both of them and spoke sarcastically. "Where the hell have you two been?"

Riley laughed.

So did Ranglen. Then he broke into tears.

Sabal looked shocked at their behavior. He said he was sorry he said anything and he returned to the barracks.

Riley admitted to Ranglen their journey might be over, but she didn't believe his *plight* had ended.

She was still concerned, maybe even more so. Ranglen looked too frightened when he was near Mylia, as if he expected fate to attack her—a tree to fall on her, the sky to break open and drown or bury her, all such destruction caused by him.

He said to Riley when they were alone, "I'm too nervous. What will I do to her *this* time?"

"Just take her away to a safe place and get reacquainted. Spend time with each other. Enjoy being together without worrying."

He nodded, unquestioning. He drew Mylia away, as if wanting to assure himself of her existence.

And Riley was left alone.

Abandoned.

Chapter 19: You Are Not of Them

After Ranglen left with Mylia, Sabal returned and pulled Riley aside. "I need to talk to both of you. Can you get him back?"

"Not now, Sabal."

"Ranglen promised to find the Clip that controls the Blight."

"I'm sure he will."

"You don't understand. The people are ready for him now. They *want* him to find it."

"We'll talk of this but not now. Do you have a room I could use? I need to clean up and get a full meal. We've been on the go—more than what you can ever imagine."

"If you have any control over him, then persuade him to do what he promised to do."

"I'll try. But, meanwhile…"

"I'll get you a room."

Riley found this Sabal not that different from what he was before, accommodating, if annoying. Maybe more agitated and less forward. Time, of course, had passed since they left, whatever "time" was and meant.

Sabal took her to a guest room and said he'd wait in his office for her. The place was luxurious after the living conditions she and Ranglen had been used to.

How did all that happen? she wondered. Was she losing memories of it already?

She washed her clothes and took a shower, donned them again when they were still a little damp. She ate in the barracks cafeteria and listened to people talking, tried to understand what they were saying. Their accent was manageable but it wasn't her nature to be talkative.

She had so many questions, but her interests went way back to when she snuck a reading of Ranglen's notebook. She wanted the dirt, the secrets, the underside.

A dark bronze and black woman with rust hair walked up to her as if she knew her, stood over her with an almost stern disposition.

Riley made a guess based on Ranglen's descriptions. "You're Barinda, aren't you?"

The woman sat down across from Riley and stared at her, tilted her head as if considering something she saw in her.

Riley said, "Please don't say I remind you of someone."

"But you do. A friend of mine from the past. You don't look a lot like her, but... Did Sabal tell you about her?"

"No. Ranglen did."

"Ah, Ranglen. I usually liked him."

Not every version of you did. "I like him too."

"He's in love with Mylia."

"I know, but that shouldn't concern you."

"I don't think it'll work out between them anyway. He's an outsider, like you and Sabal, and all of you think you know so much about us but you don't. Ranglen perhaps knows us the least."

"There's a difference. Sabal might want to 'understand' you, but Mykol wants to 'be' you."

Barinda folded her arms and smiled lightly. "That's clever. But I think you should keep *your* distance too. Stay analytic and detached. Don't fall in love with this world or anyone on it."

Riley didn't like her attitude. "Could you get to the point?"

"Ranglen said he'd find the Clip that controls the Blight. Until now, people were fine dealing with the Blight as it was. They were almost happy with it and some even admired it. Mylia was one of them. But the attitude changed after Ranglen came. His presence complicated the balance."

Riley listened, wary now.

"The creatures got worse, the hope for resurrection died, the tower was destroyed by one of his manifestations, and people took on a new dream—to escape how our lives had been determined by the Blight. It was a drastic change. They suddenly were fed up with the past, once they knew there might be a way to stop it. Sabal didn't tell anyone except me about the presence of a Clip in the mound, but the changes alone—just with Ranglen being here—were enough to get stories started. And a rumor began that Ranglen left to find a way to end the Blight. Maybe Sabal even leaked the story. But people now feel that Ranglen's the one to solve the problem."

"Didn't he return here already? Even twice?" These would have been different versions of Ranglen and, on the second visit, a different type of herself too.

"Yes, but he seemed not to be the Ranglen we knew, not interested, even cavalier. He didn't stay long. And *you*…well, you were awful. I stopped talking to you."

Riley tried to laugh. This other version of herself sounded interesting.

She would have asked about the other Ranglens but she assumed Barinda knew nothing of the teleportations.

"The point is," Barinda continued, "we're not letting Ranglen get away this time. His feelings for Mylia won't stop us no matter what happens. We'll make sure he gets the job done. I hope you understand."

Riley stared back at her coldly. "I don't control him and I can't speak for him."

"But if he wants to keep Mylia, and if you want him to stay and live on this world, you should try to persuade him."

Barinda sat back and looked belligerent. Riley stayed silent.

Then Barinda said something that caught Riley off guard. "Do you know the *real* reason why the Airafane and the Moyocks could not get along?"

"What's that got to do with anything?"

"I don't think Ranglen would understand that question. But you just might."

She understood nothing. "Enlighten me."

"Everyone assumes they hated each other. But the real problem with the differences between them—and this will sound strange—is that they loved each other."

Riley snorted. "I don't get it, and how can anyone even know? How do *you* know?"

The tall woman gave a bitter laugh. "Oh, I don't *know* at all. I'm just guessing. But I think it's…well, not quite 'logical,' but maybe a reliable, or predictable, guess."

She stood up then. But before walking away, she looked at Riley closely, almost kindly. She leaned down and said, "Your friend Mykol is important. He's being used, but for good reason."

"Excuse me?"

"Again, I'm just guessing. I think he'll survive, but he might be changed. You should be prepared." She walked away.

What the hell was that all about?

But now she was eager to talk with Sabal.

Ranglen and Mylia walked in. Everyone in the cafeteria noticed them. But the people stared at them with an intensity hardened by resentment, admiration, and envy.

The two of them didn't notice. They were in love. Riley found them equally charming and annoying with their secret understandings of each other—the small meaningful glances between them, the hands brushing as if by accident. He looked too blissful and she too proud.

Mylia introduced herself to Riley, a bit gushing. Riley assumed their chances of getting along were small. Too much sharing of Ranglen had occurred, even if Mylia was the clear winner. They would glance at each other and then quickly look away, as if they both were afraid of competition. (But Riley could always say that Mylia and Ranglen shared only *one* universe between them, while *she*...)

Ranglen broke into her thoughts, "We want you there when we talk to Sabal."

"Thank you. But why?"

"I need to do something important, and soon. Let's talk to him now and we'll explain when we get there."

"He asked to speak with all of us, by the way."

He and Mylia looked at each other, nodded, with their standard secret and exclusive understanding.

The three walked in silence to Sabal's office. The stares they got while doing so were as guarded as those in the cafeteria. Riley felt that Mykol was in the dubious role of sacrificial victim. The people radiated respect for him and yet dislike.

Sabal's private office was a relief.

Ranglen didn't wait. "I've explained everything to Mylia, and Riley knows too—how you and I got here, what I suspect is in the mound and what we intend to do with it. Mylia and I will go for the Clip. Just the two of us. I can find it, and then we'll bring it back and use your method to destroy it. I assume that method is to use my teleportation Clip to send it off to a sun and not another planet. Correct?"

Sabal looked impressed. "Very good, Mykol. Yes, I sent it to a star, not a world. I noticed the star-chart seemed to allow for that."

"And you believe you destroyed it?"

"I couldn't follow it in order to find out, but I'm sure that's why the Airafane made the distinction on the chart in the first place."

"All right. Then we'll do the same with this Clip. Which means then that afterward there should be no more Blight—at least we believe so. And people seem to want that now."

Mylia nodded, confirming this claim. Ranglen had said before that Mylia always had defended the Blight, so this change proved the general difference in opinion was valid.

"In fact," Sabal said, from behind his desk, "if you didn't do this, you'd be in trouble with everyone. But it'll be the perfect gesture if you hope to stay here. You haven't changed your mind about remaining on Alchera, have you?"

"No, of course not. Mylia and I have talked and we want our life to be here. And we agree this world would be better without the Blight."

Sabal looked at Mylia. "You're sure about this?"

She nodded again. "I still believe in what the Blight offers, but I agree that things have become too dangerous. And I won't have Mykol blamed for any more deaths. We have to think of the whole world, everything beyond this crater and not just this place, and not just the two of us. We want this cleared up so *everyone* will be free."

"I'm still surprised that you changed your mind."

"The resurrections stopped. They're not returning and people are dying. It's time we start living our own lives—*making* lives of our own. We don't need a resurrection to do that." And again that glance between her and Mykol, as innocent and appealing as it was private.

Riley believed what Mylia said, but she still was concerned for Ranglen.

"All right," Sabal added. "But why just the two of you? You could take a team to back you up."

"This should be handled covertly," Ranglen said. "A large group would just advertise our presence and maybe generate more manifestations. We think that was the problem with the other explorers. We sought them out and talked with them, just to see what they said."

"Those who survived," clarified Sabal.

Mylia looked irritated, but Ranglen said, "With too many people, I think the manifestations would begin to conflict with each other. The mound is the source and the explorers were too close to it, complicating everything that might happen. But I'll know exactly where it's located. And I'll need someone with me in case that knowledge affects me somehow. Otherwise I'd go alone. But Mylia is aware of the danger. She was hurt before by a manifestation and yet she survived."

"Barely," Sabal said.

"We insist," Mylia countered. "For then only *we* will be responsible."

Ranglen looked to Riley. "You're not coming either. So don't get any idea of following us."

"I understand," she said, with reluctance. "Be assured I won't." *Besides*—a perverse part of her said—*my spot is taken.*

Sabal added, "Maybe I should come."

"No," Mylia said. "You always hated the Blight, and everyone might think you're taking advantage of people's feelings now. I was the big supporter, so my going will seem more sincere and impartial."

He reluctantly agreed. "Okay. We all want to bring this to an end."

Riley said, "What about the things that already came from the Blight and are still around?" She thought of the jewel creatures that Ranglen spoke of, the flame beings.

Mylia answered, "We think they're independent and won't disappear. We hope not. We want to save some of the Blight's potential."

"'We'?" asked Sabal.

"Mykol and myself."

An uncomfortable silence. Riley suspected that Sabal wasn't happy over Ranglen's partiality, caring only because Mylia did.

"One more thing," Ranglen said, with firm declaration. "*No* rescue mission. If we fail, we fail. We don't want people coming after us and the same thing happening to them. There's been too much of that already."

Sabal shook his head. "I can't guarantee that. I'm not fully in charge, you know. I'll try to dissuade them, but…no promises."

"That's all we ask. I don't think they'd be willing anyway, but we really don't want anyone hurt."

"All right. Take the aircar you rode in before. It's still our best."

Again the gaze between the two lovers. Reminiscing on their last aircar trip?

As the four of them stood up, Riley hugged Ranglen, kissed him briefly, made ineffective gestures of good luck. For all they had been through, such words now seemed mannered, artificial.

But, as Sabal said goodbye to Mylia, Ranglen whispered to her, "Be careful of Sabal. He's not what he seems."

Riley, though moved by this trust, felt an uncomfortable apprehension.

And confirmation. She agreed with what he said.

The two women said goodbye in their own quiet and supportive way. Riley felt they understood each other now, with respect and acceptance.

But Riley regretted the speed of what was happening, as if things seemed out of control. She didn't like this trip at all. "You watch over him," she said to Mylia.

"I will. I wish you had seen the history of what's been happening here, the reasons for what we're doing. Mykol's told me about you. He appreciates you and all you've done. *I* appreciate you."

Before Riley could answer, Sabal indicated for Mylia to wait a minute—she was already outside—while he said something to Ranglen.

He pulled him aside, and in order to keep himself out of earshot of Mylia he had to get close to Riley. And he didn't seem to care that *she* could hear.

Sabal said to him, "You know the danger to Mylia is not just from the Blight but also from you."

"Yes, I know, but I don't know what to do about it. The manifestations will come if I want them or not."

"I just needed you to be sure."

Ranglen looked determined. "Mylia knows all this. You don't need to hide it from her."

"Still…" They said no more, and Ranglen then left to join Mylia.

Riley wondered if she'd ever see him again.

Not long after, the aircar with Ranglen and Mylia lifted away, with no fanfare. The departure was unannounced. No one waved goodbye. Only Riley and Sabal seemed to know of what they were doing.

Sabal returned to his office.

Riley paced the open deck from where the aircar had departed, as if it would return within minutes. From here she could see the landscape of the Blight, the hint of a forest beneath the mists, the rising silhouette of the central mound. All of this she had seen destroyed or transformed or reconstructed or highly altered in many different versions on many different Alcheras, though she was beginning to lose the details. Their long excursion had grown vague, Dreamlike.

Everything appeared innocuous in the Blight, even the mound, which Ranglen said once had been covered with eyes. She didn't see any. Nor her serpent.

She felt left behind.

Bitterness gradually rose up inside her, but her aloneness now was different from abandonment by parents and lovers. Now, she had things to think about. She even had been given a secret by Mykol, what he said about Sabal. She wondered about that, and how much danger she was in because of it.

She paced. Time passed.

No sign of the aircar.

She walked to the mess hall but she couldn't eat. The day ended. She considered meeting with Sabal but it seemed too soon, too obvious. In the dark she came back to the deck, watched the forest's parti-colored glow. People walked about the station, preoccupied, or studiously ignoring her.

She returned to her room, still avoiding Sabal. But she couldn't sleep.

She mused for hours.

The next day she returned to the deck. Still nothing.

The morning wore on.

About noon, she made her decision and went to Sabal's office.

She knocked, entered. He was still at his desk. "Can I sit in here for a while with you? I'm restless, and could use the company."

"Sure. I'm nervous too."

"Keep doing your work. I'll be quiet."

She sat in a chair across from him, remained silent—the pistol behind her back made a clunking noise against the seat. He must have heard it, but he didn't ask about it. He continued his paperwork, though she couldn't understand what function it served. Maybe it was just to make him look busy.

After a while, she asked how long the other expeditions had stayed at the mound before returning. He said each of them came back in under a day.

"It's now longer than that," she said.

"I'm debating what to do."

"He was emphatic he didn't want a rescue."

"It's not for him to say." But he didn't move to do anything yet.

Silence followed, eventually broken by Riley. "Mykol once said to me, rather casually, 'Sabal is not what he seems.' What did he mean by that?"

Sabal didn't look disturbed. "We all say that here. It's a kind of common social acceptance of the Blight and its potential, that we really might *not* be what we seem, that we could be resurrections or manifestations. It's just a saying, a belief in this world."

"I don't think he meant it as local custom."

"Maybe he referred to my position, my 'rank.' It's not formal, you know. The Alcherans look to me as an adviser or over-seer, but I'm not in charge."

"I don't think he meant what you *do*, but who you *are*."

At last Sabal showed his suspicion. He tilted his head downward while raising an eyebrow. "What do you mean?"

"It's just that…well, you know what to say to get Mykol to do things. You manipulate the Alcherans too. You do it very well. You say you're not in charge but in a way you are. You're almost *too* good."

He looked away from her, as if to hide his eyes. But the hard line of his smile was clear.

"According to Mykol," she continued, "you've always been critical of the Blight, apparently against everyone's attitude here. I heard about your differences with Mylia. You sent people out to the mound to try to discover why it acts the way it does, what governs it. But you didn't go yourself, and all the expeditions failed."

His expression didn't change. "Go on."

"Then along comes Mykol. And I think you decided right then that here was your chance. You never stopped him from getting close to Mylia, right? You let him become a part of this world. I think you primed him for learning what was driving the Blight, and then for getting the Clip that was in charge of it. *You're* the one behind this expedition. They believe they decided it all by themselves, but I think you planted the idea from the start."

Sabal said, "Remember, anyone you're describing would have been a different me, a separate version in some other universe. Ranglen's seen more than one embodiment. And the version he encountered the most, the original in the first Alchera, is most similar to me now but might actually be different. You still don't know for sure if this is the same Alchera he came to."

"It's close enough. And…you see? That's another thing. All these Sabals on all these different worlds, I swear you seem to know each other. I remember wondering if they could even communicate with each other. I realize that's impossible but you seemed to do it just now, talking as if you're familiar with those other selves. An average person would not be so conscious of them."

"I assure you we don't communicate. I'm not aware of them at all. And I've never harbored a scheme against the Blight. I simply don't believe in it and feel that the Clip behind it should be destroyed. Ranglen agrees with me. I didn't force him. He *chose* to go."

"Then why didn't you ever go yourself? You let *him* face danger but you don't do the same."

He looked embarrassed. "Because, and maybe I'm being overly cautious, I've always felt I'd be more susceptible to whatever manifestations might appear. I don't want to be that close to a 'creative' Clip."

"Because you're an outsider?"

"That's one reason. I don't feel I'd be as hardened to the experience as the Alcherans are."

"But Mykol's an outsider here too."

"I know. And I repeat, I didn't force him to go. But I have more 'history' here than Mykol does. And I don't want the meddling super-science of a Clip invading me, making unknown monsters from me—things I'll suddenly recognize as mine. I'm sure Mykol told you how often that happened to him, and how horrible it was."

"Yes, he told me."

"Then what's your point?"

"That what he said is true—you're not what you seem."

Sabal's face subtly became masklike. "This isn't the time for us to talk like this, Riley. I've been very tolerant fielding your accusations, veiled or not."

"I haven't accused you of anything."

"Oh yes, you *have*."

"Then answer me this…Why did you let me hear what you told Mykol before he left, that *he* causes the threat to Mylia instead of the Blight?"

"Because it's true."

"That he's responsible for the different Mylias being killed?"

"I'm not certain but I find it likely."

"You feel that way because of Barinda's friend?"

His face became stonelike. "Yes."

"And you said that I remind you of her?"

"A little. Not much."

"Yet you felt that when I arrived, didn't you?"

"Like I said, I wasn't certain."

"But…I heard that from a different version of you, in a different universe. Not from 'you' exactly."

"I still felt it."

"Almost like you 'remembered' the other one. So, maybe you do know these parallel selves."

Sabal leaned back. Riley could see a change in him. His eyes became withdrawn, guarded. "You're still wrong."

"But I teleported too. Why haven't *I* killed anyone."

"To be fair, you haven't killed anyone *yet*."

She refused to be taunted. "There's still a difference. He has Mylia and you had your friend. I'm alone here, with no one special."

He smiled. "Oh no, my dear Riley. You *do* have someone special. You might not have much intimacy with him but I'm sure you wouldn't have come here if you didn't feel something for our friend Mykol. And if what I say is true, about hurting the one you love, then that puts him in even *more* danger than what you think."

Riley said quickly, "Our relation's different. It's not like yours. I feel—"

Sabal looked smug as he waited.

But she got her reactions under control. "You're toying with me. This is how you manipulated Mykol."

"I'm not doing anything. I'm simply listening."

Now *she* waited.

Sabal said, as if trying to help or maybe distract her, "All right. *Yes.* I exploited Ranglen. Since I first saw him I maneuvered him to make him find what controlled the Blight. And now that he knows it, I'll keep him out there until he gets it—I'll keep him there forever if I have to. I'm not sending any rescue mission or reinforcements unless he says he's *found* the Clip. I've felt that way all along, but you just helped me to reinforce my decision. Before this talk I had to fake my 'brotherly' interest in him, but now I don't have to. I do expect he will find the Clip. I was certain he'd be the one."

Anger boiled inside Riley.

He said, "Is *that* what you wanted from me? Is it enough for you? Are we done now?"

Again, she felt he was trying to distract her.

But he caused just the opposite. He gave her the encouragement to proceed now with *all* her thoughts—her speculations, her discussions with Mykol, her frantic worries of the past few days. Everything came together. And she was ready—

"Both the teleportation Clip and the Blight Clip are peculiar," she said. "There's more than one teleportation Clip and they weren't buried in a planet's mantle. The Blight Clip is probably not locked in a stasis field because its actions are uncontrolled. It 'leaks.' It has power over people instead of people being able to use it easily. So there's more involved here than in normal Clip finds. We all know this. I've heard Mykol's ideas. We both believe the two Clips are somehow connected. And the light stations—where did they come from? From the Clip, or…somewhere else?"

Sabal said mildly, "There aren't many 'somewhere else's' left."

"Well, there are two, two ancient well-known contrary forces. The Airafane and the Moyocks."

Sabal's features appeared locked, inscrutable.

"Mykol believes the colony ship coming here was no accident, that it was attracted, pulled to this planet, that the Airafane wanted a group here to monitor the Clip's creation of the Blight, to maintain a watch over it and even to keep up a struggle with it. So the Airafane had to provide the towers too."

"They lived millions of years ago, not right before the colonists got here."

"But aren't the Alcherans a bit like the Airafane? They believe in possibly similar notions—the Dreaming, timelessness, living always in the moment of creation, a constant resurrection or cycle. According to some ideas of what the Airafane were like, the Alcherans are almost like miniature versions of them."

"Or pets."

"More like little soldiers in a big war, enlisted help or useful servants, pulled here because they were similar. Gate-keepers, guards."

"Maybe mindless slaves."

"No, not a bit. Believing in resurrections doesn't make them fools. Barinda's right. We patronize them too much. Neither of us really know them."

"Maybe they don't want to be resurrections so much as *sacrifices*. And instead of a Clip sitting in the mound, maybe there's a brooding primeval monster, like Ranglen's cannibal."

"I don't think so, and neither do you."

He leaned forward again, "You know, Riley, I don't believe it's me who 'isn't what he seems.' I think it's *you*."

"No, I've always been predictable. I've just been thinking a lot. I haven't much else to do. And I've hung out with Mykol on a lot of strange worlds. Tell me, what do you see when *you* look at the mound?"

This surprised him. "What do you mean?"

"Ranglen says he sees his 'Cannibal,' with many eyes or mouths, and sometimes with tentacles. He told me that Mylia saw a rainbow snake coiled into a crown. And I see—or rather, saw once—a plumed serpent straight out of some myths I've studied. This could all just be a result of different backgrounds, interpretation methods programmed into us by our personal histories. But what do *you* see?"

He didn't hesitate, almost as if glad to let his viewpoint break forth. "I see a *spider*, a huge ugly hairy beast sitting in the middle of a vast web, that ties together the entire Blight. It wants to catch us and eat up all of us."

Riley muttered, "That's 'a singular appetite hardly profound.'"

"Excuse me?"

"Never mind. Something Mykol once wrote. Do you see anything else?"

"Sometimes a nest of thorns—a tight fist of them."

"Like the plant that killed Barinda's friend?"

"Not exactly. And her name was Orani."

She took a deep breath. "Sabal, I believe that you—specifically *you*, or someone *like* you—was meant to find the teleportation Clip. Mykol just happened to get pulled in since there are more of those Clips and they were left so accessible. But you—you were 'brought' here, enticed, drawn. The Blight was built for someone like you. The Alcherans were the planned caretakers, but you were the captive, the prize, the victim. You were *meant* to be caught and held…in the web."

Sabal said nothing but his look was severe.

"Any other scenario doesn't make sense. How could the Airafane not see the problems with their own Clips? The teleportation not really working. The manifestations uncontrolled and random—even brutal, destructive. That's sloppy engineering. They were too good for that. All this somehow had to be intended. The Blight wasn't meant to be either entertaining or enlightening, not psychological therapy, and not a huge archive of a culture's deep structures. It was a *trap*....A trap to torture people like you."

Sabal said, with obvious distaste, "'People' like me?"

"The ones the Airafane wanted to hurt, their old ancient galactic enemy. Who do you *think* I mean?"

Sabal was quiet for a moment. "You impress me, Riley. You're much more surprising and perceptive than Mykol."

"Don't distract me. You know what I'm getting at."

"I'm not a Moyock."

"But it seems the Blight, or the Airafane, has assumed you're one."

"I can't see how. Aren't the Moyocks extinct?"

"So are the Airafane but that hasn't stopped them. They knew how to plan—it doesn't matter if they lived millions of years ago. I'm an Airafanologist. I don't put *anything* past them. We're still caught in their story, still a part of it. Maybe even created by it."

"But weren't the Moyocks ruthless killers? If I am one, then aren't you flirting with destruction right now—far more than what Ranglen's doing?"

"Maybe I am. But I've been through quite a lot lately so I don't easily scare anymore. And I especially don't like Mykol being used. I *know* what that's like!"

"Then maybe *you* should hate the Airafane. I certainly do."

"And why should that be?"

"Are you manipulating me now, doing what you claim I've done to Ranglen?"

"I don't have to. You'll tell me anyway. You're too proud not to."

He laughed, but with a sudden ugly expression. "Let's be honest then. It's true I'm not fully 'what I seem.' I *have* inherited some unknown traits, which I realized even before I came here. Maybe they're Moyock, but I'm frankly not certain. I do think there's more to their background, and mine. But since Mykol was dragged into this too, wouldn't that imply he's similar to me, that he also might be...?"

"No! His involvement was just bad luck. He got pulled in because so many of the teleportation Clips must exist—like bait scattered throughout the galaxy. He loves this place, he found Mylia, and he's about to take care of the problem with the

Blight. He *wants* this world. But you…you're indifferent to the rest of the planet. Your obsession is *only* the Blight."

"I could have left here if I wanted to."

"And you never did, even when you had no reason to stay."

"You mean after I lost Orani?"

"You claim you're responsible for her death, so wouldn't that make you want to leave? Or did you stay here out of vengeance? Don't you long to *get* the Blight—destroy it, punish it, in return for what it did to you?"

"I have my reasons. And, if I needed to, I could always use Ranglen's Clip to leave."

"If he let you. If he survives."

"If he dies on this mission, you're stuck here too."

"Then I'm stuck here."

"You don't have his Clip?" He seemed genuinely surprised.

"What? What do you mean?"

"I thought he'd leave it with you, to provide you a way back in case he didn't make it. I guess not. Maybe he was protecting you, making sure I couldn't take it from you if I really wanted it. I'm supposed to be a Moyock, after all—gruesome, mean, the cliché villain. But don't worry. I hardly remember where I teleported from. I'm not going back."

"But you still think this whole place is a trap."

And he looked at her fiercely. "It *is* a trap! You said so yourself. And be prepared for Ranglen not getting what he wants. Perversity is built into the system. It's typical of the Airafane. Everyone assumes they were so wonderful because of their generosity with their inventions. But it's a ploy. We're just being manipulated too. Anyone who would torture other people, and in this way, the Blight's way, should be despised. They give us what we want and then take it away. They made me pay for my decision to stay here. You *do* resemble her—I lied before—and it's hard for me even to talk about her now."

Riley didn't believe his you-remind-me-of gambit, but she couldn't help feeling sympathy for him too.

"I encountered the knife-plant on another world," he said. "The Blight stole it from my memory and used it to kill her. But I didn't surrender to the temptation that Ranglen did after his Mylia was killed. He charged off into all his universes on a nearly impossible quest. He even dragged you with him. How tactless is that? But I destroyed my Clip. They *wanted* me to do what Mykol did—to lose myself in even more hopelessness. But I resisted. And now when Ranglen gets the Blight Clip, I'll let him destroy it and free all of us. I'm not your villain, Riley. I've just been cheated by an enemy I despise. I did make Ranglen into my weapon against them. Through me, he'll learn to refuse and reject, to not be a victim. I'm doing this for all of them, liberating everyone, including Mylia and Barinda. That's *my* purpose!"

"So Ranglen gets tortured as much as you do—what's fair about that?"

"It's the only method the Airafane left me. I was delighted when he arrived here, thrilled when he fell in love with Mylia. I knew a version of her would be killed and what he'd go through. You don't cross the universe free of charge. Those equations *do* have to balance. I'm not sure if I know those other Sabals, as you claim, but I do know a lot. So don't blame me. Blame the Airafane and their selfish use of their proprietary physics. It's not my fault we live in a universe where their reality dominates, where everything's determined by everything else, where all the ruins are entangled and exactly the same. Maybe the Airafane and the Moyocks were entangled too, ensnared together, trapped together. Maybe Mykol and Mylia also. The Airafane get to manipulate and play with entropy and quantum mechanics, but it's *our emotions* that get trampled."

Riley was overwhelmed, stunned by the passion behind what he said.

"Some day we'll prove how devious they were. The Airafane had their 'Big Plans,' all right. There's a rumor that a Singularity Clip exists, one that explains everything. But unless someone finds it we'll always be controlled. Like *here*, like *now*—they use their ultra-glamorous technology to trap pitiful Moyocks into feeling pain. It's a poor joke, a cheap revenge. Their teleportation wasn't flawed. It was *meant* to take us to a different universe, where we'd be ensnared and abused—by our own imaginations, by what we bring with us. That's the Airafane way to remove the unwanted—those 'people' they don't like. Your precious Mykol got himself caught in it, brought his own demons, his killer birds and cannibal mountain and ramming hox-cars. And I brought mine, only my demons were more selective, more exclusive. His Mylia is still alive—but for how long? I *hate* them, Riley."

"And that's why you can't leave him out there."

"I'm doing *nothing!* He's on his own. And he will find that Clip. But don't expect to recognize him when he gets back. The mound can be really nasty to people."

Riley jumped up to leave. She couldn't stand him anymore.

"You're now a big part of this too," Sabal said.

"I'm not like you. And neither is Mykol."

"Not *yet*."

"And he's no Moyock."

"Neither am I."

But she had enough. She stormed out of the room and slammed the door behind her. She raced to the landing deck.

Still no arrival.

She paced, waiting. Sabal's talk frightened her too much. She asked people if they would go into the Blight and help her lead a rescue, but they were reluctant, agreeing only to save Mylia. She pushed and cajoled and finally got a small group together. Then they delayed. She became enraged. She almost left on her own but she knew that doing so would be foolish. She yelled at them and they finally got ready.

Then the aircar returned.

With Mylia half dead.

And Ranglen half insane.

Chapter 20: Deep Story

She couldn't bear to see Mykol. He writhed in his bed with a frightening half-paralyzed frenzy, his joints locked while his body rolled, shook, spasmed. He spoke, but his words were disconnected, his eyes out of control. She was certain he saw nothing and understood no one. The seizures would go on for several minutes then abruptly stop. The doctors said that the nerve cells in his brain were "disturbed," that "abnormal activity" and misfirings caused him to stiffen, jerk, shake, lose consciousness.

Sabal relentlessly interrogated him when he was briefly awake, leaned over him and repeated, "Did you find it? Where is it? Did you get it? What happened?" Riley hated him, tried to stop him. Even when Mykol slept, Sabal hung over him until he awoke and then Sabal would badger him with questions again. "Where is it? Where is it? What did you find?" This only led to more frenzy in Ranglen. Even the Alcherans couldn't stand Sabal and they tried to keep him out, but he'd sneak back and continue all over.

Mylia, in a nearby room, lay in a coma. She was physically more damaged than Ranglen, her body cut, scraped, bruised, with several bones broken. But the doctors couldn't understand her unconsciousness. For all her wounds she had no head trauma. They looked for disturbances in circulation, swelling or bleeding, pressure on the brain, lack of oxygen, electrolyte imbalance, buildup of toxins, cerebral aneurysms, but they found nothing. They finally concluded—in desperation—that her withdrawal was simply her body's way of healing its damage.

This made Riley furious. The doctors had too little experience with such cases to be certain about anything. Lives had been thrown away before, the deaths supposedly leading to resurrections. She couldn't help judging such views as lazy, foolish, cruel.

She stayed with Ranglen as much as she could, and then she'd wander back to her room and fall asleep, exhausted. On awakening, she'd return and still watch over him, while Sabal tried ineffectually, harshly, repeatedly, to get through.

One night while asleep in her room she believed she had a dream, wrought from her fatigue and emotional delirium.

But later, she wasn't sure.

The door opened and someone entered, crept into the darkness. She thought it was Barinda. But she also believed Barinda wouldn't be so secretive—she'd knock firmly and just strut right in. Yet the voice did sound like hers.

"Thank you for what you attempted with Sabal. There's more to the Blight but I understand why you feel the way you do."

Riley couldn't speak. That's why she believed she was dreaming.

"Mykol's still sick but he's about to recover. I can tell. Mylia too. It's good this is the only version of him we have."

Riley groped for meaning, something to hang on to.

"He's more important than what you know. The resurrections stopped when he arrived because, with him, they weren't needed anymore. The Blight, maybe the whole world, touched him. 'Deep Story.' No one understands yet. Think of it as a long-suspended revelation. It requires patience."

Riley tried to say that she had no patience.

"I'm glad you've helped him. You're a catalyst. It's maybe not the role you want for yourself but it's better than some. You're right he was used, but not in a bad way. I watch out for him, though most people don't see it—and they wouldn't believe me if I said I did."

Riley didn't believe in oracles, premonitions, dreams (or "Dreams"), or spirit-animals like Mykol's coyote.

"Not coyote. Law Dog, Maletji. But that's not me, Riley. And I have to go now. Get ready. He'll need you."

She woke up then, felt weak and confused. She could make no sense out of what just happened.

But she walked to the medical ward prepared for Mykol to be awake and recovered.

And he was, still to her surprise. He talked sensibly. She didn't question how she knew this would happen. He sat up in the bed and except for looking years older, he seemed alert and much more himself.

Sabal was there too, but for once he didn't ask about the Clip. "What did you see in the mound? Did you encounter anything you didn't know already?"

Ranglen's hands shook uncontrollably. He had to wait till his body settled before he could talk. "Everything I saw belonged to me. Maybe she encountered different things. The manifestations were harder on her. We often got separated and then I'd find her. She looked like she had been fighting against something that attacked her. She wouldn't say what happened. The place was...like..." And his voice cracked.

He choked and coughed. "Sorry…" Again he had to pause. "The place was a labyrinth that reacted to our presence. It changed and remade itself. We created pathways as we walked through them, like huge extensions of our pasts or ourselves. We were our own worst enemies. The humiliation…it wasn't always physical…I…I…"

Sabal waited while the nurses calmed Ranglen.

Mykol looked at Riley but said nothing to her. He passed in and out of awareness before he settled and finally continued, "Mylia never should have come."

Sabal told him she was recovering. "They claim she'll be fine now. She came out of the coma and her wounds will repair. They're even baffled at how fast she's getting better. That coma really worried them at first. They suspected she was a resurrection but I assured them she wasn't. I think you've both gotten better because you were so close to the Clip."

"It tried to destroy us."

"Maybe it also helped you. You're recovering fast. The place tries to kill you and then it saves you—typical Airafane nonsense. I hope it's not setting you up for something worse."

"It's hard to imagine anything worse. I'd never return there."

"But you found the Clip, right?"

He nodded.

Sabal's face changed. "Now we can destroy it!"

"If you're in such a hurry you can take it and do it yourself."

"No, Mykol! No! *You* have to do it, you and Riley."

"Why us? What's wrong with you?"

"I won't touch it. I'm not certain what it could do to me. Look what happened to you and Mylia. It's hard enough for me just being near it."

"But I don't think it's functioning now. It's not connected to the mound anymore, which might be just a hill from now on. I'm sure that's why Mylia is recovering— being *released* from the Clip instead of depending on it."

"Don't be fooled. This world's not free yet and your recoveries aren't natural. It has to be destroyed."

Riley broke in and told Sabal to leave Mykol alone. Sabal scowled at her.

Ranglen watched the two of them. Then, surprising everyone, he pulled himself out of the bed. "I need to see Mylia."

The nurses were reluctant but they eventually led him to her room. He impressed Riley by how well he walked while still appearing feeble and broken.

Sabal said nothing after Ranglen left. He gave Riley an outraged look and then walked out.

Riley peeked into Mylia's room. She lay in her bed heavily bandaged. She could lift an arm now and turn her body some, though the many tubes constrained her. She talked with Ranglen quietly, who sat beside her. She seemed recovered from the coma but not her many physical injuries.

By their held hands, yearning stares and hushed words, it was obvious to Riley how much she and Mykol felt for each other.

She left them alone, left the ward, went to her own room and stayed there. She dozed off, but she didn't dream.

She returned to the medical area but now she found Ranglen out of his bed and sitting in a chair. He asked the nurses if it was okay that he and Riley walk to the cafeteria and eat there. He wanted the exercise, the change of scenery. But they were afraid his seizures would return, so they warned him, "You might see and hear things that don't exist."

Ranglen laughed, said that everyone on the planet must undergo seizures then.

They finally agreed. But before leaving, Ranglen caught Riley's attention and pointed to his backpack, as if he wanted her to grab it. She picked it up casually and hoped no one noticed.

The two of them strolled out into the corridors but Ranglen stayed quiet. They didn't stop at the cafeteria. He led her past it and continued on to her own room, where he indicated with his chin they should enter. They went inside and closed the door behind him.

There, in privacy, he told her, "You and I are leaving today."

"What? Going where?"

"Back to Homeworld...or to *a* Homeworld. We left it only once, so what we return to shouldn't be very different."

"Is Mylia coming?"

"No." He added nothing more. But he looked sad as he pulled clothes from his pack. He removed the medical gown and slipped on his shirt, jacket, and slacks, even his boots. After finishing this he said, "They'll think we're eating. That'll give us some time but not much."

"Why so secretive?"

"I don't want Sabal to know. I don't want *anyone* to know. But I told Mylia, and she'll tell Barinda. Yet I didn't describe everything that happened out there."

"Mykol, what *did* happen?"

"The mound was like a castle buried in thorns, as if the Clip was in some kind of vicious self-defense mode. I saw a version of Sabal inside. He was a manifestation but not *my* manifestation. He said he only appeared to me as Sabal and that he was something else, someone trapped here, caged in the mound millennia ago. He claimed humans were brought to this planet to keep him contained, that he was the original 'outsider' and that 'a Spider' captured him. He thought I was coming to free him. I said no. So he tortured me. But he believed in death, and I was able to use that fear against him. Don't ask me how. I could never do it again. He was alone and felt nothing but rejection and despair. I think he wanted to die, and that's the reason why he did."

"Was he a Moyock?"

"I don't know. I'm not sure if it matters. Sabal once accused me of losing my rationality. I understand what he means. The Blight had no prediction, no causation, no control. It was all based on spontaneous connection. The Clip governed a universe where only *relationships* were real. That's how the Blight worked, through the ties between things and not the things themselves—that's where Sabal's 'equations' came from, and the ability of the Clip to read minds and make manifestations. When we teleport we're in a state of pure connection. My brain just got close enough to share the Clip's view of an ontic structural network of reality. I had no boundaries. Of *course* my nerve-cell activity was 'abnormal'! Ha!"

Riley listened but she didn't understand.

"Yet you can't have science if you don't believe in time. The people on Alchera replaced science with narrative, with myths of creation, where time is not specific. They have only vision, reverie, space. Maybe the Airafane were like that too. It makes me wonder if their whole dispute with the Moyocks was only a story, a desperate attempt to establish a connection defying logic. For all that you and I encountered in our chase across worlds, what I saw in the mound taught me more—and *took* from me more. I reached pure connection, but I never want it again."

Riley didn't have time to say anything. As soon as Ranglen finished, he led her back into the hallway, as if he intended to meet someone.

And Barinda before long did appear. She said, "You've made the right decision, Mykol."

"You talked with Mylia?"

"Yes, but it took a while. Sabal's around her constantly. He feels you won't leave without her so he keeps himself near. He suspects what you're planning."

Riley felt the same way, that Ranglen would never leave without Mylia. But she wouldn't speak of it with Barinda around.

She wanted to ask Barinda if Barinda came to her room while she was sleeping, but she didn't know how.

"We need to avoid him," Ranglen said.

"There are back exits. They're less busy than the doors onto the deck." She gave directions. "You're leaving now?"

"If we're not stopped."

"Mylia said she agrees with you. She wanted me to know that. I'll try to keep an eye on Sabal but I won't be able to stop him. You'll have to be quick. He's more a problem than you think."

Ranglen walked on quietly but then he added, "After I leave, please watch over Mylia for me. I asked that of Sabal once, but I ask it of you."

"She won't be alone. Everyone here feels for her now."

"I'm sorry for all that's happened."

"I'm not. I think we're better now. I should thank *you*."

But, Riley noticed, she didn't actually do so.

Barinda glanced at Riley, then back at Ranglen. She said no more and soon left.

They used Barinda's exit, encountered no problems. They gathered nothing from their own rooms and left all behind. The sky was overcast with darkness outside. They followed a little-used trail over the ridge and into the forest that led to the ruins.

Once away from the barracks, Riley couldn't hold herself back any longer. "*Why*, Mykol? Why did you come here and do all this and then decide just to leave her behind?"

Ranglen spoke evenly but with obvious emotion. "I'm helping her, Riley, not abandoning her. If I stay, I'll always feel there's a chance she'll be hurt because of me, that if I'm close to her she'll be threatened. And if I remain here at all, I *will* be close to her. I can't live with that fear. On all those worlds we went to I was trying to find her just for myself. But I see now—I have to save her *from* myself, from whatever connection ties us together. That's what I learned when she and I went for the Clip. It tortured me by how it tortured her. I couldn't bear it. And the only way I can stop it is by freeing her from me. I want her to *live!*—I can't face destroying her again. I *am* an outsider. I always will be. That's exactly what both Sabal and Barinda have been trying to tell me."

"But you have the Clip now and you can destroy it. Won't all the manifestations stop after you do that?"

"I assume, but there won't be any more resurrections either. I can't take the chance. You can remove the Clip from its universe, but you can't change the universe the Clip has defined. I think Sabal's equations are right. I'm connected to her. *Everything's* connected. So only if I'm away from this world will I be sure she's safe. And it's not just me who could cause problems. I once encountered another version of myself, from another universe who left *his* Homeworld at a different time than I did. I can't have that. I must put a stop to all of it, to remove me completely from her world. From all her worlds."

"But she's still hurt. How can you—?"

"I know. It's ripping me apart. But she and I both agreed it's best, and I have to do it *now*. The longer I stay the harder it will be. We're thinking for each other, and she knows I can't live with this. It was wrong for me to come here again. I wanted something for nothing, some *one*, and she almost died because of it."

Riley followed him in a daze, feeling caught up—as usual—in someone else's story and not knowing her place in it, not finding her own emotional niche.

Ranglen said, "I'm assuming you'll want to come back to Homeworld, but it's your choice. I'm tired of forcing people to do things."

"No, I'll come." Alchera didn't attract her in the way it did Mykol, and she appreciated him considering her choice.

They hurried through the night, reached the ruins. They warily moved along the passages and then entered the kiva room.

Ranglen examined its corners, as if expecting Sabal to be there.

But he had hidden outside—and now rushed in behind them.

Sabal grabbed the back of Riley's collar, twisted it and pulled back on her head till he gained control of her. With his right hand he yanked her pistol from her holster. He aimed it at Ranglen and said to Riley, "Keep your arms to your sides. I'm making sure you don't use this gun. I knew you had it when it bumped against the chair in my office. If you move at all, I'll shoot at Ranglen." He said to Mykol, "Do what you have to do with the Clip and do it now. I want to be certain that it all happens right."

Riley kept still. Sabal held the gun close to her side, so she didn't want to frighten or surprise him.

Ranglen said, "What am I supposed to do, Sabal?"

"Don't kid with me. You know what I want. Put the Clip into the kiva and set the location for a sun. It's all very simple."

"You didn't think I'd do that?"

"This is too important. I need to make sure. I don't want to shoot you but I *will* hurt one of you if you don't destroy it."

"I think the Clip is safe now. It can't function without a power source. I don't feel from it what I felt when I got near it in the mound. If you want, you can throw it away yourself. I'm not stopping you." He held it up for Sabal to see. But he didn't hand it over to him.

"No! I don't want it! *You* have to send it away. Just do it, Mykol."

"Did you wonder what might happen if the Clip is destroyed?"

"It doesn't matter."

"Maybe the whole Blight will disappear, the forest, the animals, the mound, the light stations."

"I don't believe so—and I don't care!"

"But what if the Alcherans disappear too? They were needed as 'caretakers.' Maybe no colony ship wrecked here at all and everyone is just a manifestation, the shipwreck created after the fact."

"You think I haven't thought of that? None of it matters."

"Maybe the whole planet too. Isn't this the place of our dreams, yours and mine, the ideal location we both always wanted? I found Mylia and you found Orani. A 'world of adventure' with ideal companions. It's too good to be true. And maybe even *myself*—I might disappear. You needed me, didn't you? So perhaps I'm just your manifestation. And maybe you were created also. The world required an outsider, someone the people could blame—a reason for things going wrong."

"Then you'd have to include Riley too. You needed her, so maybe she's unreal."

Riley felt resentment.

"Then we *all* might vanish," Ranglen said.

"But I'd still get what I wanted. Stop delaying, Mykol!"

"No one knows what will follow. And what if the Clip doesn't want to be destroyed?"

Sabal pulled back the hammer of the gun. Riley had heard him click off the safety as soon as he took it.

Ranglen was unmoved. "I won't be forced, Sabal. I've been thinking about this since we left the barracks, and your reaction now convinces me. Destroying the Clip is not our decision. The people of Alchera are the ones affected. The Blight was part of their lives, not ours. *They* should decide if they want it or not."

Sabal rammed the gun barrel against Riley's head. She cringed in pain and tried to pull away from it. Sabal aimed at Ranglen again but kept the pistol near her skull.

Ranglen asked her, "Are you okay?"

She nodded, barely.

Ranglen moved very slowly. He pulled from his pocket the teleportation Clip and inserted it into the wall.

The star chart appeared.

"Pick a sun, not a world," Sabal said.

Riley watched as Ranglen chose one. The blue column appeared.

"Now pull out the Clip, reinsert it, and throw the Blight Clip into the kiva."

Ranglen pulled the Clip from the wall, turned it over, attached it again, and the blue column returned.

But he kept the Blight Clip in his hand, staring at it. He faced Sabal and said to him flatly, "I can't throw it in. You'll have to do that yourself."

Sabal whined like an animal.

Ranglen took two steps back, stood beside the kiva. He held the Clip high and said to Sabal, "And *you* have to come get it!"

Sabal dropped the gun and leaped forward, lifted his arms to reach for it.

Ranglen yelled, "*Shoot it, Riley!*" and he tossed the Clip through the open roof.

Riley grabbed her gun from the floor and shot at the falling Clip.

The bullet struck it and it flew into the trees—out of everyone's reach.

Sabal screamed. But while still moving forward and reaching over his head, he tripped and stumbled into the kiva, into the blue light.

Ranglen reached frantically to yank the Clip out of the wall, to stop Sabal from being teleported.

But it wouldn't budge.

Sabal scrambled to get out of the pit. A burst of light engulfed him.

He disappeared.

Ranglen then managed to pull out the Clip. The column vanished.

He and Riley both stood still. They looked into the kiva, then at each other.

"I tried to pull it out," he insisted, "but it was stuck. The teleportation must have already begun."

"Or maybe the Clip *wanted* him killed."

They both tried to calm themselves.

Ranglen asked, "Are you okay?"

She nodded.

"I kept taunting him, purposely delaying. I felt safe until he held the gun closer to your head. I remembered you saying if anyone but you tried to use it, it would explode in his hand, and I thought it would hurt you being that close."

"Oh..." She then added, casually, "I lied about that."

Ranglen's mouth fell open. "You *lied?*"

"I don't know of any gun that can do that. Do you?"

"You mean he really could have killed us?"

"Oh yes. In fact, his doing so was the easiest way for him to get what he wanted. He then could have *kicked* the Clip into the kiva. I was terrified the whole time."

Ranglen shook his head. "And I was trying to force him to use the gun."

"Things worked out, though. We're all right."

Ranglen sighed, in disbelief.

Then Barinda entered the room, hurrying but cautious. "I was following Sabal but then I heard a gunshot." She looked around. "He got away from me, yet I was sure he came here."

"He's not here now," Ranglen said. "And he won't be coming back. I'm afraid he's gone."

She glanced into the kiva, where she saw that the dirt had been kicked around. She seemed to understand.

"You know how he originally came here?" Ranglen asked.

"He told Orani and she told me. I'm the only one who knew. I even was here when he destroyed his own Clip by sending it into a sun. Is that what happened to him?"

"He was fighting to get the Blight Clip and he fell into the kiva. The teleportation already started."

"So he was sent there instead?"

They both nodded, followed by silence.

After a while, Barinda told them, "He and I didn't always get along, but we spoke to each other more than we led people to believe. We weren't close, but we did talk. He surprised me because, in the end, he seemed to want only revenge."

"He loved somebody once," Ranglen said, defending him.

"But he recalled her with bitterness, not pleasure. Did you know that a resurrection of Orani *did* return? He could have loved her, but he refused, rejected her entirely. She had no memory, but it was still a cruel thing to do to her. She was one of the bodies you saw down in the forest the first day you got here."

Both he and Riley took this all in. Then he asked, "Is Mylia a resurrection?"

"No. And neither am I. Nor you, Mykol, whatever you might have heard." Then she added, in a solemn tone, "I never agreed with Sabal's claim that teleportation balanced 'equations,' or that we destroy what we love. The Blight's not a killing machine. I believe the manifestations are tools of biological progress, pulled from our minds not in order to torture but simply for convenience. I think the Blight was evolving people, moving them through the various resurrections toward something like the Airafane themselves. It's a device for evolution, I feel, not suffering. Both you and Sabal were just unlucky."

Ranglen protested. "But we *are* responsible for our actions, whatever they are. Sabal was right about that."

"Well, my universe is not as paranoid as yours. All that's happened here has been treated too simplistically. Sabal and Orani, you and Mylia. They're not just love stories. They're galactic history that's still in development. Achievements, progress, resolutions, time. 'Galaxy Time.' This is no tragedy, no matter what you might feel."

The two of them struggled with these ideas. Riley took her chance and said, "Barinda, are you an Airafane?"

She laughed. "No. But thank you. And maybe I'm becoming one."

Then Ranglen asked, "Do you speak for a certain coyote I once met?"

And Riley quickly added, "And did you once slip into one of my dreams?"

"No." She smiled. "I don't speak for animals or dreams.…They speak for me."

Heavy silence.

"Not literally, of course."

Then she held up something small and said, with an affected innocence, "Did someone lose this? It came flying through the air as I ran up to the ruins. Landed right beside me. Thought it might be important."

The Blight Clip.

Ranglen took it from her, saw it was unhurt by Riley's bullet. Even with its stasis field gone, a Clip was incredibly durable.

Then Ranglen and Riley looked at each other, as if silently acknowledging a mutual decision. Riley said, "Barinda, we feel that you, the Alcherans, should decide whether the Blight Clip is destroyed or not, whether you want it back in place and working, or whether you prefer it 'killed.' It should be your decision. Not Sabal's, not Mykol's, and not mine."

She answered, without too much irony, "So you're finally showing some respect for us, even allowing us our own choice."

Ranglen said, "We're both leaving Alchera soon, and the teleportation Clip we have to take with us, so this decision must be made before we go. You have to decide now, for all Alcherans. And if only one person *has* to do it, I think you are the best choice. Even better than Mylia. So…do you want the Clip back so you can restart it someday, or do you prefer to destroy it now?"

Barinda looked proud, and also confident. "I'm certain what the choice would be. I've heard it from everyone already. Destroy it. Now."

"Are you sure?"

"Yes, and not for Sabal's reasons but ours. Let's make some Alcherans instead of Airafane. Let's make children, not resurrections."

She said to Riley, "You see, I told you I'm not what you think I am."

Ranglen dropped the Blight Clip into the kiva. He picked a different star this time, just in case.

In a small flash of light, the Clip disappeared.

Ranglen said, "Anyone want to check to see if the world still exists out there?"

"I'm certain it does." Barinda sounded confident. "Make sure you change the coordinates before you leave. You don't want to end up where that Clip just went."

Ranglen didn't laugh. He changed the settings.

Riley said, "You're not inviting us to stay?"

"No," Barinda answered, with no trace of humor.

Ranglen pulled the Clip from the wall, and then he and Riley stepped into the kiva.

Barinda did say to them at the last moment, "Take care of yourselves."

They disappeared.

Chapter 21: Forgetfulness

And came down on Homeworld.

They landed close to Riley's campsite, not out in the dunes where Ranglen first arrived. They looked around to see if anything was amiss. The sky, the air, the rocks seemed familiar, but of course that meant little. They examined the camp. The wreckage from the storm that hit before they left was still there, the trailer tilted on a fallen support, the equipment overturned, the tools scattered.

Riley said, "So with all that traveling between Alcheras we didn't get further from our own world."

"It doesn't seem different."

"You said we'd forget details, of both where we went and where we started, that Sabal claimed the equations require it."

"He thought we might recall emotions, that little reminders might kick them off."

"So we keep the longing but not the satisfaction?"

"That's true in all worlds."

They made themselves a meal from canned food in the trailer, sat across from each other under a screen from a tent in the desert air. The breeze was cool, the sun just rising.

Riley checked her cellpad—she hadn't brought it to Alchera and had left it charging—and found the time that had passed on Homeworld equivalent to how long they had been gone, to their own subjective time at least.

She avoided information searches, newsfeeds, current events, hesitant to find what might have changed.

"Let me see it," Ranglen said. He took it and kept the screen facing himself so she couldn't view the subjects he searched. He did this for a while, then gave it back and didn't tell her what he found. Nothing showed on the cellpad but Riley's homescreen.

The mood between them reminded her of what they were like when they first met. Cautious, tentative, curious but not probing, though he was less brooding and she less distrustful. A domestic calm seemed to have settled on their relationship.

Maybe it was exhaustion.

"I'm sorry you didn't get her back, Mykol."

He nodded.

"You gave her the chance to live her life. That must make you feel very good."

"We don't have control over what we feel," he said. "We only have control over what we do. That's all we get, ultimately. I had to leave."

She understood.

"Besides, maybe I wanted only the first Mylia."

"You don't believe that."

"No," he admitted. "But maybe I've also lost my taste for uncertainty, and maybe I'd always doubt it was her."

"I don't accept that either."

He didn't answer. He seemed withdrawn and distant now. She felt she was losing him.

No surprise. I pushed myself into his life, after all.

"I'm teleporting one more time," he said, "leaving for another Homeworld, where I'll stay. Maybe it's paranoia, but I want to be one more universe removed from everything that happened."

He was leaving her.

"Do you want to come with me?" he asked.

She had almost hoped he wouldn't ask this question. Her life had taught her how to handle rejection, but she had no guidelines for offering it herself, and she lacked any pleasure in doing so.

"No," she said, more quickly than expected.

His expression changed only slightly. Maybe what she said was more confirmation than surprise.

"I can't, Mykol," she explained. "I want more now. I want someone who will love me in the same way you loved Mylia. Because of you, I saw that such a relationship is possible. And I now want that. Since you gave it to someone else, you can't rightly give me the same. And I can't expect it. I think I know you enough to say that someone like you—and maybe someone like me—can love like that only once."

His eyes looked tired and sad, but resigned. Even realistic.

"With me," she added, "you'd always be reminded of her. You said that yourself. And I'm too much a part of *this* story. You need a new story, one just for you. And, I think, at least according to what Barinda said, it's a bigger story than what you think."

"Maybe she *is* an Airafane."

"Maybe we all are."

He smiled gamely. "No wonder you impressed Sabal. What did you two talk about when Mylia and I were away?"

"Nothing in particular."

He looked at her, appraising. "You're different from when I first saw you. No more zip-ties, pistols, doubts. You're what I wish other people could be. I think the world of you, Riley."

She laughed. "*The* world, or *a* world."

"*All* worlds. And if all worlds exist, there's at least one out there where you and I are together and enjoying ourselves."

He said this with such undisguised longing that she almost broke down.

"I'm sure it's beautiful," she said. "And there's another, where you and Mylia—the original—are together again."

"I know that."

"And maybe one more, where the Mylia you just left is meeting up with another 'you' right now, so she won't be alone."

"I wonder about that too. And I'd be grateful."

But she wouldn't look at his eyes when he said this.

They sat in complete stillness for a while.

"I think I better go."

She nodded.

He gathered his things—not much was left—and walked toward the ruins.

She followed.

"No," he said tenderly, "I don't want you watching me when I disappear."

She nodded, understanding. She didn't want it either. "On the other Homeworld, will you hand over the Clip to the government?"

"No, I've decided not to. I think it's too dangerous, and its function is... compromised. What if Sabal's right and it *was* meant as a trap? Also, we don't want thousands of expeditions sailing off into different universes, especially if we have influence on how they might develop. I still worry about what we did on those worlds, that we twisted causality as we romped through time-streams. Imagine what a whole gang of people might do, what might happen to Alchera. So I'm sending it off into a sun, just like the other Clip."

"Makes sense."

"I'll feel guilty, that I'm cheating humanity, so I might have to find another

Clip just to make up for it. That's a pity, in a way. It shows how dependent on Clips we've become."

"We're not that bad."

He looked at her fondly. "You were usually right."

He glanced toward the ruins, then back to her. "Thank you, Riley. I'll remember you....Well, at least I *hope* I will."

"Thank you too, Mykol."

He left.

Well, alone again.

Though maybe not "abandoned" this time.

Still, now what?

She needed a job. She hadn't exaggerated when she told Ranglen he destroyed her profession. She wasn't interested in archaeology anymore, especially the study of Airafane ruins. She knew too much about them, and it was information she didn't want to share. Like Ranglen, she worried it all might be too big. He had said you can't choose what you feel, but you can choose what you do about it.

Besides, with the Clip gone, no one would believe her.

She used her cellpad to review jobs. The triviality of the act made her laugh.

Then...she had an idea.

She did a search, and found what she was looking for.

Is this what Mykol saw? Is this another reason why he left?

She tried to bring up the list of previous searches to check what he looked for but they all had been deleted. He always was thorough.

Or maybe he intended me to find this. On my own.

She made other searches too—to be certain no contradictions existed between her current self and anything happening on this new world. But she found things related to her to be safe. A familiar past, a person who had not been seen for a while, which was expectable, someone no different from what she currently had become. Her staying here should be okay.

There were some minor political and social changes to the culture, but nothing drastic. Apparently Earth might have tried some foolish take-over she hadn't heard about, but it was quickly thwarted. The lay of the historical landscape was just slightly different.

With one exception.

An organization that might need people.

She sealed up her camp and left in her jeep.

The Organization for an Independent Annulus didn't seem very impressive, but it occupied a large part of a building in the planet's capitol and was clearly growing.

She went inside and asked about a job.

"Why should we hire you?" asked a stern woman.

"Does your boss do all the final interviews?"

"Usually."

"Then, please, do me a favor. Tell him I liked his poem that ends with 'our longing is blind, but our longing has wings.'"

The woman narrowed her eyes and glared at her—as if Riley had turned into a sick rose.

"Indulge me," Riley said. "It can't hurt."

With a sour expression the woman marched away.

She came back looking worse, as if having lost an argument. "You can go in to see him now."

The boss's name was Michael Raglin. He had no publications yet, no poems to quote. She had learned this information earlier on her cellpad. But Riley felt sure there'd be a connection between him and the Ranglen she knew.

In the other room, that was busy with people behind data-feed screens, she identified Raglin immediately. He didn't look as "haunted" as the one she had known—a bit more stable, maybe, and a lot more open as he talked with his workers.

She could appreciate this new alternative.

She walked up to his desk and sat in the chair across from him before introducing herself. She smiled—at him, of course, but also at her confidence and feeling of control.

He examined her, openly, frankly. "You're looking for a job? We don't have much to offer and the pay isn't great. Most of us are volunteers."

"I support your work with Annulus. I support it very strongly."

"What other things have you done?"

Well, I've seen a lot of interesting universes. "I was an amateur Airafanologist. I did personal research at an Airafane ruins site."

"Really? That must have been fascinating. I've always wanted to visit one of those sites, but with all this work it's been—wait! What did you say about a poem of mine?"

"Oh, I'm sorry. I didn't mean to be impolite."

"I don't remember writing that."

"But you do write, correct?"

"Yes, but I haven't published."

"You mentioned the poem once, just in passing, I think to a reporter. You were talking about what you felt for the future of Annulus." She stopped herself before her made-up details got out of hand.

"It does sound like something I'd say. I get rather emotional about the topic. But I don't—"

A child, no more than a toddler, came running out of a back room. Her face was fresh, her eyes bright, her smile winning, and she shed a glow on everyone in the room. She obviously knew Raglin and wanted to play with him, since she jumped into his lap and expected attention.

"Abbie! I'm working. Not now." But he clearly tolerated the intrusion and would have been glad to occupy her. He yelled into the back room, "Janey! Would you come and get Abigale?"

An attractive young woman emerged, obviously pregnant, and Raglin handed her the child. The woman carried her away, admonishing her, "He's busy now. Hush."

Raglin watched as the youngster left. Then he turned back to Riley. "Sorry. We're a bit casual here."

"Is she your daughter?" She assumed Janey was his wife but she didn't want to ask directly.

"Oh no. She's my niece. I just discovered I have a distant sister—that was her just now. I never knew, and I met her for the first time just recently. So this is the only relationship I've ever had with a child. I really like it. There's an 'Isabel' on the way too."

Riley found the man's exuberance charming. She noticed that other people in the room also enjoyed his mood with the child.

He added, "Too many changes in my life lately."

"Must be rewarding to have a family."

"I had no idea. I'm enjoying it. I…Sorry, as you can see I can't stay on subject. You're here on business. A job, you say?" He straightened his back, squared his shoulders, laced his hands together in a fake pose of professionalism. His voice went deeper, mocking his own appearance, and he pronounced tendentiously, "*How* may I help you?"

She smiled. "Well, let me see now…"

And Ranglen?

In *his* world?

He sits alone at his desk before a window, in some undefined moment in a tentative future. The room is dark. The window is icy and it sheds cold air onto his hands.

Then a sudden connection brings it all back. Some spark makes a link, some Proustian taste or scent of lost worlds causes his memory to tumble, regroup, and finally recollect. Maybe his wide-rimmed coffee mug raised to his mouth, while he's focused on writing and hasn't noticed that the coffee is gone, so that only the warmth of the rim touches his lips.

And he's reminded, suddenly, of *her* lips…moist.

And he's with her again. There in the snowlight, by a powered-down aircar beneath darkness and stars. Filled with hope for a future that, alas, never came.

Does he smile as his trickster memory plays? Does he regret? Does he long for return?

Or does he, gently, place down the cup and resume his preoccupying, and sometimes even satisfying, maneuvering of words.

About the Author

An early interest in astronomy, DC science-fiction comics, and the Sunday *Flash Gordon* strip, led Albert Wendland to a life-long fascination with science fiction. (The books on the shelves behind him in the photo are all SF, and the top shelf is strictly Andre Norton.) He wrote one of the earliest dissertations on science fiction, and even his drawings and paintings had SF themes. He teaches English, and often SF, at Seton Hill University, where he co-created the MFA program in Writing Popular Fiction, which emphasizes genre fiction exclusively, an emphasis rare in graduate writing programs. His SF novel, *The Man Who Loved Alien Landscapes*, a starred pick-of-the-week by *Publisher's Weekly*, was released by Dog Star Books, and it generated the prequel/sequel, *In a Suspect Universe*, which tells a hidden story from the protagonist's past. He's now working on a collection of poems, *Temporary Planets for Transitory Days*, supposedly written by that same protagonist. A prose sequel to all these works will follow, most likely called *Galaxy Time* (though one more novel might be squeezed out before he gets to it). His other interests are geology and astronomy, landscape photography, graphic novels, film, and the "sublime" in prose, visual art, nature, and outer space

CPSIA information can be obtained
at www.ICGtesting.com
Printed in the USA
LVHW01s2300060918
589355LV00005B/935/P

9 781947 879058